ALESSANDRA

Chisholm Manor
~~ *Book One* ~~

ANN M PRATLEY

BY ANN M PRATLEY

Power Moore Investigation Tales
Hoonigan
Resolution of Happiness
Home by the Sea
Tiger in our House

Forbidden Conflicts Series
Amethyst of Youth
Ruby of Law
Diamond of War
Sapphire of Prejudice
Emerald of Wisdom

Freedom of Flight Series
Christian
Brandon
Trinity

Painful Deliverance Series
Painful Deliverance
Darkness of Heart
Friendship of Desire

Total Freedom Series
Total Freedom
Total New Beginnings

CHAPTER 1

Alessandra sat on the stone bench in front of her home, enjoying feeling the sunshine beaming down on her face. Already 18 years of age, she'd reached a point in her life where she could appreciate the life that she led at home with her parents. As a family, they weren't as well off as some people in the village, but she knew they also weren't in such a dire position as others.

Her young puppy, Fern, lay at her feet. He basked in the warmth they both knew was coming to an end. It was autumn and the trees before Alessandra were almost bare of leaves. The ground nearby was intensely covered with the colours of orange and yellow.

Day to day, Alessandra spent her time obediently doing whatever chores her mother or father placed on her shoulders. When she wasn't sewing, feeding the chickens or helping in other areas of their home, she indulged in reading novels. It was exciting to let her mind wander to lives and places far more exotic than her own. She'd been fortunate to have been raised with a tutor and a governess. Both had taught her skills in language, etiquette, and music. What her mother had taught her throughout her whole life to date was what she'd need to know when she would one day go off with a husband to a new home.

Whenever Alessandra had thought about marriage, she'd always been excited by the idea of it. Almost all of the girls in her immediate area were already married and in homes of their own before they had turned eighteen. Having attended one wedding ceremony after another,

Alessandra had started to believe that marriage might not be the chosen path for her after all. It wasn't that she had no opportunity to meet young men. A year earlier, she'd found herself quite enraptured with Tom Missinger. A handsome young man, he'd danced with her at many village assemblies over the preceding year or so. Alessandra had let herself believe that he loved her and would want to marry her. That was before she had found out he'd gone away and married another.

She still couldn't identify how she'd so mistakenly read his intentions. She didn't understand why he hadn't told her if he'd had no interest in her as a potential suitor. He seemed to have sought her out on the evenings of the balls. He'd complimented her and made sure she always had places for him on her dance card. It had thrilled her to be close to him, even just in dance. To her, he was the most handsome young man in her acquaintance, his easy-going manners effortlessly making her laugh and feel much at ease.

Since realising she had greatly misread his intentions, Alessandra had built a more solid resolve around her. She'd raised an armour to make sure she wasn't so easily misled for a second time. She would never again misconstrue any man's feelings towards her.

Having a different ethnicity blend compared to other people in their village, with her Italian mother and an English father, she knew in her heart that she was plain. She expected she would never turn any man's head through prettiness. The question that played on her mind was simply that of wondering what her life would entail if she truly was not intended for marriage.

"Alessandra," she heard her mother call from inside the house. "Can you come and help me please?"

Alessandra abruptly stood up, waking up Fern in the process. The young puppy jumped to attention. They looked at each other.

"Sun time is over for me, Fern," Alessandra said

before walking into her home.

She found her mother, Isabella, in the kitchen, looking busy as she looked through the storage of jars and boxes.

"Oh, Alessandra," Isabella said on seeing her daughter approach. "I think it is a good day for you and I to head out to the garden and harvest as much as we can. We need to ensure that whatever is out there is adequately stored for winter. It feels like a cold front is coming so we need to be prepared."

Alessandra nodded at her mother. She'd often quietly wondered how her mother and father were both so handsome and yet had made her - someone so plain. She quickly dismissed the thought from her head. Such thoughts fell under the umbrella of vanity - something she'd been taught she shouldn't let herself fall victim to.

The two of them walked out the back door and into the sprawling area behind the house. Alessandra imagined that sometime in the past it must have been wonderfully well kept, tidy and structured. Now, with only the family plus one married couple to help in and around the house, it always seemed like there was never enough time to keep on top of everything that the property demanded.

As Alessandra walked alongside her mother, she felt particularly plain and dull. In her mother, she saw beauty, confidence and such a sense of power. Alessandra knew her parents had presented the world with four children. The first two hadn't survived past infancy. Now there was only Alessandra and her older brother Nicholas, and he was already married and well settled with his own family underway in their own home.

Watching her mother begin to harvest what was left of the late fruit, vegetables, and herbs, Alessandra began to suspect there was more to their time outside together. She waited patiently as her mother seemed to gather her words and then finally spoke.

"Alessandra, you know that we have always told you that one day you will marry," her mother began, making Alessandra's heart skipped a beat at the words. "You also know that we do not have such a level of land or income that may have presented you with suitors to choose from as you wished."

Alessandra nodded. She had no idea of their financial situation as a family but guessed money wasn't too readily available, given how they lived. She remained silent as she saw her mother stop walking and looked at her.

"We have found a young man who you are to become betrothed to," Isabella said, surprising Alessandra all the more. At the astonished look on her daughter's face, Isabella continued. "This young man lives on a large family estate near Bath. It is a good match for you."

"But why should he want to marry me, knowing that I have nothing to offer him?" Alessandra asked. She was confused about how such a thing could have come about, given how hopeless the idea of marriage had seemed only minutes earlier.

Her mother looked at her deeply.

"Because you do have something to offer him, Alessandra," Isabella said before pausing to wonder how her daughter would receive the news about to be delivered. "Although we have never advertised it, your father and I have had money put aside for you all these years for your dowry."

"We are not poor?" Alessandra asked meekly, still not understanding. On hearing what her mother had just said, she felt like she was in shock.

Her mother took her hand and led her to a stone bench in the sunny corner of the garden wilderness.

"Your grandparents - my mother and father - were distantly related to the royal family in Italy," said Isabella. "They were very wealthy. When they died, they left a considerable amount of money in trust for your dowry. It has never been touched as you had to wait till you turned eighteen until you could access it. Now that you are of age, it can be used for the purpose it was intended."

"So this man who wants to marry me - what he actually wants is this money?" Alessandra asked her mother. She could still not see what the attraction would be for this other mystery family.

Her mother looked at her and took her hand.

"Alessandra, it is every woman's right and duty to marry, set up their own home, and start their own family. This family is a farming family. They have much land and many tenants. What they do not have is the level of ready money they would like to keep their estate well cared for. So, yes, they wish for this match due to the size of the dowry you will take with you."

Alessandra considered the situation being presented to her. She'd known this was how marriages were formed, of course. Marriage was a recipe of two parties needing something from each other, but as Isabella spoke, Alessandra felt like she was simply an item, being put up for sale.

"What if they take this money and then they do not want *me*?" she asked. "Where will that leave me?"

"You seem more worried about the issue of the money than the issue of getting married," Isabella replied.

Alessandra took a moment to think about this news. Some man she didn't know wanted to marry her. Only, he didn't necessarily want to marry her because he had never met her - or had he?

"Have I met this man?" she asked her mother, who shook her head.

"No, you have never met anyone in this family," Isabella replied. "They live far away and have only contacted us via post."

"How does he know that he wants to marry me? He

might see me and then run away," Alessandra said, making her mother laugh softly.

"Oh, Alessandra, he will not want to run away when he sees you! But it is his father and mother who are initiating this, not the young man himself. I suspect he has as little to do with this decision as you do."

"Have you already accepted?" Alessandra asked her mother, not at all certain how she was feeling about it all.

"No," Isabella replied as she shook her head. "Your father and I agreed that we would talk to you first, and see how you felt about it. We will not force you. With the kind of money that was left to you, you do have the power to make your own choice. But this family seems honourable and well known. They will introduce you to good social standing. I also understand the estate is vast, which will be something for you to pass on to your children."

"But will it be in any way good for you and Father if I do this?" Alessandra asked.

"It will mean security for *you*," Isabella said, nodding. "Your father and I will not be around forever. We would like to see you settled. We want to know you are being taken care of, and you are old enough now to be married and starting your own family."

At the thought of that, Alessandra blushed. In the few novels she'd read, there had been mention of what happened between husband and wife in the dark of night. It equally frightened her and intrigued her. To dispel such thoughts, she looked at her mother and nodded.

"Mother, if you think this is the right thing for me to do, I will marry this man. I should like you and Father to be there with me when I meet him, however. Will you be?"

"We will all go to their family estate and spend some time there before you are officially betrothed," Isabella replied, smiling. "If you do not wish to marry him, you can tell me or your father why and we will consider what is to be done then."

Alessandra leaned in and hugged her mother. She'd long wondered if such a day would come. Now she had to prepare herself for the reality to happen.

"But what will happen to Fern?" she asked quietly.

She received no response.

CHAPTER 2

On a broad, wide land a little to the east of the town of Bath, a young man called Edward Chisholm was out riding on his beloved Beauty - a beautiful black horse with an almost dark blue sheen to it. Edward grinned as he rode up the steep incline and reached the summit of the tall, broad hill on their land. There he climbed down and secured Beauty's reins to a tree before sitting down on the ground and looking out over the estate. From that point on their land, all of what his family owned could be seen. It constantly brought out in Edward a source of great pride.

For more than 200 years, the Chisholm family had lived on the land as farmers who provided tenants with opportunities for somewhere to live and to work. Edward had grown up among the tenants. He regarded them all as extended family, as they did him. For as long as he could remember, they had spoken to him with affection as they called him 'Young Master'.

Now 20 years of age, Edward felt like he was neither a boy, dependent on his parents, or a man, completely independent. He was the only living child his parents had after several miscarriages. Following his birth, his mother had been told she should never end up with child again. All responsibility would be on him one day to manage the entire estate. For the moment, both of his parents were alive and active in the management of the land, buildings, and tenants.

He wasn't a sociable person but had been well brought up with good manners. Because of this, he did seem to make friends easily, although there were few instances where he could see them. Everyone he knew, he'd met through his parents. Being the future master of the estate, it had been explained to him very early on that he wouldn't go to school like other children. Instead, he'd remain at home and be taught everything there was to know about the land before him. His father regarded that as infinitely more valuable than any schooling could be.

With a mother who'd been well educated, however, even being confined to the estate, she'd ensured Edward had a tutor who could teach him as well as any teacher in the school system. As a result, not going to school was no loss to him academically. He'd grown up well versed in literature, language, music, and bookkeeping.

Sitting on the summit, pondering the many aspects of his life, Edward could feel the chill of winter beginning. The grounds were beautiful with leaves of various colours scattered around. It wouldn't be long before winter truly set in. He knew it would then get frightfully cold. He was thankful that he was fortunate to live in a home that was solid and warm once all the fires were going. They would have enough people around in winter to be able to keep a good supply of firewood coming into the house, ready for use at all times.

The only negative thing he occasionally felt about his life was the aspect of sometimes feeling so lonely. There were always many people he could see and talk to but now and then he did feel alone. His father had been telling him for a long time that he needed to get on and meet someone who could provide an heir for the family. It seemed to have been left in Edward's hands to find that 'someone'. Nothing had changed so far. He never met anyone new, so no courting had ever taken place. Because he believed his parents weren't too old to leave this world yet, he didn't consider there was any rush.

~~~~~

After enjoying the tranquillity and beauty of the
~~~~~

summit and its views, Edward stood up and started down the hill again toward the main house. As he approached his home, he dismounted and watched as Beauty was led away to the stable by the stable hand. Having grown up with horses, Edward sometimes considered them as good a friend as any man could have. Certainly, he'd seen and heard of horses doing things that saved men's lives. They were a constant source of wonder to him, despite him having been around them every day of his life.

Walking into the house, he immediately went up to his room to freshen up and change before going to find his mother. As he entered the drawing room, he was confronted with his mother looking agitated while talking to his father.

"Charles, he needs to get married so our line - *your* line - can continue. Why do you object to this so much?" his mother was saying to his father.

Both parents looked up as they noticed Edward had entered.

"What are you talking about?" he asked his father, who shook his head in reply.

"It does not concern you, Edward," his father replied.

Edward could see the dismay on his mother's face.

"Are you sure, Father?" he boldly asked. "Who else needs to get married around here?"

His father was silent. It seemed like his mother was hesitant to speak up also. Edward went and sat beside her. She appeared visibly upset whilst an angry vibe seeped from her.

"Father?" he prompted, one more time.

Finally, his father looked at him and spoke.

"Edward, you know that it will be your duty to marry and carry on the family line and business," he said.

Edward quietly nodded in response before his father continued.

"Your mother has found someone who she considers suitable for you to take as a wife."

Edward looked at his father, his mother, and then back again. He felt somewhat perplexed at the rather unusual conversation.

"And you do not consider her suitable?" he asked.

"She is a nobody, with no land or social status," his father said.

Edward was surprised to hear a sound of almost disgust in his father's voice.

"She has money! Exactly what we need! How can you call that nothing?" his mother said forcefully.

"Oh, Mother," Edward began to ask. "How has she come to have money if her family has no social status?"

"She is descended from a well-known family in Italy, with connection to Italian royalty," his mother replied. "She is hardly a nobody."

At that point, his father jumped back into the conversation. Edward immediately began to see why they were disagreeing so much.

"They aren't known or respected!" his father exclaimed with passion in his voice. "No-one has even heard of them!"

Edward looked at both of his parents. He could see their individual levels of stubbornness that he'd witnessed on many previous occasions. He knew they could have a stand-off for days or even weeks if they both felt strongly enough about their own points of view.

"Mother, tell me how you have learned about this young lady and why you see her as a good match for me," Edward suggested in an attempt to calm his parents down. He watched as his mother took a moment to consider her words.

"I know that they are a family who do not live in society and they have very little land," she said. "They live as though they are common people, but in this girl's heritage there is history and honour. They have contacts who are the equivalent of dukes and duchesses, even if they do not live like that themselves. The young woman is to inherit a very large dowry now that she has turned eighteen."

Edward could see his mother's point of view. She was a romantic soul. She'd ideally prefer a marriage to be more than just an exchange of money or land. In this instance, however, he could see that money appeared to be a major contributor to her enthusiasm.

"And Father?" he asked. "What is your argument against this young lady?"

"I have no particular argument against her," his father replied, beginning to look worn down. "I have never even met the girl or her family. But your mother's argument that her ancestors had some kind of standing in Italy makes no sense to me. She would bring a cash injection to the estate, but she won't bring land or social status to you. What real purpose would she be?"

Edward looked at his father and could see the stress on his face. That worried him.

"Would her real purpose not be to be my wife and to give me children?" asked Edward. "I do not think that she needs land *or* a title for that. All I could wish for is someone who I can get on well enough with, and who will work with me to keep our home together and running smoothly."

As his parents looked at each other, Edward saw softening on their faces as they started to relax.

"I know that you have tried to leave it to me to find someone I want to marry, but I am simply not in any position to meet new people," he said. "To be honest, I would be happy to marry anyone who can think and speak and is as eager to work at marriage as I will be. So, Mother, if you think you have found someone suitable, even if just to secure more money for the estate, can we at least meet her? What harm could there be in inviting her and her family to stay here for a few weeks, so we can all just simply meet?"

CHAPTER 3

Alessandra spent the next two weeks relishing what would possibly be the last time she'd be home. Although her family lived simply, it was the house and township that she'd grown up in. It was somewhere she had a deep sentimental appreciation for. She'd known for a long time that one day she would have to leave. Knowing that didn't make it any easier for her as she packed up her few belongings into trunks, ready for the journey she would soon make with her parents.

During the final days in her home, Alessandra leaned on her mother. She appreciated that her mother was talking to her as a wife, sharing with Alessandra the last information that Isabella felt her daughter would need to know. Of the intimacy between husband and wife, all she would say was that it was a wife's duty to do as her husband wished for. She should do it without argument, regardless of how uneasy she may feel about it.

Alessandra pondered her mother's wording. The choice of words made it sound like the marriage act was, for some, a completely unenjoyable thing to experience. And yet, when she watched her mother and father together, she'd only ever seen affection between them. They'd never been overly intimate in front of her, but she remembered seeing small moments when they would look at each other in such a way that would make her mother blush. She could also remember moments when her father would touch her mother. Sometimes he'd straighten up a small area of hair that was determined to not stay tidy. Sometimes he'd take her hand and hold it in his while looking into her eyes. It was difficult for Alessandra to align their level of affection to something horrible being done to her mother night after night.

She knew that thinking about that aspect of marriage was something she shouldn't be focusing on. It was wicked to think such thoughts so often but, until she met the young man who would be her husband, she found she couldn't think of any other aspect of it. Her role would be, after all, to have children. It would be her responsibility to provide an heir for the family she was possibly going to be a part of.

~~~~~

Finally, the time came when Alessandra and her parents were on their way to the estate of her possible betrothal. Alessandra could see tension on both of her parents' faces. They each appeared to be in their own thoughts about it all.

Looking at her father as they travelled, she wondered what he was thinking. He'd said nothing. He wasn't a man who was completely cold to his children, but he was less inclined to speak to her than her mother was. The days of Alessandra being able to enchant him with a hug or a smile seemed to have ended long ago. He'd grown increasingly withdrawn from her in recent years as she'd evolved into a young woman.

Having never left her home town before, Alessandra became excited as she saw the landscape change. She saw views she'd never visualised even in her dreams and imagination. For one night mid-journey, they stayed in an inn. It was something else that was also new to her. The inn owners were a married couple who appreciated the custom with it being a very quiet time for them. They also enjoyed viewing the excitement Alessandra exhibited in being able to eat and stay overnight in the establishment. To Alessandra, it all was starting to feel like such an adventure - so much so that she almost forgot where they were heading, and why.
~~~~~

CHAPTER 4

In the manor house near Bath, staff were instructed to clean everything excessively. Under the instruction of Edward's mother, to everyone it seemed almost as if royalty must be visiting. Edward's father, Charles, found himself exasperated at her. That didn't stop him fondly teasing her about her excitement.

"They are not of society, my love. They really will not find anything wrong with our home, I am sure," he said to her, over and over. Despite his teasing, still she flitted around like a little bird, issuing orders and trying to get everything just right for her upcoming guests.

Edward watched it all with amusement and fondness for his mother. He felt calm about the prospect of possibly meeting a woman who would become a part of his future. He knew that if he was very unhappy with her as a potential wife, his parents wouldn't force the marriage but he'd also been raised with the understanding of duty. He knew how much his getting married would mean to his mother. That was enough for him to be resolved that no matter who the young woman was or what she was like, he would go through with the marriage. He would see it through and he would make the most of it. To him, his mother was the utmost example of womanhood. He considered it impossible for any other woman to match up to her.

Early in the evening on the night before the guests were to arrive, Edward was sitting in the last of the sun before it would disappear, when his mother came and sat next to him. Turning to look at her, he noticed that over the previous few days she seemed to have become more youthful in her looks. He wondered if it was due to her getting excited about the possible upcoming wedding, just as a bride might do.

"Are you at peace, my son?" she asked, looking at the young man who'd begun life inside of her. He'd never been a handsome boy. In the eyes of many, he would possibly never be regarded as a handsome man. Regardless, she was proud of the person he was and the kind and loving nature he possessed.

Edward looked closely at his mother with the sudden awareness that as he moved closer toward marriage, they all were getting older. One day she wouldn't be there for him anymore.

"I am at peace, Mother," he replied. "I am looking forward to meeting my potential wife to be, and marriage after that if it is meant to be."

He saw his mother take a deep breath, as if to consider what she wanted to say before words came from her mouth once more.

"Edward, be kind to her," she finally said. "I know you have a good heart and would never be intentionally cruel to anyone, but I remember how afraid I was when I was sent to meet your father."

"Oh, but you love Father, do you not?"

His mother smiled with a slight blush on her face.

"Oh, yes! Now I love him with all my heart, but the day that we met, we did not know each other at all. It was a difficult time for me, trying to fit in with his family while trying to get to know him. It is always the way things go but it is not easy, particularly for the young woman." She paused a moment before continuing. "Be patient with her. Give both of you plenty of time to relax with each other before ruling her out of being a possible partner."

"Everything will be well, Mother," Edward said, smiling to reassure her. "You have taught me well in what to expect of a wife, and I am beginning to understand how things are run on the estate. I want you to now relax and not worry so much," Edward said as he put his arms around her in an embrace.

"You are my son and I love you. Of course I worry. That is my job as your mother."

CHAPTER 5

"Isabella, Alessandra, we are nearly there," Alessandra's father said to his wife and daughter. They were nearing the estate they expected to be guests in over the following three weeks.

Already Alessandra had experienced so much excitement in previous days, she didn't think she could become any more anxious. When she heard her father explain how close they were, she felt a new level of nerves appear. Inside of her was so much self-doubt about what the young man would think of her, that she hadn't given any thought to whether she would like him. She hoped that he wasn't expecting someone beautiful or pretty. They were expectations that, in her mind, would most certainly result in his disappointment when he saw her.

"Look, Alessandra," she heard her mother say.

They both looked over the land to see the large home that looked as though it was getting closer. Alessandra was in awe, never having seen a home quite so big. The front façade alone looked like it would be four times the size of the small home she had grown up in. She found herself wondering how she would ever be able to find her way around it.

When they finally arrived in front of the manor house, they were greeted by strangers that none of them had ever laid eyes on. Fortunately, with there being only three family members on the doorstep of the home, it was easy to identify who was who.

The first person Alessandra noticed was the young

man. At first sight, she didn't see any handsomeness at all. In fact, there was something about him that was very *unattractive*. That contributed to Alessandra's heart sinking. At that moment, she realised she'd been assuming he would be the most handsome man she would have ever seen - perhaps even more handsome than Tom Missinger. The year before, Tom had indeed swept her heart away with his good looks.

Catching her mind wandering, she cursed herself inwardly for being so silly. She only had a moment to think such thoughts before Edward's parents were moving forward toward her own. They both held out their hands and gave a customary kiss on each cheek.

"And here is our son, Edward," Edward heard his mother say, breaking him out of his thoughts. He'd been looking at the young woman who was intended to be his wife. On seeing her, he instantly had similar thoughts about her as she'd just had about him.

At the prompting from his parents, he stepped forward and greeted Alessandra's mother and father. He then moved right up to Alessandra and gently took her hand and raised it to his lips.

Alessandra was momentarily stunned before remembering her manners and giving a small curtsey to Edward and his parents. They took some time for introductions and friendly greetings, all the while subtly looking at each other and assessing each other. Soon they were all ushered inside the great home, and Alessandra and her parents were shown to their rooms.

Inside the bedchamber that would be hers for the following three weeks, Alessandra sat on the bed and looked around before going to stand at the window. As she looked out, she felt her breath catch as she realised she was facing a view more beautiful than she had ever seen. For as far as she could see lay different shades of green, orange, red and yellow over flat land and a tall hill. From her angle, the hill looked like it might almost reach the sky.

After she'd stood like that for a time, taking in the land's beauty, she heard a light knocking at her door. When she opened it, she saw an older woman deliver her a friendly smile.

"Miss, the mistress has asked me to invite you down to the drawing room, where the family is assembling before their evening meal. Is there any way I can be of assistance to you?"

Alessandra was taken aback, wondering if there was something she was supposed to be doing, or to have done. The woman in front of her looked at her kindly and then spoke again.

"The family is relaxed this evening," she said. "You will fit right in."

"Thank you," Alessandra said, smiling. "I would appreciate it if you could show me the way."

Walking into the drawing room, Alessandra felt a new set of nerves come on. This time it wasn't because of Edward but rather the uncertainty of how she was supposed to act in the great house with such grand people. She desperately tried to remember all the rules of etiquette she had been taught growing up. She wanted so much to not put her parents to shame.

She was still deep in thought when she realised Edward was in front of her, saying something. She looked at him, flustered for not having been giving him her attention.

"Oh, I am so sorry," she stammered. "What were you saying?"

She could feel herself falling deep into blush, knowing her face would become deep red in her flustered state.

"Would you like to sit with me?" he asked, finding her blush in one way endearing but also a little uncomfortable.

"Yes," she stammered again, feeling like she had

been reduced to mumbling at a level that he probably wouldn't even understand. She felt the blush grow deeper and deeper. Despite her discomfort increasing, she pushed herself to follow him and sit down near him.

Edward looked at her, remembering his mother's words from the night before about making a young lady try and feel at ease. He was uncertain what was the best way to approach the young woman in front of him, given that she was looking so terrified.

On the other side of the room, the two of them could both see their parents talking amongst themselves. Now and then, one or more of them would glance at Edward and Alessandra. They seemed to be talking about them. That realisation compounded the distress Alessandra felt even more.

Edward was dumbfounded about what he should do. Should he keep trying to talk to her, to draw her out and relax her or would that make her feel even more uncomfortable? Would it be better to not speak, and let her have more time to relax instead?

Alessandra could not raise her eyes to look at the man she was intended to marry. It had all seemed so easy and even a little bit romantic when she'd thought about it in her mind. Being in his presence, she couldn't summon even the smallest amount of confidence in herself. Edward tried to ask questions about her and show an interest in her. Alessandra found herself answering automatically but without thinking enough to provide any additional information to her answers.

Soon dinner was announced and both young people were relieved. They would be separated as both families gathered around the dining table and everyone talked together.

It wasn't an easy evening for anyone. When Alessandra retired that night, she was overwhelmed with emotion. She wasn't unhappy to be in the grand home but she did feel like she'd let her mother down by not being anywhere near as eloquent as she'd been taught to be.

In another part of the house, Edward also was thinking about the evening and the young woman who could become his wife. He knew he wasn't a handsome man but the way she hadn't wanted to talk to him made him feel even more unattractive and unwanted. In his heart, he knew the most important thing was that he wanted to make his mother happy. If the marriage was what she felt was best for him, he would do his best to make it work.

CHAPTER 6

After a restless night, Alessandra was woken by the older woman who had been kind to her the night before, lighting the fire in her room.

"Oh, Miss, I am sorry to have woken you. I was hoping I could do this quietly so the room would be warm before you woke," she said quietly.

"That is alright. I wake up at this time each day anyway. Is the family already up?" Alessandra asked and saw the woman nod as she smiled.

"Yes, they have just gone down for breakfast, Miss, but they do not rush meals so you have time to wash if you wish. I have put some hot water on your dresser there."

Alessandra followed her eyes and saw the welcome sight of the warm water to wash with.

"Thank you," Alessandra said. "I am sorry, I do not even know your name. How should I address you?"

"You can call me Margaret, Miss."

"Thank you, Margaret. I will get dressed now and go down."

"Do you need some assistance, Miss?" Margaret asked.

Alessandra shook her head. "No, I shall be fine. Thank you."

The woman nodded, smiled and left the room to let Alessandra have her privacy.

After climbing out of bed, Alessandra took her time to enjoy the warm water as she splashed it on her face. She made herself presentable and ventured downstairs, wondering if she would remember how to get to the dining room.

After a while, she came across an older man in livery that indicated he was a service staff member. She timidly asked him where the family was. He smiled at her softly and asked her to follow him to doors that he opened before removing himself and disappearing again.

Inside the room, Alessandra could see everyone else was already up and enjoying what appeared to be a banquet of breakfast in front of them. It was so far removed from the quiet little breakfasts she and her parents shared in their home that she felt like she almost wanted to cry at the stark difference. Looking around the table, she could see that the only seat left was between her mother and Edward's mother. Alessandra was relieved until she realised she would be sitting directly across from Edward. The shyness, and resulting embarrassment about the shyness, began all over again.

Edward saw his mother begin a conversation with Alessandra. It seemed a bold attempt to subtly make the young woman feel at ease. After a while, he saw his intended betrothed start to relax a little. While they talked, he watched Alessandra. He tried to figure out whatever he could about her, to file away for further attempts at conversation that would happen later. She was quite plain in looks, but that would not bother him. All he had hoped for was someone he could talk to and be friendly with. So far that was looking unlikely but, for his mother's sake, he was determined to give his best effort.

To the side of him, Alessandra's father was beginning to engage with Edward, asking him about the estate and his life to date. Edward's father had earlier said that Alessandra's family had no social standing, but Edward found Alessandra's parents to both be well-spoken, knowledgeable and very comfortable in their surroundings. There was nothing about them that said they were 'nobody', as his father had said.

The family chatted among themselves until breakfast was cleared and Edward's mother suggested he take Alessandra for a tour of the gardens. Both Edward and Alessandra looked up at that, surprised at the suggestion that they go anywhere alone, but he nodded in response. As they both stood up, Alessandra looked at her mother with a pleading look on her face. Instead of her mother coming to her rescue, she smiled at her and encouraged her to go. The two young people walked out of the room quietly. Alessandra looked at Edward only enough to see where he was leading her. Passing through passageways and doorways, they ventured outside.

Edward led her through different areas of the gardens, chatting as easily as he could about each one's history as he knew it. He wanted Alessandra to feel comfortable and relaxed, but even with his soft nature, he was starting to feel like it was all a bit of a pointless effort. For whatever reason, the young woman quite simply persisted in not talking to him.

They returned to their parents in the drawing room, not having gotten to know each other any better at all.

CHAPTER 7

After another two days and nights of similar feelings and efforts having been made, Edward felt like he had no choice but to assume that Alessandra had no desire to marry him. He spoke to his mother privately about it.

"Edward, you must be patient," she responded to her son's words of sadness.

"Mother, can you not see that she does not want to even be around me?" Edward replied, feeling defeated. "You know as well as I do that I am not handsome and I do not believe I am the kind of man that she wants."

His mother looked at him, distressed at the declaration that his self-esteem was being lowered by the discomfort of the young lady that she had chosen for him.

"Please give her one more day. If she does not soften after another day, I will talk to her and find out what she is thinking," she said, trying to put his mind at rest.

"Yes, Mother," Edward replied sadly. He didn't relish the thought of continuing his efforts for another day or so, only to be rejected again and again.

~~~~~

After dinner that evening, the family again gathered together in the drawing room. Edward and Alessandra sat close to each other at one end of the room while their parents settled at the other. He looked again at the blushing and flustered young woman in front of him. It seemed so useless to put in any effort but he did have determination inside of him, knowing how much it would please his parents.
~~~~~

"Alessandra," he said quietly to her, wanting so much for her to look at him.

At the sound of him saying her name so intimately, Alessandra dared to raise her eyes and look at him.

"Yes?"

"If you do not wish for this marriage, it is quite alright. My parents will not force it," he said.

As soon as he said the words, he saw a brief look of alarm on her face. He also saw worry and a deep blush appear over her skin before she looked down again and she appeared lost to him once more. At that point, he was ready to give up completely. If they couldn't even talk to each other, how likely was it that they could go on to have a happy life together?

The evening passed. That night in bed, Alessandra felt ashamed at herself for having let her nerves take over so much. Now Edward was ready to cancel the arrangement that could otherwise have been suitable for them both if only she could have done better in her efforts to be friendly. With that thought on her mind, she finally went to sleep, determined to make a better effort the following morning.

~~~~~

In his room, Edward stood in front of his looking glass, understanding why Alessandra did not want to know him. He'd never felt he was handsome, but the level of her not wanting to talk to him was taking him to a new level of dislike for himself and what he looked like. He felt caught in a horrible place, wanting to do the right thing for his mother, but wondering at what point he should stop doing that and consider what was right for *him*.
~~~~~

CHAPTER 8

At breakfast the next morning, little had changed. Alessandra was still quiet but did seem to be making somewhat of an effort, at least with Edward's parents. After breakfast, she left the room to find somewhere to be alone and gather her thoughts and her confidence. She found a pleasurable spot inside an enclosed glass room. The space appeared to be used for growing plants but had seats set around inside of it, like seats inside a small jungle.

She was so deep inside her thoughts that she didn't hear the door open.

"Alessandra," said the voice she immediately identified. She forced herself to look up at him.

"Edward," she stammered back at him, feeling the blush coming on again, and cursing herself on the inside once more.

Edward watched her, sitting still and looking stubborn in her effort to not speak to him. He knew he'd reached his point of no return. He could not keep putting in any more effort that only resulted in pain for him. His mother would have to accept that it would never work between them. Taking a deep breath, he started to leave.

"Wait," Edward heard her quiet voice say before he reached the door.

Halting his steps, he looked back at her and saw her standing, facing him. She had such a look of determination on her face that he remained quiet and still, and gave her the time to speak he felt she was due.

"Please," Alessandra pushed out. "Please, sit down

with me."

She moved along so there was room for him on the bench she'd been sitting on. She waited as Edward did as she bid, looking at her with obvious surprise.

"Please, let me speak," Edward heard her say quietly as he watched her face go a darker and darker shade of red. "Although my parents have always told me that this would happen - I would one day go and marry someone I did not know - now that I am here, I am finding it … very difficult…"

"We do not have to get married," Edward said softly, trying to reassure her.

Alessandra stopped him from speaking more.

"Since I came here, you have been nothing but attentive and kind to me, and I am very sorry about this silly insistence my face has to turn into a beetroot so often. It causes me vexation and then I get more frustrated at myself for being so silly…" she continued, determined to say what she wanted to say.

As Edward watched her, he began to feel not only relief but also some light amusement at her words. It seemed a new side of her was starting to reveal itself all of a sudden.

"Please do not think that I wish I were not here, or even that I do not like the thought of marrying you. I…" Alessandra started to say before taking a breath. Finally, she found the strength to look right into his eyes. The move surprised him in her first flush of boldness. "We live in a very small area and I do not remember the last time that I met new anyone new. My skills in conversation are greatly lacking but if you could please be patient with me a little longer, I promise to try harder to relax more around you."

Alessandra stopped speaking for a moment and realised that Edward was watching her face intently. Seeing that resulted in her becoming flushed all over again so she smiled shyly at him.

"See, you do not even need to do anything for my face to go so red," she said, trying to sound light-hearted and make him smile too.

Edward had listened to her and now watched her. As he saw her force herself to look closely at him and smile at him, he was thankful he hadn't rushed to dismiss the idea of marriage to her quite so quickly. He thought she'd finished speaking, and was enjoying just looking at her for the moment, but then she spoke again.

"Could we perhaps start again?" she asked, looking at him, smiling at him despite the extreme redness in her face. She held out her hand to ask for a handshake. "Hello, I am Alessandra and I am very pleased to meet you."

Suddenly Edward felt enchanted by her, as if she had just woven a spell over him. He placed his hand in hers, happy to begin again as she was.

"Alessandra, I am very pleased to meet you too," he said. "I am Edward."

They smiled at each other and at last a moment of relaxation came for both of them at the same time. They were both unaware that from a window nearby, they were being watched by their mothers who were huddled together, having decided between them that they needed to come up with a plan to get their children talking.

"I think we shall not be needed after all," Edward's mother said to Alessandra's, who nodded in return.

"I think you are right. All will be well now."

They both looked on toward their children as, in their minds, they each remembered when they'd met their husbands-to-be. They remembered as clear as day how awkward that had been for each of them. Despite those awkward first moments, both had gone on to spend their lives to date with someone they had grown to love dearly. They could only wish for the same result for their children.

~~~~~
~~~~~

For the rest of that day, Edward and Alessandra started relaxing more and more with each other. They loosened up like a thread being pulled from a very tight cloth.

That evening, they sat near each other in the drawing room, just as they had done each night since Alessandra and her family had arrived. As Edward studied her, he finally saw before him a young woman who had knowledge, dreams, and a desire to do right by her parents.

"Alessandra, I did mean it when I said that we do not have to get married if you do not wish it. I would not want to force anyone to be my wife..." he started to say. Their conversation was finally completely relaxed between them and they had begun to talk like friends who'd known each other for a long time. It pleased and relieved him greatly.

Alessandra looked at him and smiled while reaching out and taking his hand. It was a movement that was new but didn't seem unnatural to her.

"Edward, I thank you for that but I do want to marry you. But if you do not wish it..." she started to say.

Edward instantly squeezed her hand, looking at her in a very different light from what he had done before that day.

"No!" Edward exclaimed. "No, Alessandra, this marriage is a gift from our parents. They all want this and it is important to me to regard their wishes. I want to be married, but I want it to be with someone who wants to work at marriage as much as I do. I think you and I could be happy if we are both willing to work at making each other happy. I *want* to make you happy."

They sat, holding hands and simply happy to have found each other.

From the other side of the room, two sets of parents smiled at each other also.

CHAPTER 9

The next day, Edward and his father excused themselves immediately after breakfast, saying they had to go and attend to some business in a nearby town, taking with them Alessandra's father. The men's absence left Alessandra with her mother and Edward's mother.

"I have asked Cook to prepare a picnic lunch for us. I thought we could enjoy it out in the garden since it is such a lovely day. Soon it will be too cold to enjoy time outside," Edward's mother said.

Later they settled outside on the grass, relaxing with good food and conversation. During that time, Alessandra said little, happy to listen to the two mothers comparing stories as they talked about her and Edward as children. When their conversation turned to their initial experiences with each of their husbands, Alessandra listened intently. She enjoyed the stories they had to tell about their individual levels of determination to make their marriages happy with the men they did not even know.

In the late afternoon, they entered the house to find the men back from their journey. When the woman saw them, it was clear the men had embarked on something enjoyable, judging by the smiles on their faces.

"What mischief have you two been up to?" Edward's mother pressed them in a teasing tone until they gave in.

"Edward has chosen a gift for Alessandra," Edward's father said, smiling at his son.

Alessandra blushed and looked down, making Edward smile now that he understood her blushing was a positive thing, not a negative one.

"Alessandra," Edward said softly to her. "I wished to get you a gift to show you how much I look forward to being your husband. Please come with me."

He stood up, as did his parents, all welcoming Alessandra and her parents to follow. Edward led them all out toward the stables. When they got outside, he looked exceptionally happy and proud as he signalled to a groom to walk out a beautiful white pony that he as a horseman, knew was well suited to Alessandra's petite size. While he expected Alessandra to look surprised, the look on her face wasn't quite one of horror, but it was something indefinable and unexpected.

"This is Misty," he said, uncertain he had done the right thing in buying it for her.

Edward saw Alessandra look desperately at her parents, who equally had indefinable looks on their faces.

"Do you not like her?" Edward finally asked her, confused.

Alessandra stepped up to him so that she was right in front of him. Looking into his eyes, she reached out and took his free hand in one of hers.

"Edward, you are so kind, and she is a wonderful gift, but…" she started to say.

Edward waited patiently for her to continue, fearing that she was going to reject the gift because she wanted to reject *him*. After a long while, he saw her smile sadly at him as she spoke again.

"I can only accept her if you promise to be patient with me as you teach me how to *ride* her," Alessandra continued.

Finally, Edward comprehended what she was saying, and why she had looked uncomfortable.

"You have never ridden a horse?" he asked with a tone of disbelief. He had grown up on horses. He'd ridden since he was a toddler. It hadn't occurred to him that she hadn't done the same.

He saw her smiling with a look of amusement that relaxed him.

"No, never," Alessandra said. "But I am happy to learn if you are happy to teach me."

After the initial shock had passed, Edward smiled brilliantly at her.

"I will gladly teach you to ride," he said happily.

Everyone clapped, reminding the two of them that they were not alone and had an audience.

Alessandra heard Edward's mother call to her and summon her over to her.

"Alessandra, if you do not ride then I suspect you will not own a riding habit?" she asked and saw Alessandra shake her head. "Tomorrow, you and your mother will come with me to my dressmaker and we will get one made up for you. After *that*, Edward can teach you to ride."

~~~~~

Later that evening, in their usual spot, Edward apologised to her.

"I am sorry, Alessandra," he said. "I did not even think to ask if you liked horses…"

"Think nothing of it, Edward," Alessandra said, laughing softly. "I am looking forward to learning something new. You do not have to apologise. I can see you have grown up with horses, so of course you would expect everyone else has too. I look forward to the lessons you are going to give me."

As Edward watched the animation of Alessandra's expressions, he noticed that his appraisal of her had changed. Before, he had considered her quite plain. The more he saw her smiling, he enjoyed looking at her more and more.

"But you must be patient. To me, horses are very large and quite scary," she continued, looking directly at him now that she had begun to force herself to.
~~~~~

In his mind, Edward couldn't imagine being afraid of a horse, but took her at her word and nodded. "I promise. It is not essential for you to know how to ride. If you do not care for it, you do not need to persist in trying to learn."

Alessandra smiled at him softly, enjoying that finally she was finding some confidence to be around him. Although she still blushed often, she was relieved that she no longer let it affect her quite so much.

CHAPTER 10

The following day both mothers escorted Alessandra to get measured up so a riding habit could be designed and prepared for her. In their home she'd had dresses made, of course, but not with the detail or cost that she imagined was currently being invested in her. Her mother was surprisingly relaxed about it. It made Alessandra realise how little she knew about her mother's background. They lived so quietly and simply day to day but as she looked at her mother she could see perfect calm and harmony with being in such surroundings, and with every little thing that happened.

Later that day she approached her mother and asked her to walk in the garden with her. It was an invitation that surprised Isabella as her daughter so rarely asked for anything. As the two of them walked, Alessandra suddenly found herself somewhat shy and afraid to ask the many questions she wanted to.

"What is it, my daughter? I can see you have things on your mind. Are you worried about the marriage? Do you not wish to go through with it?" her mother asked and Alessandra shook her head.

"No!" Alessandra said. "I am very happy to be here, and now that I am getting to know Edward, I think we can both be very happy as husband and wife."

"Then what is it, my child?"

"Before you and Father leave I want to make sure that I know about you. I would like to learn about how you grew up and what kind of life you have lived."

Her mother stopped and looked at her. "You speak as

if we shall never see each other again."

Alessandra looked sad. "Mother, this estate is a long way from home. It might be a very long time before we see each other again. Please tell me about your family, and the home you grew up in."

They sat down on a bench in the sunshine and her mother began to speak. In the two hours that followed Alessandra learned about her mother's childhood in Italy. She learned about Isabella's brothers and sisters, her parents, and the process of becoming betrothed to Alessandra's father. For the first time in her life, Alessandra could see her mother as a woman and not just as her mother.

"Your father has always been very kind to me…" her mother was saying.

"He loves you," Alessandra replied as if it were the natural answer.

"Now, yes. When we met we did not know each other. I was like you - shy and sometimes flustered with myself but he was not deterred," her mother continued, starting to look youthful and blushing herself. "He is a good man. I always knew that, from the moment I first saw him," she said and turned to look at her daughter. "I believe Edward is a good man too. There has been nothing so far that has made me question how he will treat you if he marries you."

Alessandra nodded. "I think so too, Mother. He certainly has been patient with me so far."

The mother and daughter hugged each other and continued to sit quietly, each in their own thoughts.

CHAPTER 11

Over the next week, Alessandra found herself being drawn into more conversation with Edward and both of his parents. Even though they came from such different upbringings and lifestyles, she found that they were both friendly toward her. They didn't seem to judge her for the quiet life that she'd lived till now.

As time passed Alessandra also became aware that, inevitably, one day soon her father and mother would leave and return to their home. They would leave her behind and she would not know when - or even if - she would see either of them again. In pondering that, she found herself becoming morose even though she knew she should only be happy to have been accepted so well into such as family.

"You do not look happy, child," Alessandra heard someone say in the glass room that she had come to enjoy solitude in. When she turned, she saw Edward's father approaching her.

She took a moment to consider how to reply, before speaking. "I know the time is approaching when my mother and father will leave, and I do feel sad about that."

Edward's father sat down beside her and she heard him take a deep breath. "Ahh, one of the saddest things about marriage for a young woman is having to leave her family behind. But Alessandra, your parents are welcome here and can come to stay anytime they wish to," he said with only kindness in his voice.

"Thank you, Sir, but they have little money.

Everything that was left in trust to me will go to Edward when we marry, so they will still have no means to travel this far," she replied. Instantly she regretted having said it, knowing the words could have been interpreted as an offence.

Edward's father only smiled and spoke softly again. "I will let them know that whenever they wish to come, the estate will cover the cost. There will be no need for you to not see them as often as you like. Do not worry about such things." He sat in silence before continuing. "I remember when Edward's mother came here, how upset she was when her father was leaving. Such is the circle of life, but it makes it no easier, does it."

They sat together in silence for a few minutes longer before he stood up to leave. As he approached the door it opened and in walked Edward. Alessandra saw his father whisper something in his ear before he left. Finally, Edward approached the bench she was sitting on and sat down.

"I shall not tell you not to be sad about your parents leaving. I know sadness is not something we can control, but Alessandra, please believe that I will do my best to make you happy," he said quietly.

She smiled at him softly. "I do believe that."

They sat together comfortably until Edward took her hand and brought it to his lips, a show of physical affection that moved her heart unbearably. When she looked at him she started to feel such a longing for him. It was something new that she'd never felt before. As if feeling it also, and needing it to stop, he stood up quickly.

"I think it is time I got you on your horse! Mother said your riding habit has just arrived, so what do you think? Are you feeling brave?"

She stood up as she laughed quietly. "I will certainly give it a go, Edward."

CHAPTER 12

As Alessandra dressed in her riding habit she felt the strangeness of it compared to her usual daily attire. Looking at her reflection in the looking glass, she also appreciated how she looked in it. Edward's mother had chosen a dark burgundy as its colour, with gold trim and accent. To Alessandra it felt luxurious.

Heading downstairs she met Edward waiting at the bottom of the stairs. His face revealed exactly what he thought of the vision before him.

Looking up at her, Edward thought she looked like she had been made for the outfit, rather than the other way around. The colour brought out the brown of her eyes, far more so than her usual clothing. He felt stunned as he looked at her, but was brought out of his thoughts as she approached him, stood at his eye level and smiled at him.

"I am so thankful to your mother for her kindness toward me, as I do love this," she said, running her hands over the front of her new clothes. "Do you?"

He took a deep breath and looked at her full length before meeting her eyes again. "Yes. You look beautiful in it."

Seeing her start to blush again, Edward smiled at her in amusement as they both relaxed once more. "Come, Alessandra, my wife to be. It is time," he said and led her out to the stable.

Outside, the groom had already prepared her pony for her. Alessandra saw the groom walk it forward so it was closer to her. She continued to watch as Edward took the reins.

"Before you learn to ride, I think it might be best if you simply get used to being around her. Come closer," he said, prompting her to move forward to the animal that, to her, looked like a giant. "She is quite calm and peaceful, but always approach her from this angle and quietly so she can start to get used to you as well."

Alessandra moved closer to Edward and the pony. She stood so that her back was to Edward, and he was standing close behind her. They were both aware of it but it only felt right and not at all uncomfortable.

She reached up tentatively, moving toward touching the great animal in front of her, but found herself nervous again. Her hand stopped midair. She felt Edward lean forward to take her hand and gently place it on the pony's neck, guiding her in stroking softly. As he did so, he moved closer to her so that his front was lightly touching her back. Alessandra felt comforted by his presence so close. Inside she could feel herself shaking, due to both the regal animal in front of her and Edward standing so close to her. She determined to try to not let her anxiety show.

Both sets of parents looked on from where they stood. Mothers looked knowingly at each other and smiled. Even if the young ones had no idea how they were affecting each other, their mothers could see it clearly.

<center>~~~~~</center>

After what seemed like a long time, standing close to her pony and adjusting to being in such close vicinity to it, Alessandra heard Edward ask if she might like to just sit on the saddle. She looked at him with fear showing on her face but she smiled at him and said she would try. He admired her braveness whilst making sure he would not get ahead of himself in teaching her to ride.

He demonstrated to her what she needed to do once he lifted her up. As he did so, she followed his instruction, as the studious student she was in all that she learned. Sitting up on the horse she felt like she was on top of a mountain. She felt so high, even though at a logical level she could see the ground wasn't too far away. She let Edward put her feet in the stirrups, while he never let go of the reins. He watched her just sit there momentarily, not knowing what to do next.

"Are you alright?" he asked her. She kept her eyes on his while she nodded.

He smiled up at her with his hand on her thigh, a small gesture that meant nothing but felt extremely intimate to her. Alessandra looked over at her mother. Isabella was smiling the broadest smile Alessandra had ever seen on her. Alessandra delivered a small, scared smile in response.

"Hold on to this," Edward said, placing her hands where he wanted them to be. "I am going to walk her just a little bit. If it scares you, you need to let me know."

She nodded at him, doing as he instructed but now feeling a greater fear inside of her.

The pony suddenly started moving. Alessandra held on tight, finding the new sensation of sitting on a moving animal very strange indeed. As she forced herself to relax and look into Edward's eyes when he turned to face her, she found herself adjusting to it and her fear relaxed off.

Edward kept looking at her, even as he slowly walked the pony around the stable yard. He could visibly see her face changing in its level of relaxation. He considered how brave she was as he tried to think of the last time he'd tried anything completely new that he had never done before.

Alessandra sat and rode the pony for as long as it took before Edward stopped and looked up at her, again with his hand on her thigh.

"How are you feeling, Alessandra?" he asked,

smiling but at the same time looking concerned that she might not be enjoying it after all.

She took a deep breath and smiled down at him. "I am fine. With this I feel alright," she reassured him. She could visibly see him let out a breath that he had been holding.

"Do you want to take the reins?" he asked but she shook her head.

"Could I try that tomorrow? I would very much like to get used to only one thing at a time," she said, letting out a little, frail laugh.

Edward smiled up at her and made sure the pony was secure before lifting Alessandra down to the ground again. As he did, her knees almost gave way to her when her feet touched the ground. He laughed with her as she almost fell with nervousness. His quick responses ensured he caught her before she fell.

"Remain still for a minute, Alessandra. Let your legs adjust to being on the ground again," he said.

Alessandra did as he instructed, revelling in being so close to him. With both of his arms supporting her, she felt secure and safe.

"Thank you for being so patient with me," she said, almost in a whisper, they were so close. She was looking at his face so closely - his eyes and his mouth. In that, she felt like she did not want to stop.

Edward felt her eyes intently focused on him. He fought to control his emotion as he looked at their parents standing not too far away. "You are going to be fine. We shall do a little bit each day, and I am sure you will be a confident horsewoman in no time," he said, tearing his eyes away from her lips.

CHAPTER 13

The next day Alessandra went through a similar ritual again. After putting on her riding habit she walked with Edward out to the stable. There he helped her up onto her pony and led her around, helping her to feel more comfortable.

"Are you ready to try taking the reins yourself?" he finally asked. She looked so afraid that for a moment he thought he'd made the completely wrong suggestion to her. Then he saw her she smile through that fear.

"I can try. But she will not be able to run off with me, will she?" she asked, timidly.

Edward smiled at her. "We are in an enclosed space and the gates are all closed. I am sure she will not run, but if she does you need to hold on and relax. Soon enough she will stop."

He had meant to relax her but instead made her feel more afraid than she had been. When he handed her the reins and talked her through what to do with her hands and her legs, to guide the pony, she found herself automatically in student mode again, set on learning and practising what he was teaching her.

As she started to move off by herself, putting her theory into practice, Alessandra felt a blend of fear mixed in with pride as she realised she was riding a horse! When she wanted it to move left, it was moving left. When she wanted it to move right, it was moving right. She found it exhilarating. She didn't want to trot or move quickly in any way so she was happy enough being on the pony as it walked slowly around the stable yard. She didn't dare look up at anyone else. She wanted to just maintain her concentration purposely on the pony and her alone.

"Can you walk her back to me?" she heard Edward call out. She looked up briefly to see where he was from her. With confidence slowly growing, she moved the pony closer to him.

As she neared him he came up to her and smiled brilliantly up at her. "You are a natural," he said to her and saw her instantly blush. "After a few more days of this we shall take the horses out for a slow walk together up to the summit," he continued, pointing up the hill not far from the house.

Alessandra looked at Edward doubtfully and he laughed at her.

"We will go at a pace you are comfortable with. Do not worry," he said, helping her down from the pony again.

Today their parents were not nearby, watching. Knowing that, Edward took longer before he set her apart from him, enjoying being so close to her again. In the evenings he'd started to feel himself thinking about her in her future role as his wife. He knew things were changing inside of him, as he considered her in a much different way from when she'd first arrived.

CHAPTER 14

A few days later Alessandra rose and made her way down to breakfast, as had become her usual daily routine. On entering the room, everyone smiled at her in a way that made her certain something had been discussed about her, without her there. After a few minutes of sitting at the table, her assumption was proven correct.

"I hear Edward is taking you up to the summit today, Alessandra," Edward's mother said. Alessandra looked across the table and saw her future husband grinning broadly at her. His smile was combined with a look that also showed his wonder at whether he was rushing her into something she wouldn't want to do.

"Oh? Is today that day?" she asked him, teasing him and making him smile even more.

"Yes, if you have no objection. I think you are confident enough for us to walk the horses up at the pace you wish to set," he said, with his look of amusement well set in now. "Do you have any objection?"

She looked at him, aware that four parents were also at the table, and kept silent for a moment to tease him in anticipation some more. "No, I look forward to it," she replied after teasing him with her silence. His relief was evident by the loud exhale of breath that immediately came from him.

"I shall ask Cook to prepare some picnic food to take with you. Since the weather looks fine enough you can luncheon up there also," Edward's mother said, a satisfied smile very evident on her face.

~~~~~

Two hours later Alessandra sat on her pony, nervous about leaving the confines of the stable yard but also excited at again having something new to try and do. She watched Edward expertly and confidently mount his horse and slowly come up beside her.

"Are you ready?" he asked, with that smile of happiness and doubt blended together.

She nodded at him, so nervous she was unable to speak. Off to her side, she could see her parents standing together, arms around each other's backs, watching. She nodded to them and then focused on Edward.

"Stay behind me. All you have to do is look at my horse, and follow me," he said, smiling at her one more time before he walked ahead slightly.

The gate was opened and both of them walked slowly through it, allowing Alessandra the view of Edward's back. She found herself wishing she could talk to him, but she was so nervous that she knew she had to concentrate heavily on what she was doing, otherwise she would make a mistake that might take her off in a different direction - literally.

Edward looked back at her now and then but for the most part, kept his eyes forward whilst ensuring his horse remained at a slow pace. He could feel Beauty wanting to move much faster. He understood the desire completely.

Up they climbed. To Alessandra, it felt like it was going on forever, but then all of a sudden she heard Edward's voice.

"We are here," he said. "Look."

As she looked up Alessandra realised they were very high above the level of the house. Around her, she could see land for miles.

Edward dismounted and tied the rein of his horse to a nearby tree that had on many occasion served that very purpose. He then moved next to her, helped her down,
~~~~~

and walked her pony to the same tree to be secured. Alessandra stood and looked out over the land. In all directions the view was beautiful. As a result, she found herself awestruck.

"Are you hungry?" Edward asked as he started to unpack the compact picnic bag Cook had presented him with before they had left.

Alessandra nodded and moved to help him set out the large blanket and selection of food on the ground. They both sat, in awe of the view from where they were.

"I never tire of this spot, Alessandra," Edward said. "All of this land that you see, right to the bottom of those hills over there, is part of the estate."

She turned to look at him and instantly saw the incredible level of pride on his face. She'd never known anyone who owned land of such size and was in awe of having found herself in the position she could potentially be in.

Edward felt her looking at him and turned to face her. For a moment they stared openly at each other's faces and into each other's eyes before manners told Edward he should stop. He looked down at the food and laughed. "My mother seems to have requested enough food to feed us for a week. Do you think she had plans of us not coming home today, perhaps?"

Alessandra laughed with him, also looking down at the many types of food in front of them. "Well, I am quite hungry, truth be known. These strawberries, in particular, look delicious," she said, holding one up. "Were they grown here?"

He beamed at being able to respond so positively to her. "Yes, all of this was grown or made here. We are quite self-sufficient on the estate, which we are very lucky for," he responded. He picked up a small piece of cheese and popped it in his mouth as he watched Alessandra devour the strawberry she had been holding. They ate in silence for a while, just looking out over the view while both indulged in their individual thoughts.

"Alessandra, do you still want to marry me? If there is any reason why you do not, please do tell me," Edward said softly, surprising her.

Alessandra looked at him but he had his head down, seeming to purposely not look at her directly as he asked the question. She sat silently and waited for him to look up. Finally he did after not having heard any response from her.

"I very much want to marry you, Edward. Why would I not?" she asked, wondering why he was asking such a question when they had been getting on so well in recent days.

"I know I am not handsome like other men..." he started, for the first time sounding flustered in her presence.

Alessandra placed her hand on his and brought it to her lips, just as he had done to her not too long before. "Edward, I do not want to marry anyone because of what they look like or do not look like. I want to marry a good man who I truly believe will work with me to create a good, happy marriage as my parents have. I see how your parents are with each other and I believe that you have had the same good example that I have. You too have grown up seeing how a husband and wife can be toward each other - kind, generous and loving," she said and he nodded at her words.

"My parents have always seemed very happy together," he replied. "I have always hoped I could find someone who I could have the same thing with, but of course marriage is more about transactions than anything else. Truth be told, I would accept anyone my parents felt was right for their purposes."

He was silent as they both considered what he'd just said. "It's important to me that you know that although my parents found you, Alessandra, having you here has shown me that I know I can love you, regardless of their wishes. It is not just to please my parents that I am eager for us to wed," he said, looking more intently at her. Inside he felt a strength of longing for her that he had never felt before. He saw her look at him just as intently, as though she could see right into his soul through his eyes.

"I am eager for that also, Edward," she said as they looked deeply at each other.

"Alessandra, may I kiss you?" he asked, slightly embarrassed but not so much so that he would not ask.

"Yes," she replied, nervous but excited at the prospect of receiving her very first kiss.

Edward looked at her, aware that he'd never kissed anyone before and didn't know how it worked. It had to be enough that he just knew inside of him it was something he needed to do.

Slowly they both moved forward toward each other and tentatively placed their lips together. They took time to move their lips against each other's and explore how it felt in reality, after reading and thinking about such an action. They sat like that for a long while, not touching in any way other than their lips lightly caressing. Edward could feel reaction elsewhere too. It was another new feeling he'd not experienced before. He was embarrassed by it but hoped it wouldn't show through his clothing. He had woken like that from time to time - hard - but it had never happened during daylight hours and in the presence of anyone else.

Alessandra relished the feeling of his lips on hers and equally felt other parts of her body responding to their shared kisses. She wasn't even sure if she was meant to be allowing him to kiss her, given that they were not yet husband and wife, but the feelings it was invoking in her were exquisite. She didn't want them to stop.

Edward, feeling his embarrassment heighten, pulled away from her slowly and looked at her before moving his eyes down to the food again.

"Perhaps we should eat," he said simply.

Alessandra laughed at his effort to relax the moment, resulting in him smiling and laughing softly also.

~~~~~

That evening, after their journey to and from the hill summit, it was evident to all parents that something had changed between their children. At the evening meal, the parents broached the subject of the wedding.

"Should we perhaps set a date, if everyone here is happy about this marriage?" Edward's father asked, throwing surprise at all gathered around the table with his unexpected candour.

Alessandra and Edward looked at each other, each of them hoping inside that the date would be sooner rather than later. Everyone was quiet, not sure who should speak and who should not, so Edward's father continued.

"Alessandra, are there any particular considerations you wish to have noted for your wedding day?" he asked her, making her blush furiously with the attention such a question brought upon her. She looked at Edward and saw him silently prompting her.

"Only that my parents are here, Sir, and that if my brother and his family would like to attend, they are welcome to," she replied quietly.

"You have no other wishes for the wedding ceremony itself? No luxury chariot to bring you to your husband to be? No groups of friends from your home to attend?" he asked, playfully. She relaxed in seeing he was open to whatever she asked for.

"No, thank you. I need only my family."

Edward's father turned to Alessandra's parents and they talked among themselves of possible dates that suited their own needs. It was decided.

"Two weeks from today then," Alessandra and Edward heard his father say. They both turned to him, feeling excited inside. "We shall host it here in our chapel. I shall leave it up to you to invite whoever you
~~~~~

wish to attend," he continued, addressing Alessandra's parents, who nodded in return.

~~~~~

After the evening meal, they all made their way to the drawing room again. It felt like a well-established routine now, with Alessandra and Edward at their one end of the room and their parents at the other.

"Are you sure this is what you want, Alessandra? It is not too late if you have any reservations," Edward asked again.

She took his hand and held it as she smiled at him. "I am sure. Are you sure you wish to marry me?" she counter asked him, wondering if his questioning was in some way an indication of him not wanting to marry.

Edward looked at her, finding his eyes again and again wanting to return to her lips. The memory of their first kiss instilled in him another yearning of longing for kissing her again.

"My only regret is that we have to wait two whole weeks," he said quietly, not realising he had said it out loud. Alessandra giggled quietly at him, causing him to blush in the realisation that he had indeed voiced his thoughts.

As he shyly looked at her, Alessandra saw before her the man who would soon become her husband. She felt herself blush at that thought also. Aware she was still holding his hand, she looked down at the two hands intertwining, and found her fingers lightly moving over and around his. They said nothing. The only way they were touching was through their joined hands, but once again such beautiful feelings occurred inside Edward and Alessandra both. They sat like that for a long time, mesmerised by just two hands getting to know one another so intimately.

From a distance, Alessandra's mother watched them quietly. Seeing the looks on their faces she silently remembered how that felt - the getting to know one
~~~~~

another physically stage. It had been so long since she and her husband had been intimate in any way, not for any reason other than it seemed to have just fallen away from them. When she turned away from the young couple and focused on the conversation at hand once again, she caught her husband's eye and knew that he knew what she was thinking about. She could also read that he was thinking about the same thing.

CHAPTER 15

Over the following two weeks, Alessandra felt like she was in a whirlwind, being asked so many questions by so many people. While the household took care of the physical aspects of the wedding, for Alessandra it meant being fitted for a wedding dress, among other things. She found herself quite overwhelmed by it all.

During that time she and Edward escaped when they could to head up to the summit. It was expected by everyone that the weather would soon be bitterly cold. They both felt determined to embrace the freedom they presently had to escape outdoors.

Two days before the wedding, they sat up on the summit again, noting the change in the landscape already as real winter was due to set in.

"Are you nervous about being married?" Edward asked her, looking at her face as she looked out over the land.

She considered the question as she turned to face him. "There are aspects of it that make me nervous," she said demurely, casting her eyes from his for a moment.

He watched her look away and then bring her eyes back to his before he leaned in and kissed her. Over the previous two weeks, they had become quite accustomed to kissing. He indulged in it again, loving the feeling of the softness of her lips. Always the result was the same for him, embarrassingly, but he had come to realise that when he grew hard, she had no awareness of it, so it no longer worried him as much. He always made sure that he had relaxed again before they stood up to return home. He knew the mechanics of mating. Growing up on an estate like his, with so many farm stock, he couldn't have missed it. He believed that the core of conceiving was the same with humans so it wasn't that part of marriage that he looked forward to. It was the kissing that he found himself yearning for more of.

He pulled away, knowing they would have to head back to the house soon and wanting to be relaxed before they did. He didn't think the way she affected him was visible to others through his clothing but he didn't want to take the risk.

"It won't be long and we will have winter upon us," Edward said, breaking his chain of thought. "When that strikes, we are often snowed in here for weeks," he continued as he watched her face recover from her emotions that seemed to strike when they kissed. "Will you be comfortable with that, do you think?"

Alessandra refocused on him and his question and took time to answer while nodding. "I think so. Will I have to learn how to run the estate also? I know your mother has her responsibilities. I do not know if I am expected to step up and learn them also, or if I am to leave them to her still," she said, thinking out loud.

He looked surprised. "I do not know, to be honest. I will ask her if you like."

She nodded at him. "Yes please, Edward. I would not like to cause any offence to your mother by doing something I should not, or not doing something I should."

He looked at her, appreciating the ease of the relationship building between his wife to be and his mother. He'd never had many friends but he was certainly aware that those particular relationships did not always go smoothly at all.

"You must guide me, Edward, as this is all new to me. Please do not ever assume that I will just know what I am supposed to be doing."

"You have my promise. And you must promise me that you will tell me if I do anything to make you unhappy, for I have never been a husband so it will be a learning experience for me also."

They both sat silent until the cold reached a point where it was time to leave.

~~~~~

That evening Edward sat with her and held her hand again.

"I will be leaving soon to go and stay with my aunt and uncle in Bath. I will not see you again until our wedding day," he said, with a slight emotional tinge to his voice.

"I look forward to then," Alessandra replied quietly.

When Edward looked into her eyes he could see she had the same look that she had when they kissed. Instantly he felt fuelled in desire again so quickly turned the conversation away to mundane topics so he could relax before having to leave.

~~~~~

"Edward, it is time," Charles said. He was eager to get on the road to escort his son to Bath, where he would see the brother he did not often see anymore.

"Yes, Father," Edward responded before lifting Alessandra's hands to his lips, bidding her farewell and walking out.

After he left, Alessandra's mother came and sat next to her. "Alessandra, you do still want to get married, do you not?" she asked, surprising her daughter.

"Yes, of course, Mother! I regard Edward very highly, and I look forward to being his wife."

Isabella was relieved. She had been worrying that perhaps her daughter was moving forward with the wedding plan purely to satisfy others. She could see from the way Edward and Alessandra had been acting towards each other that they did like each other. It was a great relief after the first few days of discomfort when they'd first come to the estate.

Edward's mother and Alessandra's father joined them. Between them, they moved the conversation on to neutral topics to help each other feel relaxed about everything.

CHAPTER 16

Two days later, Alessandra sat in her room with people all around her, fussing over her hair and her gown, making everything look perfect. Inside herself, all she could think about was seeing Edward again. The strongest thought was how she would soon sleep beside him as his wife. The idea both excited her and scared her.

Before leaving to go to the chapel, her mother requested everyone leave the room so she could have some time alone with her daughter.

"Are you worried about tonight?" she asked quietly.

Alessandra shook her head. "No, Mother. I know it is my duty to bear children."

Her mother looked embarrassed and like she was trying to formulate the right words in her head, before speaking. "The … act … it is something that I know many women do not enjoy and do only for their husband's pleasure or to conceive a child, but Alessandra, it can be pleasurable also. There is no shame in enjoying what you will share with your husband, and if it is not pleasurable, do not keep quiet about it. Talk to him and work together in that part of your marriage," she said, looking extremely flustered in herself. "Many would disagree with me telling you this, but I have had too many friends who have talked about it as though it was the most disagreeable thing in the world, and yet I know that it does not have to be that way. I will say no more about it as it is making you and I both uncomfortable. Edward will be good to you. I know he will."

Alessandra hugged her mother and enjoyed what she knew might be the last time she would see her for a long while. "Mother, you have chosen well for me and I thank you for not pressuring me, but I am happy."

~~~~~

Two hours later Edward and Alessandra stood at the altar in the small chapel, both eager to get through the ceremony so they could be pronounced husband and wife at last. Finally, it was all over and they were walking out of the chapel with dried rose petals being thrown over them by the bucketful, making them both laugh in their happiness. With the chapel being on the estate land, it was a short walk back to the house. Edward and Alessandra walked side by side while holding hands.

Alessandra looked at her husband and felt a desire and need to spend time with him alone, away from the masses of people who had watched the ceremony. She regretted it would be hours before she and Edward would be able to be in private.

Edward felt the same inside of him. Even holding her hand was enough to make him feel somewhat excited at the prospect of the two of them being alone and in the private confines of what would be their marriage bed. Desperate to not let those thoughts keep taking over his mind, he had to keep talking to people about anything but his wife and upcoming marriage night.

~~~~~

After much feasting and festivity, the time came when the young couple would leave everyone else and be alone together. Alessandra was taken to a new room, away from what had been her bedchamber since she'd arrived in the manor house. There, Margaret helped her to undress from her gown and get into a nightdress. She had become a regular support and help to Alessandra in previous weeks, and, despite their age difference, the closest person Alessandra regarded as a friend.

As Margaret stood behind the young woman and brushed out her long hair, Alessandra let her mind wander to the night ahead. Margaret could sense everything and so remained quiet. Finally, she helped Alessandra into the large bed in the room, said goodnight, and left the new bride alone. Alessandra sat up in the bed with the covers pulled up over her chest, not sure what she should do, if anything.

In another room, across the hall, Edward was similarly prepared and put into a nightshirt, before being led into the marital room and the door shut behind him silently. He felt vulnerable in only a nightshirt. When he laid his eyes on Alessandra, he could see she was just as apprehensive.

He climbed into the bed and lay down beside her. He faced her as she moved downward and lay facing him also. They didn't touch. For a long while, they just looked at each other.

"My wife," Edward finally said, taking in what she looked out with her hair out.

She smiled at him meekly. "My husband."

He returned the smile and they both thought of ways to remedy the discomfort they felt.

"You are so beautiful," he said, reaching his hand out to touch her cheek and hair.

She felt an overwhelming surge of emotion and leaned in slowly to kiss him on the lips, just as they had already done so many times. They didn't move for anything more, just enjoying kissing as they lay facing each other but not touching any other part of their bodies.

Edward felt that part of him grow. He understood it was necessary for the conception of a child, but still disliked that his body reacted so harshly when he wanted to take things slowly and find his way as they both felt comfortable with.

Kissing him more and more, Alessandra felt a strong longing to be closer to him. She moved forward so that she could put her arms around him and hold him while they kissed. As the gap closed between them, she felt it, rigid and hard against her stomach.

"Oh!" she said before thinking. She saw Edward blush considerably, even in the dim light of the room.

Edward remembered that she hadn't grown up on a farm and possibly didn't know the mechanics of how mating was performed. He then found himself wondering what to say or do, but with her inquisitive mind, he wasn't surprised to find she was completely open in her questioning and wonder.

"Are you always like that?" she asked timidly, but also with the confidence that told Edward she would view joining just as she did learning to ride a horse or learning to run a household. She had an amazing ability to compartmentalise learning as something to ask questions about until she understood it.

He initially found the discomfort at his embarrassment unbearable. He then remembered how she had been when she'd first come to his home, and how hard she'd fought with herself to get over that.

"No, but always when I am kissing you," he said quietly, stroking her cheek and watching her face.

"That is what … you will … put into me, to make a child?" she asked, blushing profusely herself now, but with determination on her face to question and learn.

"Yes."

"Can I look at you?" she asked, shocking Edward in the process. After a moment he realised he didn't want his body to always be a source of embarrassment so he should view her question as an opportunity to help things seem easier after this night.

"Yes," he replied and gulped heavily. He watched her face as she pushed back the covers that were over him. She raised his nightshirt enough to be able to see him.

Alessandra had read novels so she had gained some understanding from them at how the baby-making process worked. When she looked at that part of Edward, she was surprised at how it looked.

"Can I touch you?" she asked, tentatively.

"Yes."

Alessandra reached down with her hand and let her fingertips run over him, until a moan escaped from him, making her pull her hand back.

"I'm sorry! Does that hurt?"

Edward felt awkward but surged ahead in his feigned confidence. "No, quite the opposite, Alessandra. When you touched me it felt wonderful, like I have not felt before."

She put her fingers back on him, and moved them over him while watching his face and listening to him moan again. She saw him open his eyes and look at her before he leaned in and kissed her. She boldly closed her hand around him while she enjoyed the kissing he was indulging her in. They didn't stay like that for long before he pulled away from the kiss.

"Oh … Alessandra, I do not know what is happening, but I feel … oh … do not stop," he moaned at her and closed his eyes. She continued her fondling and then all of a sudden he seemed to experience great pain, as he moaned loudly and his body seemed to convulse. She realised that a considerable amount of wetness had escaped him and was all over her hand and nightgown.

She watched his face, worried that she'd done something wrong and hurt him. When he opened his eyes, she saw him look content and then smile.

"Are you alright?" she asked and he laughed softly.

"I have never felt anything like that. I do not even know how to explain it. It was like a volcano building to an eruption, and then a release."

He kissed her again, making her melt in her longing before she pulled away. She brought up her hand, which was covered in moisture. "Then this is what makes a baby?"

He looked at her hand, very embarrassed, but nodded. "I think so."

She touched him gently again but he pulled her hand away, wiped it with his nightgown and then raised it to his mouth to kiss it.

"Do you think you could have the same feeling in you as you just made me feel?" he asked, now wondrous about her body also.

"I do not know. Do you think it can be as nice for a woman?" she asked, remembering how her mother had told her that some women found the act distasteful and awful, while at the same time implying that it was not like that at all.

"Alessandra," Edward found the confidence to ask. "Can I see you?"

She nodded slowly at his question and watched him as he pushed the cover back on her side of the bed now. He slowly raised her nightgown to above her hips. He had no idea about the female form and wanted to explore.

"Can I touch you?" he asked and she nodded again.

He tentatively reached his fingers out and touched the top of her thigh and the hair that was visible. It was all tucked away, he realised, so he did not know what he could touch - if anything. He slowly caressed the area as he could, and heard her breathing change.

"You will tell me if I hurt you," he said to her and she nodded.

As he caressed more, Alessandra felt a natural desire to open her thighs slightly. Edward moved his hand between them, feeling more and more down and around where the hair was growing. As he let his fingers move inwards of what felt like lips to him, he heard a quiet 'oh' escape from Alessandra's lips. Edward looked at her face. She was looking right into his eyes, with the same look he had seen on her face sometimes when they had kissed.

"There," she whispered. He looked to see the location she seemed to want him to touch and moved his finger back and forth across the small pea-like piece of skin he could feel. He watched her face and could see her excitement.

"Keep going," she whispered, encouraging him to continue. As he did, he felt himself growing again in the excitement that he was also experiencing.

"Oh, Edward ... something is ... oh!" he heard her moan as she seemed to also convulse before him. He watched her face as she relaxed back and finally opened her eyes and looked at him.

She suddenly started to giggle, making him smile more. "I guess that can happen to men and women," she said between giggles.

They lay together for a while in silence before she spoke again.

"It will be expected that I will get pregnant, to give you an heir," she said to him and he nodded.

"Yes, my parents would expect that," Edward replied.

"But this is not how we can make a baby," she said and he nodded again.

"That is true."

"Edward?" she asked and he looked at her closely. "Do we need to rush for me to become with child? Can we take some time to just get to know each other like this first? When my brother's wife conceived I overheard him talking about how he then had to sleep apart from her until some time after the baby was born. Could we perhaps not rush to that?"

Edward heard her words and pleasantly agreed with her. "I would like to get to know you more before we bring another little person into the world," he said and kissed her again, making her melt and move closer again, to find him hard once more.

"Can I touch you again?" she asked and he laughed at her.

"I think so," he said quietly before she resumed touching him with her hand once again, making him excited until he again climaxed.

Both of them felt the effects of such a long day. Edward pulled her into his arms and held her, until he felt her drift off to sleep, after which he did the same, silently thanking his mother once again for choosing his wife.

CHAPTER 17

The following morning Alessandra woke up to find herself intertwined in Edward. He had his arm over her, while her leg seemed to be thrown over his. He was still asleep and she was alarmed when she heard someone else in the room, making up the fire. After initial surprise and shock at the discovery, she realised that the bed she was sharing with Edward had curtains around it and they were not at all visible to whoever was also in the room. She lay quietly and looked at her husband. She loved the word. Her husband! Her mind drifted back to the nice things they had learned about each other the night before.

As she listened, she could hear the person outside the curtain finishing up the lighting of the fire and the laying of hot water on the dresser. The door opened and closed quietly and there was silence again. Alessandra extracted herself enough from Edward to be able to peek out from the curtain. When she did, she could see that no-one else was in the room and the fire was starting to warm up. She huddled back to the spot she had been and felt Edward start to stir.

When he woke up he opened his eyes and was happy to see Alessandra there still. He pulled her close and kissed her.

"Good morning, my beautiful wife," he said.

Alessandra melted against him, kissing him with a fervour that woke him up immediately.

He lowered his hand to touch her as he had the night before and she moaned in his arms as she moved her hand and touched him at the same time. They kissed deeply, touching each other until one and then the other exploded in blissful pleasure, after which they continued kissing.

Finally, Edward pulled away, breathless but smiling. "We do have to leave this bed today, you do know," he said as Alessandra smiled shyly at him.

She suddenly remembered that her parents were leaving that day.

Edward saw a shadow pass over her face. "What is it?" he asked.

She looked very sad as she replied. "My mother and father are going home today. I shall miss them very much, Edward."

He pulled her to him and held her tighter. "You can see them whenever suits you all. They are welcome here, Alessandra, anytime they wish to visit, and we can go and see them too."

She pulled back and looked at him with a glimmer of hope in her eyes. "Really? You would be happy for us to go and visit sometimes?"

He laughed with her. "Of course. You have seen where I grew up, so of course I am curious to see where you grew up," he said. Alessandra suddenly felt ashamed of her home, uncertain and embarrassed that he should see it. She changed the subject quickly.

"We definitely should get up," she said and after kissing more, they began their first day together as husband and wife. They found a new adventure in seeing each other dress and do things in the quiet privacy of their marriage room.

~~~~~

After breakfast, Alessandra prepared to say goodbye to her parents, but not before her mother had pulled her aside to talk to her quietly. "Are you alright, my daughter? He did not hurt you?" Isabella asked quietly, looking at Alessandra's face to read how it was for her.
~~~~~

Alessandra smiled. "All is well, Mother. You do not need to worry," she said, putting her mother's mind was put to rest. "Edward and I shall be well together. He has also told me that you and Father are welcome to stay here whenever you wish to. Please do come back and see me."

Her mother and her father both hugged her before leaving, and even her father surprised her in his words before he left the manor.

"If he treats you in a way that makes you unhappy, you must send word to us immediately and we will help you to come home, Alessandra. Too many women stay in situations they should not. Promise me you will ask for help if you need it," he said, in the most solemn voice she had ever heard her father use.

She nodded at him. "Father, I will be fine but, yes, if I need help I shall be certain to ask you for it."

Soon they were off on their way back home, leaving Alessandra standing on the manor doorstep watching after they had long disappeared from view.

"Alessandra, come. The weather is too cold to stay out here. Let us go indoors," Edward said, putting his arms around her completely in a full standing hug, openly for the very first time.

She responded by putting her arms around him and kissing him deeply, not caring who would see them. Through their clothing, she felt him press against her, hard. She giggled as he looked sheepish in the realisation that she had woken him up again.

"Perhaps we do need to stay here for a few minutes after all," he said, making her giggle more. They stood like that until he felt it was safe to be walking around again.

CHAPTER 18

Over the next few days and nights, Edward and Alessandra indulged in further getting to know each other. It wouldn't be long before they would both be engaged in their ongoing learning about efficiently running the estate together. The prospect was frightening to Alessandra but she already knew that Edward's mother was accepting of her, and a patient and kind woman. That knowledge helped reduce her fear of expectations about her.

Each night the newlyweds eagerly awaited the time when they could go to their room and pleasure each other. Always it was the same, but for those first few nights, it was enough.

On the fourth night of their marriage, Edward entered the room, expecting his wife to be in bed as usual. At first sight, not seeing her, he was alarmed. When he turned his head he saw her, standing in her nightgown in front of the fire.

He walked up to her, concerned something might have happened. "Are you well, my love?" he asked. She turned to look at him with such an intense passion that he was overwhelmed with his desire for her.

"Edward, will you look at me?" Alessandra asked. Edward was confused as to what she meant. When he didn't reply but only gave her a look of not understanding, she continued. "We have started to know each other's bodies, but we have not completely seen each other. Will you look at me?" she asked again and he nodded, still not entirely certain what she wanted but sensing it was important to her.

"Will you remove this?" she asked him, holding one section of her nightgown.

Edward felt his throat and mouth go dry as he finally understood what she wished for. He moved forward to her and kissed her while taking the fabric in his hand and starting to lift it. She pulled away from him slightly and lifted her arms, providing him with the opportunity to lift the nightgown completely from her. He saw her stand before him, naked. She had thought about it and had not been certain how she would feel, being in such a vulnerable position. With the way he was looking at her, she felt confident and not afraid at all.

Edward drank in the sight before him. He had never seen the female form naked before. He was overcome by an intense longing to touch, kiss and explore. As he moved closer to hold her and kiss her again, she welcomed his hands and mouth moving over her.

His hands explored her breasts and touched her nipples, making Alessandra moan. It thrilled Edward to realise that he had found another pleasure point. He guided her to the two-person seat near the fire and lowered her so he could kneel in front of her. Once she was seated he began kissing her everywhere. Her neck, her breasts, her nipples and over her belly all received his attention. His lips needed to touch everywhere on her body. He kept kissing downward, even to the inside of her thighs. Tentatively he tried to kiss her where she had guided him on their wedding night with his finger. As soon as his mouth touched her there, she seemed to melt completely, with her legs spread wide. He could feel himself stretching with a level of hardness he hadn't experienced before.

"Yes," he heard her moan as his mouth pleasured her. It wasn't long before he felt her explode as his lips were still on her. He realised he had just found new things about her, and a new way to give her pleasure. Taking his time, he kissed his way back up her body, particularly enjoying her breasts again before kissing her on the lips.

Alessandra had thought the pleasure from his finger was joy enough. As strange as it was to feel him kiss her in such a private place, it was also something of a new level of pleasure for her. When she was recovered and kissing him, she turned her mind to him, knowing he was also highly aroused. She pushed him away and invited him to stand up with her. She pulled his nightshirt up and over his head until he was standing before her unclothed. They moved together, embracing for the first time completely naked. She marvelled at his shoulders and chest, touching him all over and learning that he too liked his nipples to be touched.

She did to him as he had done to her - edged him back until he sat on the seat. His arousal stood up fully and looked different in the light of the fire rather than in their bed. She acted as he had, kissing him around his neck, and over his chest, hearing him moan as she kissed his nipples, and working her way down until she, too, ventured to pleasure him with her mouth. As soon as her lips touched him he moaned. She didn't hesitate to move her mouth right down over him, enjoying the exploration.

"Oh, Alessandra," she heard him say, pushing her on to keep kissing him like she was doing. After a few minutes, he spoke again. "Oh, it is going to happen, my darling. Remove your mouth or I will fill you."

Alessandra did not know whether it was safe to drink his fluid or not, so removed her mouth and touched him with her hand. In only a few seconds he was climaxing, groaning heavily in relief. She looked up at him and watched his face change from the tautness of the climax, to relief. She then saw him open his eyes and look at her. She sat up on the seat beside him and they kissed passionately before he stood up and held out his hand to her.

"My darling wife," he said, pulling her into a standing embrace. "I want to sleep with you like this, without our nightgowns. Your body enflames me and I want to see you like this when I wake in the morning."

Alessandra walked with him and climbed into bed. Instead of going straight to sleep, he instructed her to lie back while he moved over the top of her, kissing her everywhere again and again, well into the night.

CHAPTER 19

When Edward woke up the next morning he was immediately alert and aroused at the feeling of Alessandra's skin next to him. He put his arm around her from behind and his hand found her bare breast, making her moan softly and push back her hips against him. She moved her back closer to him so he was hard up against her buttocks.

Both realising the other was awake, Alessandra turned and found herself looking at a breathtaking sight that was her husband's naked form. She immediately started kissing him everywhere, taking him to the heights again as she pleasured him with her mouth. He returned the pleasure before they even spoke to one another.

As they lay in bed afterward, looking at each other, he smiled at her. "I did not know there was this much pleasure to be had. I thought married couples did this to make children, and no other reason," he said, idly caressing one of her nipples.

She sighed and enjoyed the caress. "I did not know either," she said quietly. The look on her face made him kiss her again and move on to pleasuring her yet again, this time with his finger while they kissed. It was a pleasure neither could imagine they would ever get tired of.

~~~~~

Some time later, finally they knew they had to get out of bed.

"Today I have to go with Father to visit some of our
~~~~~

tenants so I shall be out most of the day," Edward said as he dressed.

Alessandra dressed as far as she could herself and then Edward helped her to secure the back of her dress, an action he was learning to enjoy greatly each morning. As he did so, he kissed her on the back of her neck, an area she now loved him kissing while he assisted in her dressing ritual each day. She moaned again. The sound induced his body to become aroused once more.

He laughed softly at her. "I wonder if I shall ever get anything done, wanting to be close to you like this all the time."

She smiled at him and pulled herself away, readying herself as presentable for company finally. "Come then, Husband. Let us leave this room of privacy to go be with your parents, and I shall simply look forward to tonight," she said as if to tempt him into arousal again, before laughing with him as they headed to breakfast.

Entering the breakfast room, they greeted Edward's parents who exchanged a knowing look but refrained from chastising them for their lateness of rising from their bed.

"Eat quickly, Edward. We have an appointment we must get to," Edward's father said with a slight tinge of sternness in his voice. The tone told Edward that possibly from that point forward, it might be best to not indulge in quite so much pleasure early in the morning, which seemed to consistently make him late for breakfast.

"And you and I, Alessandra, are going to spend some time today going over some household management learning," Edward's mother said. Alessandra smiled and nodded back at her.

CHAPTER 20

Over the following week, the two young lovers were both busy with assignments given to them by Edward's mother and father. Every evening they fell into bed with each other, exhausted from the day's events but still eager to please and be pleased.

On the Sunday after church service, Edward informed his father that he would spend the rest of the day with his wife, and he and Alessandra made their way up to the summit. The weather had been too cold for such activity but it was a rare winter day when the sun was out and it was fairly warm. They seized the moment and took the horses up. It was the first time they had been up there since their wedding. They sat down on the blankets and held each other while they looked out over the land around them. As they kissed again Alessandra felt the same longing as she always did.

"Edward," she seemed to breathe out. "Touch me, please."

He looked at her, surprised, knowing they were in the open, but was overcome with arousal also, and did know there was never anyone else up on the summit to see. He discretely placed his hand on her calf, and ran his hand up her leg, inside her dress, until he could feel where she liked to be touched.

"Yes," she said. Edward watched her face as she was taken away into the world of pleasure. It lasted only a few minutes before it was over for her, breathing heavily as she recovered.

She looked at him, her eyes deep with passion. "And

you?" she asked him but he held her hand and kissed it.

"Later my love," he said, wanting more than anything to be touched by her but knowing he couldn't be pleasured quite as discretely as she could. He decided to put that thought behind them. "Tonight, when we are in the privacy of our room."

After she kissed him again in response, they ended up lying down with him on top of her. It felt natural for him to be positioned so that her legs were spread and he was lying between them. Even with all of the clothing they both had on, it felt thrilling.

Alessandra felt like she couldn't get enough of him. She knew they both had so much work they should be doing, all day every day, but what she wanted to do more than anything else was just be with her husband. They stopped kissing and lay unmoving, looking at each other.

"I do love you, Alessandra," Edward said, his face full of emotion.

She looked at him, acknowledging that he had no traditional handsomeness on his face, but yet was still a man who she regarded as truly beautiful.

"And I love you, Edward."

As they started to feel cold Edward stood and helped her up. "My beautiful wife, we need to get home and in front of the fire. It is getting too cold to be out here," he said, kissing her again and feeling her respond with the passion that she seemed to have an unending supply of.

He laughed and pushed her away from him.

"Later!" he exclaimed. She laughed at him before they mounted the horses and made their way back home.

CHAPTER 21

The next morning they woke to feel a different chill in the air. After they dressed they looked outside and saw it had snowed in the night. They were going to be confined to their home until the weather passed.

"Could we perhaps stay in bed all day then?" Alessandra asked him, with a small suggestive smile on her face.

Edward laughed at her. "No! There is still a great deal to be done. At this time of year it is harder to keep fires going and the house warm, so we all have to pitch in and work to make it possible. Even you and I! After breakfast I will show you where we keep extra stocks of everything we may need to get through this time if we are stuck here and unable to get outside at all," Edward responded, even though inside he did indeed like her idea of staying in bed.

Before making their way to breakfast, he walked up behind her and held her while they both looked out the window. Both considered how much their lives had changed in recent months from what each of them had individually expected.

"Come," Edward said as he pulled away from her and held out his hand for her to take as they made their way to the breakfast room. "The sooner we begin our day, the sooner it will be bedtime again."

~~~~~

Later that afternoon Alessandra felt a familiar sensation, that being of her monthly bleeding arriving. She excused herself and headed toward the room she
~~~~~

now shared with her husband, not sure how to handle the situation without the comfort of her mother around. When almost there, she ran into Margaret.

"Oh, Miss, are you unwell? Is there anything I can do for you?" she asked. Alessandra looked perplexed. She did not know how to act with her 'monthly visitor' now being here. She looked at Margaret, judging her to not be as old as Alessandra's mother, but possibly old enough to know a great deal about etiquette and what people did in their marriage.

She tentatively spoke. "Margaret, may I ask you about something of a rather private nature?" she asked quietly.

The woman before her smiled softly. "Of course, Miss. Let us step into your room for privacy, and you can ask me whatever you like."

Once inside the bedroom, Alessandra turned to Margaret. "I do not wish to cause any offence when I ask but are you married?"

The woman before her smiled and laughed. "Yes, I have been married for over ten years, Miss. What is it that you wish to ask me? You will not offend, and you have my confidence."

Alessandra only hesitated a moment. She wouldn't see her mother again and the thought of talking to Edward's mother did not appeal at all. She needed to find the courage to keep speaking. "I … today my …" Alessandra started, finding herself blushing.

Margaret was perceptive and made everything easier. "Is today the start of your monthly cycle, Miss?" she asked.

Alessandra nodded. "I do not know what I am to do, as a married woman…" she tried to continue.

Margaret looked at her, now suspecting what Alessandra was worried about. "Are you concerned about what to do during these days, with regard to your husband?"

She heard Alessandra let out a sigh of relief, as she saw her nod her head. "Do ... things ... continue ... during this time?" she asked, feeling her face go to its dark red tone once more.

Margaret looked kindly at her. She remembered the first months of her own marriage and how timid she had also been.

"That is for you to decide, Miss. I believe some women do not wish to engage in that way with their husband during the time of bleeding, but for other women it does not bother them in the slightest. It is something that will come to visit month after month unless you are with child, so it is something you can decide with the young master if your communication is open."

"Did you talk to your husband about it?" Alessandra asked, hoping she was not overstepping any boundaries. Instead of seeming offended, Margaret only looked happy to talk about the subject and started to laugh quietly.

"Oh, Miss, the first bleeding I had after I married, I was so embarrassed that I made up excuses for almost a whole week about how I could not sleep beside him. After that week was over and we re-met in our marriage bed, he was so concerned about it that I ended up telling him it had been my week of bleeding. He told me there and then that that would be no excuse for not sleeping with him ever again. He didn't mind if we did not engage in our intimacy for the week, but he would not have me sleeping in a different bed from him ever again."

Alessandra watched the older woman as she seemed to be remembering the time with fondness.

"After that conversation, I never slept apart from him again, and I found it easiest to just tell him when it was starting. He was very patient and accepting of it, as I am sure the young master will be also."

Margaret stopped and now looked right at

Alessandra.

"He is a good boy, the young master. Everything is new for both of you but I have found that the more and the sooner you can talk about everything, the quicker the relaxation about it comes."

Alessandra looked at her with gratitude. "Thank you. I hope I have not made you uncomfortable."

Margaret smiled broadly at her. "Miss, it takes a lot to make me feel uncomfortable. You can ask me anything, anytime. I may not always be able to answer, but I will always be happy to try."

~~~~~

That night as Edward climbed into bed with Alessandra, she found herself suddenly very shy around him, and not like her usual forward self at that time of day.

"You seem distant," he said to her, watching her for some sign of what was going on in her mind. By now he knew she sometimes thought about things very deeply before doing or saying what she wanted to.

"I have my monthly bleeding today," she said quietly, avoiding looking in his eyes.

Edward was momentarily confused. He remembered his mother had talked about such things but he equally noted that he might not have listened well enough to know what he should say or do in such a moment.

"Alessandra, I am not too aware of the workings of a woman's body, but am I right in thinking that you will bleed for a few days every month and that if you do not bleed, that is a sign that you are with child?" he ventured to blurt out, feeling certain that he probably had gotten something wrong. His words encouraged her to look up again, into his eyes.

"Yes! I thought you might not know, and I was worried about what it might mean for us and ... this time of day," she said quietly and he smiled at her.

"Does it make you feel different, like you do not
~~~~~

want us to touch each other?" he asked, now very curious about how things were.

"No, I do not feel like I do not want to touch you, but I am … a little bit …messy."

He kissed her on the lips and caressed her nipple before moving his hand down, making her feel embarrassed but also trusting of him. She felt him touch her there, with his finger, as he had done so many times before.

"Does it hurt, now that you are bleeding?" he asked and she moaned in pleasure.

"No," she breathed out at him, looking as she always did in these moments.

"Shall I keep touching you?" he asked.

"Yes, please."

Alessandra relished the feelings again, realising that the time of month did not need to equate with no pleasure for them. She appreciated that he wouldn't want to kiss her there at such a time, but the pleasurable caresses were quite enough for them both.

CHAPTER 22

In total, the family was snowed in and confined to the manor for three weeks. It was near the end of that time that Edward's mother discretely veered Alessandra off so that they could talk alone.

"Alessandra, you have now been married for almost two months. Have you bled?" she asked directly, making Alessandra blush. Immediately she felt guilty about the decision she had made with Edward to not yet have children. She was uncertain if or how could she tell her mother-in-law that.

She nodded her head in response. At least in this, she could be honest.

"Then you are not with child yet," Edward's mother continued, and Alessandra shook her head, not wanting to respond in any way at all. "It is of no consequence. It is still early days," she continued and then changed the subject as if it were nothing. The memory of it having been spoken remained with Alessandra right through the day, until she was with her husband alone again.

In the privacy of their room, Edward knew immediately that something was different about her. He lay beside her in their bed, the two of them huddling together to keep warm in the cold of the night. "What is bothering you, Alessandra?" he asked, worried that she was going to give him some kind of bad news.

"Oh, Edward. Your mother asked me today if I had bled," she said, revealing her concern in her voice. "She was asking in a roundabout way if I was with child yet."

Edward sighed. "Oh, I see. But you told her you were

not?"

"Yes, of course. I have no desire to lie to her but I also did not tell her that we have not tried yet. Do you think we are being selfish, wanting this time for ourselves?"

He held her tight and they looked into each other's eyes. "No, but I equally do not want you to feel pressured by my parents."

"Edward, do you think it is the right time for us to try?" Alessandra asked and she heard him let out a deep breath.

"Do you?"

Alessandra considered their situation for a moment. She knew that she would feel guilty if they continued to be selfish and keep from his parents something they so desperately seemed to want.

"Yes."

He kissed her passionately while they pleasured each other with their hands. After they'd both climaxed and he'd become hard again, they moved naturally so that he was on top of her, between her legs. He looked into her eyes, not wanting to hurt her.

"Are you sure?" he asked one more time. She nodded and kissed him deeply, preparing herself for whatever feeling was about to come.

Edward moved closer to her, kissing her so much and moving with her in a way that it all happened naturally, surprising them both. Alessandra felt him enter and while it was a strange sensation, she only felt a mild discomfort before she realised he was fully inside her.

"Oh, my love. Are you alright?" he asked, staying still and not moving while fully inside her.

"Yes, I can feel you. Oh, Edward. I like how you feel," she said. He slowly moved out and then back into her, trying to control how he was feeling. After three such movements, he came inside of her. She felt him convulse and slump on top of her. He stayed there, unmoving while looking at her face and continuing to kiss her.

Alessandra kissed him eagerly in wonder at how babies were made. She considered that a life may have just begun to grow inside of her. If so, it had come from the wonderful act that produced so many good feelings in her.

CHAPTER 23

The next morning, although determined to get out of bed as early as was expected by his parents, Edward found himself once again late to breakfast after waking and finding his wife eager to repeat the previous evening.

As he slid inside her, she spoke to him, asking him how it felt to him. The question was enough to take his mind off it for a moment and enable him to stay in her for a bit longer.

"Oh, Alessandra. It feels warm, like a fine fur coat wrapped around me tightly. It is exquisite - you are exquisite," he said in reply to her question as he stayed still deep inside of her and kissing her.

When he felt her move slightly, he let himself go with the feeling of physical pleasure as they started to move together, before he let go completely.

Alessandra revelled in the feelings that came from the new connection she'd found with Edward. The feeling of joining took her to another level of happiness. She found it difficult to comprehend how other women could not enjoy it.

She watched his face as she saw him recover from the moment of bliss. Focusing on her once again, Edward gave her a shy smile.

"My parents are going to tell me off again," he laughed quietly, making Alessandra smile.

"Yes, sorry," she said, teasing him.

"I think you are not at all sorry, my beautiful wife. I think you are enjoying getting me into trouble almost every morning!" he laughed back at her as they pulled themselves from the warmth of their bed and readied themselves for the day ahead.

~~~~~~

"Edward!" they both heard as they entered the breakfast room. The sternness of his father's voice made the two of them jump. "This has to stop. You have responsibilities that need to be attended to. Eat quickly as we are expected at the lawyer's office … now!"

Edward grabbed what portable food he could in a napkin and ate as he walked out of the room, only having time to give Alessandra a quick kiss. After he and his father had left, Alessandra remained at the breakfast table with Edward's mother.

Expecting a similar reprimand, Alessandra sat quietly while choosing a selection of food to eat but could feel the eyes of Edward's mother on her.

"I remember how it is in the first weeks of marriage, Alessandra. Do not worry so much. Edward's father is eager for Edward to take over the full running of the estate, so he wants him to prove his sense of responsibility. He has forgotten what mornings were like for us also at the start," Alessandra heard Edward's mother say quietly. When she turned to look at her she noticed a slight blush on the woman before her.

"Enjoy this time and make the most of it. Once a baby comes along, something changes between a husband and his wife and things are never quite the same again. Work hard to hold on to what you now share."

Alessandra nodded while quietly eating, not sure how to move forward with the day from such a conversation. Edward's mother resolved the uncertainty, beginning a conversation about the storage of linen that relieved Alessandra's mind of having to think about pleasure anymore.

"Come, Alessandra. Today you and I are going to visit and talk to every staff member who works in this household. It will help you know who everyone is by
~~~~~~

name, and what their role is. I know it is not a common practice but since I have been the mistress of this estate, it has always been important to me that the people who work for us are all treated with respect and appreciation. For some of them, us simply remembering their names shows them how much we need and respect them," Edward's mother said as the two of them began walking through the large house. It was quickly becoming home to Alessandra, even though she was sure she had still not been into even half of the rooms.

Alessandra spent most of the day in the company of Edward's mother. When she was dismissed later that afternoon, she made her way to the glass room she had come to love so much. Sitting behind the glass in complete solitude in the late afternoon sun was something she appreciated doing every day when she could be spared. Always there was so much for her to remember from what she considered her daily lessons in the manor management. It was invigorating to someone who loved learning and viewed everything as being a possibility to discover new things. That invigoration didn't stop her from becoming overwhelmed when she took a moment to consider that one day she would be running it all.

Determined to not put herself in a panic, Alessandra turned off her mind, closed her eyes, and let the sunshine warm her face. She sat like that until she heard the door quietly open and close and then felt a presence sit beside her.

"You look so tranquil," she heard Edward say. She turned to see him smiling at her.

"I do love it here in this room," she replied, loving looking at him. Almost instantly she was transformed into a woman of desire again, even without him touching or kissing her.

Edward moved closer to her and leaned in to softly kiss the side of her neck while taking her hand and holding it in his.

Alessandra moved her head so she could grant him access to her neck completely. She sat with eyes closed once again as she felt him softly move his lips slowly but steadily all over her accessible skin.

~~~~~

From a distance, Edward's mother watched the interaction and felt a huge sense of sadness. On the one hand, she was sad because she felt like she was losing her son - the one person who she had always felt needed her. On the other hand, she was sad because she had lost that level of physical interaction so long ago. Even though she had put that aspect of her marriage out of her mind in recent years, she found the memories resurfacing at a rate that was starting to affect her greatly.

Suddenly she was aware of her husband moving up behind her. She briefly turned and smiled at him before resuming her stare at the young lovers.

"You miss that, I think," he said to his wife.

She knew him well enough now to know there was no point in not being honest.

"Yes. I had forgotten for so long but when I see their faces when they are like that, I do miss what you and I shared." She was silent before continuing. "I am sorry that I was restricted from the possibility of conceiving. I know that you have missed out..." she started to say before he cut her off.

"I have not missed anything. I have you, I have Edward, and now we also have a daughter who I believe we both highly regard," he said and saw his wife nod in acknowledgement.

He turned her slowly so they could look fully at each other.

"I did not know you missed our physical closeness so much. Come with me," he said to her softly. Taking her hand, he led her to the room that he now slept in alone.
~~~~~

She stayed quiet, not sure why she was in the room that was foreign to her.

"You are still the most beautiful woman in my acquaintance," he said.

Upon recognising that he was in the mindset to make love to her, the thought made her fearful.

"I know that we agreed that we would keep apart all those years ago, as a way to ensure you did not get with child," he continued, as he began to undo her gown. As nervous as she was, she did not stop him. "We are older now, and we can better control what we do. Let me help you to feel like the desirable woman that you are. I will not put you in danger of a child, but we can still give joy to one another."

He continued undressing her until she stood naked before him. He drank in the sight of his wife of so many years while he removed his clothing.

She fell into his arms, realising then how hungry and lonely she had been in body. She let him kiss her all over, including that special spot he had found all those years ago. Once he'd settled there, he teased her until she experienced the first release she'd had in almost two decades.

After her climax, she became worried again. It was always after that moment that he would join with her. What she didn't know was that in the time they had spent apart, he had learned, as a way of managing his desires, the art of self-pleasure. He took her hand and placed it on himself. She had never pleasured him in such a manner. It was as new to her as it was to him, to have her touch him in such a way. They kissed as she did as he showed. It was not long at all before he found that release came.

They lay together, holding one another, relishing the contact of their bodies once again.

"I did not know we could both find pleasure without joining," she whispered, feeling tears come to her eyes for all the years they had stayed apart from one another in body. He held her even closer.

"Oh my dearest love, I love you as much now as I did when we began our marriage, and I have always desired you. When you miss this, you only need to let me know," he said, and suddenly, with remembering how it was, he was more understanding of how his son could have been so distracted and late to breakfast every morning.

CHAPTER 24

Over time Alessandra found herself learning more and more about the running of such a grand household. Almost all of every day was spent with Edward's mother. There was much to learn and so many things she had assumed would only be the responsibility of the household staff. She was surprised to see the level at which Edward's mother - someone she now regarded as her mentor - knew what was happening in each little corner of the great home.

At times when they were confined indoors, Alessandra was introduced to some other rooms in the house. Due to it being so cold, there were places that Edward's mother told her she wouldn't see until the weather warmed up once again when a full spring clean would be undertaken.

One afternoon her mother-in-law took her to the steward's room, where Alessandra was pleased to see Edward going over the accounts with his father.

"And this, Alessandra, is where you will find your husband often when you cannot find him anywhere else!" she said in a teasing manner as she looked fondly at Edward's father.

Edward's father responded by smiling at Edward's mother shyly. "Now, my dear, you know how important this part of the house is," he said to her before turning his attention to Alessandra. "This is where we monitor the success or failure of the estate, Alessandra. It is important to keep on top of the business accounts and paperwork, and this particular job Edward will take over from me in the not too distant future. He must know it completely. If you are good with numbers, it would not hurt for you to learn also," he said. Edward's mother exclaimed a sound of surprise but he continued regardless. "Would you like to learn about the business also, Alessandra?"

His question placed Alessandra in an awkward position due to her knowing it was not standard for women to have any place in financial matters. Hearing his words resulted in her face once again showing the depth of her embarrassment. As she felt all eyes on her, including those of Edward's mother who appeared horrified at the question, Alessandra settled her eyes on those of her husband. She saw in them extreme amusement at her having been put in this position. While looking at him she also found a small amount of strength to hold her head up high and answer confidently.

"If my husband would have no objection, I should like that very much. I am confident in my abilities with figures, and would enjoy working with Edward in this aspect of the estate management," she said. She immediately saw Edward respond with approval at her choice of words.

She turned to look at Edward's parents, hoping the question had been sincere and that she had not read more into something that his father had not been serious about. The only person in the room who did not seem impressed with the idea was Edward's mother.

"Well, Alessandra will have plenty of other work to do every day so this must not be treated as a priority for her," Edward's mother said more abruptly than Alessandra had heard her speak before. After a few minutes of everyone feeling slightly uncomfortable, she spoke again. "And now, Alessandra, let us visit the kitchen." Alessandra timidly fell in step behind her mother-in-law as they left the men behind in their work.

That evening as the young married couple lay

together in the privacy of their room, Alessandra spoke up, full of her natural curiosity once more.

"Why is this house so big, Edward? It feels like it is a castle, and yet only three of you live here," she said, full of wonder at why she hadn't asked the question previously.

"There are only three of us now but this house was built more than 100 years ago. The families then were large, and the social need for guests and entertaining much greater."

"But do you have brothers or sisters? You have not mentioned any."

Edward shook his head.

"No, my mother told me once that she was informed by the doctor after I was born that she must not have any more children, so I was all they had. I do think my parents would have preferred that they could have a large family."

Alessandra processed what he was saying. Her parents had only her and her brother as offspring. Until now she had never wondered how they felt about that, even though she knew that in the village she grew up in, other families were much larger.

"We must have many children then, while your parents are still alive," she said, making him laugh softly while looking into her eyes.

"Oh, must we?" he teased her as he saw that look come over her again. "Best we get on with that then," he continued before kissing her and once again indulging in further pleasure.

CHAPTER 25

Two weeks later Edward approached Alessandra as she was looking through store cupboards with his mother, making what seemed to be endless lists of things they would need to have delivered in the coming weeks.

"Mother, I would like to take my wife away now, if you do not mind," he said. The words caused his mother to experience equal amounts of love when she looked at her son, and frustration at his timing when she felt she was teaching her daughter-in-law something important.

"Edward, things need to be learned…"

He nodded and kissed her on the cheek, playing on his ability to charm his mother, and making Alessandra smile at him knowingly. By now she was very used to seeing how he could turn both of his parents to his way of thinking so that he could do what he wanted, when he wanted.

"I know, Mother, but today there is a smell of spring in the air and this sunshine might not last. I would like to take Alessandra out for some fresh air while I can."

Edward's mother sounded resigned as she gave her consent for Alessandra to finish what she was doing. Soon Edward was walking Alessandra up to their room as she laughed at him.

"What are we doing, husband? You are not going to pull me into our bedchamber so blatantly at this time of day…" she teased him and he smiled back at her.

"No! Although…" he started to tease her back, before laughing and continuing. "Put on your riding habit. I need to ride and I shall enjoy it infinitely more if you are with me."

They quietly changed in each other's presence, both too focused on the sunshine they could see outside to be tempted into anything else. Soon they were on their horses again, after what seemed like such a long period of time stuck inside the house.

As she sat on her quiet little pony, Alessandra could sense the power of Edward on Beauty, and the desire of both of them to not only be out but also to be having a good run.

"Edward, you and Beauty look like you are ready to run a race, but I cannot accompany you on that," she said to him, worried about where she was going to fit into this excursion.

"Worry not, my love. Once we are beyond the gate I want you to make your journey to the summit as you feel confident to. I will let Beauty run as he needs to, but I will keep coming back to you so you will not be alone," he said, and she could see the excitement on his face as he spoke. Always when he had been out on his horse since she had come to the estate, he had forced himself to remain slow and steady beside her. She found herself now looking forward to seeing him enjoy his horse riding to the full degree she had not seen before.

"Alright," Alessandra replied tentatively, not certain about the plan that had been presented to her.

After they passed through the main gate to the yard, Edward positioned himself beside her, looking at her with almost the same look he had during passion. The brilliant smile he delivered to her made her melt.

"Just take your time, going the same way as we normally go," he said and saw her nod and smile at him.

Once Edward left her side, Beauty carried him at a speed that took them far away as Alessandra and Misty began their slow journey toward the hill. For the duration of Alessandra's journey, now and then she would see Edward riding not too far off in the distance, running at what seemed like a frightful speed to Alessandra. The sight made her thankful that Misty did not seem in any way inclined to move with such fervour.

She made her way up the hill. When she reached the summit she secured Misty and spread out the blanket to sit down and watch her husband's horse skills from the distance. Soon he was riding up toward her and then slowing, finally, to dismount and secure Beauty next to the timid pony who always looked like a dwarf next to him.

Alessandra looked at Edward and remembered how she had always thought him not in any way handsome. With his face full of excitement and passion, as he was in that moment, she regarded him in a new light as a most handsome man indeed.

He sat down beside her, grinning so much that she laughed at him.

"If you get this much joy from riding, you must have been missing it greatly since I arrived," she said and he smiled at her.

"Yes, but it has been a great pleasure seeing you learn and develop your horse riding skills, Alessandra," he said, taking her hand and kissing it. "On the other side of spring, when summer truly arrives, Father organises a hunt that brings many people. Then you shall really see some horse-riding skills!"

Alessandra drank up the vision in front of her. Her husband looked excited and full of life. It made her wonder what kind of father he would be. As she let her mind wander there, she realised that she had not had her monthly visitor, which by her calculation should have already arrived.

Edward saw a look of confusion pass over his wife's face and immediately felt concerned himself. "What is it, Alessandra?" he asked, revealing his concern.

She looked at him, still trying to count weeks in her head, but wasn't entirely certain.

"I'm not sure, Edward, but I think I should have bled…"

Edward briefly had a thought in his head that she was saying that she was bleeding and so would be a bit distant over the next week. Then he seemed to register exactly what she had said. She saw his eyes go wide.

"Alessandra, are you saying that you … might be with child?"

She continued to look uncertain.

"I am not entirely sure, Edward, but I do think I am late," she responded. Instantly she watched his face transform to a similar level of excitement that she'd seen on his face just a few minutes earlier as he had come to her from his ride. "Oh but Edward, I am not certain so please, can we not say anything yet? Just for another week or two, to make sure I am not simply mistaken?"

He pulled her to him and kissed her hard. "Yes, of course, my darling. Oh, but if it is true, we are blessed, are we not?" he asked and smiled at her.

She sat quietly - very quietly for her, he knew. He also knew that for her that meant she was processing things in her mind. He sat quietly and watched her, waiting until she would speak her thoughts.

"Edward, if I am with child," she said quietly. "I should very much like to see my mother."

Suddenly he sensed a seriousness about her; even a slight sadness. He could only imagine how difficult it might be for her to be far away from her mother if she were to be with child. He also gave thought to how it could affect his mother, given her sadness at having been prevented from having more children.

Alessandra saw his face change in response to what she had said. For a moment she regretted having spoken at all.

"When would you like to see your mother?" Edward asked. "Father will be happy to arrange for your mother and father to come here, or we can go and visit them," he said, putting his wife's worries instantly at rest.

"Thank you. Let us wait another week or two so I can be sure," she said and saw Edward nod in reply. "If it does look like I am with child, I shall like to visit my mother and father soon, and go and see my brother also, who lives close to them."

"Very well, we shall arrange our travel when you are ready to do so," he said before giving her another look of joy and kissing her so deeply.

Immediately Alessandra felt herself melting against him. Soon they were lying down with him on top of her, enjoying being nestled between her legs even with the level of clothing they each had on.

She pulled away from him and looked into his eyes, as always enjoying the feeling of his weight on her and his arms around her.

"I do not want to sleep away from you. I know it might be expected…" she began and he kissed her again.

"I do not want that either. We shall do things as we want to do them, Alessandra, not by what other people expect us to do."

"Even your mother and father?"

He took a deep breath before he spoke.

"I respect my mother and father, but in this, I think you and I are the only people who should make such decisions. You will be able to calculate your comfort levels, and you will let me know if you wish to be alone," he said to her, with the tone that made it into a question.

Alessandra nodded in reply. "I will. I promise," she said.

"Well, my wife, if there is a chance that you are with child, we should return to the house before the weather changes again," Edward said, pulling off her and helping her up.

Once settled on their horses, she turned to him.

"Shall I see you back at the house?" she asked,

expecting him to want to run again but he shook his head.

"I will ride beside you now," Edward replied. She suspected that he was naturally moving into possible father mode, wanting to be protective over her. She greatly enjoyed the feeling that thought produced.

~~~~~

That evening as the family sat in the drawing room, enjoying the warmth from the roaring fire, Edward held Alessandra's hand particularly close to him. Edward's mother noticed but said nothing to them, waiting until she could speak to her husband when she was alone with him later.

"Do you sense that Alessandra might be with child?" she asked him and he looked surprised.

"Do you?"

She looked apprehensive, as though she didn't want to believe it could be true, given her history of miscarriages and the resulting instruction to not have any more children after Edward had been born. When she didn't reply, her husband approached her and took her hands in his.

"If they have an announcement to make, they will make it. Until then we must not assume anything."

She looked at him and knew he was right. She was determined to not let her own condition affect how she looked at or treated her daughter-in-law if she was in fact on her way to starting her own family.

Since the afternoon weeks earlier when she'd found herself re-engaging in the simple art of pleasure with her husband, they had spent some more time together in a similar way but still lived in separate rooms. Thinking about that, she turned to him.

"Stay with me tonight," she said simply.

He happily put his arms around her and held her tight. "Of course."
~~~~~

CHAPTER 26

Over the following week, Alessandra and Edward put the possibility of her being with child out of their minds while they continued with their individual and joint learning and responsibilities.

One morning after breakfast had finished and Edward had gone off with his father, Alessandra returned to their room to rest alone for a short time. She was startled when Margaret walked in.

"Oh my, Miss! I am so sorry. I did not expect you to be here," she said as she began to walk back out the door.

"No, actually Margaret, please come back in," Alessandra said to her, making the older woman turn and close the door behind her so that they had privacy. "You have been assisting me long enough now that I wonder if you would have noticed..." she started to ask. As always, the older woman successfully anticipated what Alessandra was thinking and feeling too shy to say.

"Miss, I have noticed that perhaps you have missed a bleeding," she said quietly and Alessandra nodded and put her head down.

"Yes, that is what I wanted to ask you about," Alessandra replied, sounding relieved. "I was trying to work out the days but every day seems to be like the last so I am not sure..."

Margaret moved closer to the young woman before her, who she had come to respect and appreciate as her future mistress.

"Does it seem to you that I have missed one?"

Alessandra asked quietly, finally looking at the older woman in front of her.

Margaret nodded. "To me it does, Miss. In fact, you almost should have had two bleedings in the time since your last one."

She watched Alessandra, wondering if the thought would bring joy to her or not. A few minutes later she saw Alessandra's face transform into a smile.

"Do you think it is too soon, though, to be sure? I would not like to give hope if I am wrong," Alessandra asked.

"Oh, Miss, whenever a woman is with child, there is a possibility that it will not come to full term, as sad as that is. So some women do choose to keep the realisation to themselves for as long as they can, so they do not let anyone down. Only you can know if you want to share the news or not, but if you are asking me if enough time has passed for it to seem like you are with child, then yes, I think you might be," Margaret replied. She almost instantly felt Alessandra jump up and put her arms around her, before Alessandra pulled away again, looking like she might have offended.

"Thank you, Margaret. You cannot know how much I appreciate your openness in talking to me about such personal things," she said quietly.

The older woman took that as an indicator that the conversation was now finished and Alessandra wanted privacy. Margaret curtseyed and silently removed herself from the room, leaving Alessandra alone.

Alessandra stood at the window and looked out over the land, wondering what to do. Part of her wanted to shout out to everyone, full of joy, about the possibility. As always, she found herself thinking of Edward's mother and feeling like it might not be a cause for happiness for her, to have her daughter-in-law carrying a child. It was expected, of course, but how to bring the news out without causing any vexation or hurt to her mother-in-law?

~~~~~~

Late in the afternoon, she was studiously focusing on not thinking about the issue when Edward found her in her favourite spot in the sunshine of the enclosed glass room.

"What are you deep in thought about, my beautiful wife?" she heard Edward say. Alessandra was startled at the realisation that she had not heard him enter the room.

He approached, sat beside her and took her hand before kissing her and waiting for her reply.

"I think I am ready to go home to visit my mother, Edward," she said quietly, hoping she would not be offending him or his parents for asking. He only nodded and kissed her hand.

"I will talk to Father and arrange everything," he said, realising what she might be saying. "Do you still think there is a chance that you might be with child, my love?"

She nodded at him and smiled shyly. "I do. Would you be happy if it is true?"

He smiled brilliantly at her as his mind ventured far off into the future, imagining being a father to a child.

"Yes! But whatever happens, I shall be happy, Alessandra, as long as you are with me," he said. She melted against him, happy to just sit and hold hands and lean on him.

~~~~~~

Edward later sat in the steward's room with his father, having purposely lured him there so he could speak privately with him and tell him what he and Alessandra suspected.

"I can arrange this for you and Alessandra, Edward, but why is there no announcement, if she thinks she is with child?" his father asked him and Edward found himself trying to be very careful in his words.

"Father, Alessandra knows the difficulties for Mother in not having been able to have more children after I was born. Even for me it feels wrong..." he started to say but his father cut him off abruptly, startling him.

"Edward, your mother's time of having children passed long ago, and she expects, as I do, that you and Alessandra will produce children to continue our family line. I appreciate that you are sensitive to how your mother may feel, but please believe me when I tell you that when that news comes, she will be as joyous about it as I will be."

Edward nodded in response, not feeling like any words were required.

"How certain is she?" his father asked.

"Well, she wants to see her mother. I am sure that will clarify anything she is uncertain about."

His father nodded to him. "Very well. I will arrange for the two of you to travel tomorrow afternoon. Once you are there you can send word to let me know when you are ready to return," he said.

Edward nodded and left him to go and find Alessandra and give her confirmation of her ability to go home.

~~~~~

"We are going tomorrow?" Alessandra asked, finding it difficult to hide her excitement to the news. "To see my mother and father?"

Edward laughed at her. "Yes! It is all arranged for tomorrow afternoon. We shall travel halfway and stay overnight in an inn before continuing the next morning. You shall see your mother day after tomorrow," he said, feeling great power from his parents' situation in life that made it so easy to make such arrangements at such short notice.

Alone in their room, Alessandra threw her arms around him and kissed him passionately, instantly stirring him. They quickly undressed and indulged in pleasuring each other.

"Should we still be doing this, Alessandra? I mean, if
~~~~~

you are with child?"

Alessandra looked at him with such a suggestive look in her eyes that he laughed as she said to him, "But we do not know for certain that I am, so we have to keep trying, do we not?"

Edward smiled, held her tight and kissed her more, very happy to do just that.

CHAPTER 27

The next day Edward and Alessandra stood on the steps of the manor house and hugged each of his parents as they said their goodbyes. Neither Edward's mother nor his father had spoken of the possible pregnancy. They wouldn't until Alessandra felt sure that she could announce it but they both felt certain that they would have a grandchild soon enough.

After what seemed like a much longer journey than the one she'd originally made to the estate, Alessandra was shown to the room that she would share with Edward. They were staying in the same inn she had stayed in when she had headed in the reverse direction previously.

When they closed the door behind them after eating and readying themselves for the night, they immediately closed the gap between them, hungry for each other. It felt different, being in a different place and it being just the two of them with no parents at all anywhere in their vicinity.

Edward felt like he couldn't get enough of his wife. She continued to surprise him in her eagerness to be so close to him so often. After satisfying her with his mouth more than twice, and he had been satisfied three times, they both lay back in the foreign bed and smiled indulgently at each other.

"I do think I shall need sleep at some point tonight, Alessandra, if we are to face your parents tomorrow," Edward said in his teasing manner. She giggled at him with a sound that to Edward was simply delightful.

As he looked at her, he was again thankful inside for the choice his mother had made. It may have been made for an entirely different purpose - that being the money that came with her that had been able to be injected into the estate. Regardless, after their initial unease with each other, he could not have asked for a more giving and loving wife.

"I just want to make the most of our time together," she said, smiling as her giggling toned down. "I am so happy to be with you, Edward."

Edward could feel the emotion coming off her. He pulled her close to kiss her over and over before they finally let themselves fall asleep.

~~~~~

The following morning they made their way to Alessandra's home. On the way there she started to feel nervous about Edward seeing where she had grown up. Sensing her anxiety, he questioned her to find out what she was so worried about.

"Edward, I did not grow up like you. My parents' home is very small, and we live on the edge of a small village. In fact, I think your estate might be larger than the whole village!"

He looked at her closely and tried to understand her concern, having not given any thought to their different upbringings.

"Alessandra, I enjoyed getting to know your parents and I love you. What your house looks like does not matter to me. I just want to be with you," he said, holding her hand tightly and kissing her lightly. "Stop worrying."

~~~~~

Later that day Edward was introduced to the small village that his wife had grown up in. He realised then that not only had he never visited the village before, but he had never even visited anything like it before. She had not been stretching the truth. The village did seem much smaller than the estate that he had grown up on. He kissed her hand and smiled at her in affection.

Almost immediately after arriving at Alessandra's family home, they saw her mother running out to greet them. Isabella pulled them both into a hug, with tears in her eyes.

"Oh, you are here! Oh, Edward, thank you to you and your father for bringing my daughter home to me," she gushed as she gave him an extra hug and made him laugh. "Come in, come in," she continued, ushering them both inside, where Alessandra's father joined them.

"Edward, it is good to see you," he said, shaking Edward's hand. "I trust you are taking good care of my little girl."

Edward and Alessandra smiled at each other and her parents could both see the happiness of their daughter.

"I certainly am trying, Sir."

As they entered a small room, Edward, although he didn't want to be, was surprised at how small the room and the house were. He hid his feelings, in the wonder of finally seeing where his wife had grown up.

"Sit down, Edward," Alessandra's mother insisted. He did as he was bid before she continued. "I shall make some tea. Alessandra, please come and help me."

Alessandra looked at her mother, surprised, but did as she was instructed and followed her mother out of the room and into the kitchen. Once away from everyone else, Alessandra saw her mother take her hands and smile broadly at her.

"You are with child," she said, without any hint of a question at all. Alessandra felt surprised. "I am your mother, Alessandra, and I can tell."

"I am not sure, Mother…" she started to say, relieved that the subject had come up.

"Have you bled in the past few weeks?"

"No," Alessandra replied and her mother looked pleased.

"Oh, my daughter, you are going to have a baby," Isabella said, clearly excited.

"But Mother, can I be certain enough to declare it? I do not know when is the right time."

Her mother looked at her and held her hands tighter.

"Alessandra, babies come when they are meant to. Some look like they are meant to but then they do not. We never know what is going to happen, but if you find out you are expecting a child, you do not need to hide it. It is a joyous thing - something to be celebrated. Do Edward's mother and father know?"

Alessandra shook her head. "No, I wanted to see and talk to you first to be sure."

She watched her mother as she started to make tea and prepare the tea tray.

"As long as there is no bleeding, I think you can be certain that a baby is growing inside of you. Oh, my darling daughter, I am so happy for you. Does Edward know?"

"He knows that I think I might be with child," Alessandra replied.

"Good," Isabella said as she nodded and looked closely at Alessandra. "Is he treating you well, my daughter? Is all well between you?"

"Oh yes, Mother, he is wonderful," Alessandra said. The dreamy look on her face told her mother that all indeed was well in the marriage that had been arranged purely for money.

~~~~~

That evening Alessandra and Edward lay alone not in the room Alessandra had grown up in, but in a guest room with a bigger bed. Alessandra was too aware of her parents being so close, to be able to summon desire. She'd suspected Edward might have been upset about it but all Alessandra saw on his face was his look of amusement.

"I think we can probably be good while we are here,
~~~~~

do you not agree? Especially after last night..." Edward said, teasing her. He saw her face blush deeply while remembering how much they had made love well into the night during their stay at the inn.

They lay facing and looking at one another, content to do just that.

"Did your mother talk to you?" he asked and she smiled at him.

"Yes. She told me I was with child, even before I said anything. I think now I can let myself believe it. Edward, we are having a child!" she said.

Edward smiled brilliantly at her. "I am going to be a father, and you shall be a mother," he said with a shallow indication of excitement revealed in his voice.

Alessandra looked at him in wonder, thinking about how much her life had changed in only a few months. Prior to the day she'd learned of Edward, she had questioned if she would ever get married, or would end up being at home with her parents and then alone.

"Do you think this could be the first of many?" Alessandra asked.

She saw Edward's face begin to beam, revealing his wishes.

"If that is what is intended for us, then we will welcome it, but you and I both come from small families. We must not forget how things can go sometimes. If we only have the one - even if we have none - we shall be happy, Alessandra."

Alessandra cuddled into him and let herself drift off, thinking about the prospect of not only having to learn how to run an estate but also now having to learn how to be a mother.

CHAPTER 28

The next morning Alessandra had some more time alone with her mother while Edward was kept busy by her father.

"Would you like to see Dr Rothguard?" her mother asked, startling Alessandra.

"Should I, Mother? Do I need to?"

"It cannot hurt to have a check-up with him, and then you can ask him any questions you might have," her mother replied. She was silent for a moment before continuing. "You do not have to, Alessandra, but I am happy to arrange for you to see him if you wish."

Alessandra considered the possibility. She had grown up with Dr Rothguard as the family physician. The thought of talking to him about bringing a child into the world seemed very odd to her. After she considered that she could learn new things that she needed to know, she nodded at her mother and smiled.

"Thank you, Mother. Yes, I think that would be good for me."

~~~~~

Later in the day, Alessandra made her way into the village with Edward beside her, to show him around what little attractions there were in her home town.

Edward looked around in amazement that such little townships existed. He could now fully understand how it had come to be that his wife had never learned to ride. Wherever he looked, everyone seemed to be walking. There was no horse to be seen.

Alessandra watched her spouse's face and found great
~~~~~

amusement in it. When she had originally thought about taking him to her home she had worried and been embarrassed. Now she was glad that he was there with her. She considered that he also had lived a confined life, having been kept largely on the estate as his parents prepared him to one day be master of it. His face expressed that he too was now living a new adventure, just as she had when she went to his home.

After walking around for as far as they could go before the edges of the village were reached, they returned to Alessandra's family home and found her mother talking to the family physician. The speed of his arrival immediately flustered Alessandra.

Edward was introduced to Dr Rothguard before Alessandra was swept away to her childhood room along with her mother and the physician, where she spent some time with both of them and then further time alone with the doctor.

"All seems well with you, Alessandra," the doctor said. "I expect you will indeed find yourself as a mother in months ahead. Do you have anything that you would like to ask me?"

She looked at the man before her and wondered how much he knew about pregnancy. Facing up to her discomfort she considered there could be no harm in asking what she wanted to know.

"Will the baby be hurt if..." she started to ask. She then blushed so heavily that the physician smiled at her softly in anticipation of the question he had found almost every mother-to-be asked.

"If you continue your marital relations with your husband?"

At that point, Alessandra could feel the heat of her face, but she nodded, determined to continue.

"Yes."

"That is something that is often debated. What I can tell you is that I have had patients who have continued intimacy right up till close to giving birth. Others have decided to stop immediately when it was confirmed the wife was with child. I do not believe any harm can come to the child, at least not for many months yet. When you get close to the time to give birth, you may find a level of discomfort that will naturally prevent you from wanting it. It is something you need to decide with your husband, but for at least several months yet, you will be fine," he said as he packed away his few medical instruments. "Is there anything else you would like to ask, Alessandra?"

"What can I no longer do?"

"Just look after yourself and the baby will be fine. Your mother mentioned that you ride a horse at your new home," he started to say and she nodded. "That is fine, but be careful not to fall. That is what seems to be a common contribution to babies being lost, I am afraid. Is there anything else?"

She shook her head, having had the most pressing questions answered.

"No. Thank you for seeing me, Dr Rothguard."

"You will need to ask Edward's parents about their family physician, and if they will be able to locate a midwife for you. That is not urgent. When you are in your fifth month will be sufficient, but a midwife will help you with the birthing process."

Alessandra thanked him and walked him downstairs again, where he made conversation with her parents before saying his farewell and leaving.

Edward stood up and went to his wife immediately. "Is all well?"

She nodded at him and smiled softly. "Yes, the doctor recommended that I find a physician and a midwife when we return to your parents' home but he said everything appears well."

She then thought about the doctor's confirmation that she could continue being intimate with Edward. As he looked at her, he saw her look of desire come over her face. It immediately affected him so the two of them stood close while Alessandra contained a small, quiet giggle. The two of them faced one another in a light embrace until he had relaxed, smiling bashfully.

"You cannot look at me like that when we are in company, Alessandra!" he said, teasing her with a mock voice of sternness and making her giggle harder.

Just then her parents returned and they all sat down to begin normal conversation and see the rest of the day out.

~~~~~

In bed that night they enjoyed each other with humour, finding a different level of enjoyment without the passion they had indulged in so regularly since their wedding night.

"Curse this house being so small, with paper-thin walls," Alessandra teased him openly. "I do much prefer your house. Those nice thick walls contain the wonderful noises you make when we are alone and undressed," she said openly, not at all shy now in saying such things to him.

He laughed quietly at her. "Oh, the noises I make!"

Alessandra looked at him and realised how much she loved the openness they had about their lovemaking. He'd never said as much but she'd assumed since their wedding night that it had been as new for Edward as it had been for her. She considered that if he had already been experienced, there was a great chance that they would never have been able to be as they were with one another, as he wouldn't have been as curious as she was. It was the curiosity, she believed, that had brought them so close together.

When they quietened, she let her mind wander to other things that had to be considered.

"When should we travel back, Edward?" she asked.

"I do not mind, my love. When would you like to
~~~~~

leave?"

"I think I am almost ready to go home," she said, making Edward feel warm inside at the realisation that she did now consider his home hers also. "Perhaps day after tomorrow?"

"I will send notice to Father tomorrow morning and let him know."

CHAPTER 29

The following day Edward received confirmation of travel arrangements for the day after. After receiving the news, he and Alessandra spent more time walking around her little township once again.

After seeing her peer inside the window of a store on the main street, he made a note of what had caught her attention. When she was preoccupied elsewhere he excused himself and ran back to purchase it and arrange for it to be sent to the estate as a surprise for her.

As he stood inside the shop, arranging things with the shop owner, he looked out the window again and saw Alessandra approached by someone. His first instinct was to run out of the shop and instantly be at her side. Then something held him back and he decided he would rather stay where he was and simply watch the interaction from afar.

~~~~~

Outside and across the road, Alessandra was peering inside the window of another shop. She jumped in alarm when a voice behind her called out to her.

"Alessandra?" the voice said. As soon as she heard it, she was instantly reminded of another time, before she had heard of Edward and his family. When she turned she saw Tom Missinger standing nearby, looking intently at her. "It is you!"

Alessandra curtseyed to him and felt her heart become heavy. She realised now that he had never been in love with her. That idea had been a childish assumption and wish on her part. Still, she could not

<div align="center">

115

</div>
~~~~~

deny the level of outward handsomeness that he held, even now.

"Tom," she seemed to breathe out his name. "It is good to see you."

She watched as he came closer. For a moment it looked as though he might put his arms out to her and around her, but then seemed to remember himself and stood back. It wasn't unnoticed by her that he was looking at her in a way even more intent than he had on the occasions when they had danced together.

Alessandra looked him in the eye. Tom felt slightly taken aback by the level of confidence she now seemed to have. He had thought her endearing before but now she seemed to be exuding a different kind of self-awareness.

"You look beautiful," he said, almost as if he was thinking those words but had not meant to say them.

They looked at one another, for a moment both forgetting their spouses.

~~~~~

Edward watched his wife stand before the man in front of her. He could see the man's face clearly and knew he was what any woman would call very handsome. It momentarily played on Edward's confidence, knowing that he was the complete opposite.

He looked at the face of the man, and then the face of his wife. Although she had never mentioned any previous loves, he suspected from looking at them that they must have had some acquaintance previously, and some fondness for one another.

~~~~~

"I have not seen you since..." Tom started to say as he began to recover from his surprise.

"Since you married," Alessandra replied for him and saw a slight blush appear on his face.

Tom became tongue-tied before finding the words to be able to speak. As he stood in front of her he was reminded of their time together. They had only danced together on occasion. Nothing had moved forward from that because he'd known from a very young age that he was not allowed to give his heart to anyone other than the person his parents had chosen to be his wife.

"I could not love you, Alessandra. I had been betrothed by my parents since I was born," Tom said as he moved closer to her, now within intimate speaking distance. "Please do not think that I did not wish things could have been different for us."

Alessandra looked into his eyes and expected to see deceit but all she saw was what appeared to be sincerity. The discovery relaxed her.

"Tom, I am pleased that you are happy in marriage…" she started to say to further relax things between them but he cut off her sentence.

"But I am not," he said, startling her in her thoughts and words.

Tom looked at her and knew it was true. He also realised this might be the only moment he would ever have to speak to her alone.

"I am not happy in my marriage," he continued. "I do not love her, and too often I have thought about you," he said, speaking only the truth that he knew at that moment.

~~~~~~

From across the road, Edward watched the interaction continue. It lasted a short time but everything seemed to be moving in slow motion. He saw the man move closer to Alessandra, and yet still he could not bring himself to move from his spot and return to his wife. He felt eager to see what would happen between them, if anything. He had no reason to doubt her feelings for him, but looking at her standing and talking to a man with such a level of attractiveness played on his confidence greatly.

Behind him, the shop owner approached.
~~~~~~

"Your parcel shall be delivered in three days, Sir," he said.

Edward thanked him before resuming his view across the road, bringing his stare to the awareness of the shop owner.

"Ahh, young Miss Alessandra has captured your eye, I see. She has always been a polite young lass who everyone respects. She and her family are loyal friends in this part of the land."

Edward heard him and took the opportunity to learn something new about his wife.

"But who is the man she is talking to?" he asked bluntly.

"Oh, that is young Tom Missinger. It looked for a time to many of us that they would marry but he up and went off to marry another young lady. This is the first time I have seen him back." After a moment of silence, the shop owner continued his conversation. "Do you know the young miss?"

"Alessandra and I are married," he said quietly and the shop owner looked overjoyed.

"Oh, Sir, I apologise. I did not realise. Congratulations," the owner replied, holding out his hand to shake Edward's.

"Thank you," Edward replied as he shook the hand of the man in front of him, and then turned back to resume his view. The shop owner turned away respectfully and moved on with his day as if nothing out of the ordinary had happened at all.

~~~~~~

"You cannot say such things to me, Tom," Alessandra said to him quietly.

"And why not? I have said I do not love my wife, so why should you not know how I still feel about you?" Tom replied. He knew he was being disrespectful to his wife but was not at all prepared for the look she gave him then. It was a look that pierced him completely.
~~~~~~

"But I am married, Tom, and I do love my husband. He is the greatest man I have ever met and we are very happy together," she said. Instantly she saw Tom take a step back from her with a look of surprise and realisation on his face.

That is why she looks so confident, he thought to himself. She is not like my wife, hating everything about our intimate time and cringing when I touch her. Alessandra has learned how to share intimacy and enjoy it the way it is meant to be enjoyed. The thought passing through his head resulted in his heart feeling heavy. The regret that then set in that made him blunder on without thinking about what he was saying, or how he sounded as he said it.

"But I know that you loved me, Alessandra. I do not believe that you could have moved on to love someone else..."

"Tom, please listen to me," she said, moving closer to him. "I am in love with my husband. Did I think that I loved you then? Yes, I did, and if you had asked me to marry you I would have accepted you. But you did not ask me and now we are both married to other people. There is nothing more to say about that."

Tim looked at her in surprise at the level of assurance in herself that was flowing from her. It left him utterly speechless.

~~~~~

Across the road, Edward told himself that enough was enough. For Alessandra's sake, he should have been standing next to her as her husband, supporting her in whatever was going on. He walked out of the store and reluctantly started to cross the road. Out of the corner of her eye, he saw Alessandra notice him and smile. She held out her hand for him, giving him the confidence to walk forward and come right up to her. Once he reached the two of them he let her take his hand in hers and heard her speak up as Edward could feel the eyes of the
~~~~~

other man upon him.

"Edward, please allow me to introduce to you an old friend of mine, Tom Missinger. Tom, this is my husband, Edward."

The two men shook hands, neither of them wanting to but both falling under her spell of making happen what she wanted to happen. Alessandra then turned completely away from Tom and toward Edward.

"Are you ready to return to my parents' house?" she asked, looking at him directly in a way that reassured him. Edward nodded in return.

She looked back at Tom one more time. "Take good care of yourself, Tom. It was nice seeing you again," she said and led Edward away, holding his hand firmly and not wanting to let it go.

Tom watched the two of them move away, aware of the way she had looked into her husband's eyes. He noticed how she was holding Edward's hand and looking up at him now. Even from his angle behind them, he could see the way they looked at each other. Inside of him, Tom regretted deeply that he had not stood up to his parents and told them how much Alessandra had meant to him.

~~~~~

The rest of the afternoon and evening was spent with Alessandra's parents, talking about arrangements to be made later for them to come to Edward's parents' home to stay when the baby was almost due.

"Are you sure your mother will not mind, Edward? We would not want to cause any imposition," Alessandra's mother said. All found her words amusing. Everyone in the room knew that she wanted more than anything the opportunity to be close to her daughter when her time would come to lie in.

Edward laughed at her fondly. "It will not be an imposition, I assure you. We have more than enough room for you to come and stay with us for as long as you
~~~~~

wish to," he said and paused, looking at his wife. "And I know Alessandra would like you there too."

~~~~~

Later, lying in bed, finally Alessandra spoke about earlier that day. She'd thought that Edward might want to question her about Tom. On hearing no question, she wondered if he'd put his appreciation for privacy ahead of his curiosity, even if it meant he would get twisted inside.

"Tom and I were close for a short time, long before I had heard of you, Edward. I did think for a time that I was in love with him and that he might ask me to marry him," she said. She could see the relief on her husband's face as the subject was opened up.

"And what happened?" Edward asked.

"He married someone else. At the time I felt very let down, and such a child for having read his intentions so wrongly," she said, her memory of that time showing on her face.

"But if he had not married someone else, and he had asked you to marry him?" Edward probed.

Alessandra looked at him, not wanting to be anything except completely honest.

"Then I would have married him," she said and his face revealed the hurt of that. "But then I would never have met you, and I do not believe that you and I were not intended to meet and be together, Edward. I know that you are who I am meant to be with, and the only man I want to be with."

Edward lay quietly, not speaking, and she let him until he was ready to speak.

"I watched the two of you from across the road," he said, looking ashamed in the process.

"As I am sure I would have, had it been you talking to a woman," she said, making him look up at her in surprise.

"Would you?" he asked.
~~~~~

"Yes. I think anyone would take notice of their loved one talking intimately with someone as I was with Tom today," she replied honestly. She put her hand up to his face before kissing him softly. "Do not think about him again. He is from my past. You, and the dozens of children we are going to have, are my present and my future."

He was quiet for a moment before he realised what she had said, and laughed softly.

"Dozens?"

CHAPTER 30

The next morning Alessandra and Edward said their farewells to Alessandra's mother and father, with the promise that both parents would come to Edward's estate in the coming months.

Once on their journey, Edward and Alessandra both started to think about the night ahead, staying in the same inn once again. Edward found himself fuelled at the thought but now also worried about her being pregnant. He was desperate to not do anything that might harm her or the life growing inside of her.

After greetings at the inn, they calmly followed the innkeeper up to their room and immediately closed the door behind them. Once there, Edward found his desire to maintain control was forcefully counteracted by his wife wrapping her arms around him and kissing him passionately.

Alessandra heard him groan deeply but then felt him pull away from her.

"What is it?" she asked him and could see conflict on his face.

"Are we going to hurt the baby?" he asked shyly. She smiled broadly at him and pulled him closer to her again.

"No, the doctor said that everything will be fine for months yet," Alessandra said. When Edward didn't say anything she continued. "Edward, all is well. My body is hardly changed at all yet."

She leaned in to kiss him tentatively, to feel her way and make sure she wasn't pressuring him. Slowly he melted against her, having missed her warmth so much in previous nights.

~~~~~

Lying in bed, still connected to his wife, Edward relaxed after the vigour of their lovemaking. He relished the feeling of being so close to her, lying on top of her as he rested inside her. As she kissed him all over his face and stroked his hair, he felt at rest.

"I love you so much," he whispered to her, wondering how he was going to get through months without such intimacy if she carried the child to full term.

Alessandra kissed him deeply, knowing that he was still concerned for her.

"I love you too, Edward. Please stop worrying. You and I both know that babies do not always survive through to birth, or after birth. I do not want that thought to stop us from enjoying our love for one another."

Edward said nothing in reply, instead quietly moving beside her, cuddling into her further, and holding her tighter.
~~~~~

CHAPTER 31

As they approached the manor house the next day, they could see Edward's mother run out the front entrance, already extending her arms to hug them as soon as they could reach her.

"Oh my son, it is good to have you back," she said, holding him tightly before turning to Alessandra. "And you too, Alessandra. Are you well?" she asked, expectantly.

"Yes, I am well, and yes, I do now believe Edward and I are going to have our first child," she said, smiling at Edward's mother, who let out a shriek of happiness.

"Oh!" she said, seeming unable to say anything more as she gathered her son and her daughter-in-law into her arms once more. "I am so happy for you both."

She ushered them into the house. They were then greeted by Edward's father, who came forward to shake his son's hand and kiss Alessandra on the cheek.

"Alessandra is with child," Edward's mother informed him. Alessandra saw Edward's father's face become visibly emotional before he contained it and a look of determination came over him again.

"Congratulations to you both. We must all work now to help you rest, Alessandra," he started to say.

Alessandra laughed lightly at him. "I shall be well, I am sure, but thank you."

Edward spoke up, to bring attention back to the fact that they had only just arrived home.

"Father, I should like to get Alessandra settled. Shall I then join you for anything that needs attending to?"

"Yes, please. If you can come to the steward's room when you are free I would like to go over some paperwork with you," his father replied and then walked off in that direction.

"Mother, we shall see you soon," Edward said, dismissing his mother and taking Alessandra's hand to lead her upstairs to their bedroom.

Once in their room again he pulled her close and held her while softly kissing her.

"I have to leave to go and see Father. What shall you do? If you want to lie down to rest, I can let Mother know…"

"Edward, I am fine. Stop worrying. I will go down and see your mother once I have freshened up," Alessandra replied, kissing him and then ushering him out the door.

Once the door was closed she took a moment to lie on top of the bed and just be silent and alone for a few minutes. She moved her hands over her stomach, feeling highly protective of the little person trying to grow inside of her. She suspected it would be something that was all thought-encompassing for the entire household in months to come.

She was deep in thought when she heard a light knocking on the door. Upon opening the door, Alessandra saw Margaret curtsey to her.

"Good afternoon, Miss. I just wanted to see if you need anything," she said. Alessandra smiled at her.

"Now, Margaret, be honest with me and tell me if someone sent you here to fuss over me," she said.

The older woman smiled back while nodding.

"Mistress has asked me to stay close by in case you need help with anything," she replied. "Do you need your case unpacked, perhaps?"

Alessandra nodded and opened the door wider to allow Margaret access into the room.

"Thank you. I would appreciate that," she said and

watched as her items were carefully removed from her case and laid out for sorting. "And thank you again for our conversations." She paused as she saw Margaret look up at her with a wondering look on her face. "I do now believe that I am with child, so I may lean on you more in the coming months."

Margaret smiled broadly and then toned it down in remembering her place.

"Of course, Miss. I am always here."

~~~~~

Alessandra made her way downstairs to find Edward's mother. Upon not seeing her in the drawing room, she ventured further back in the house, through the kitchen and into the garden. Still unable to find her, she decided to go to her own preferred place for sitting and thinking. As she entered the glass room, she saw Edward's mother sitting there, looking like she was deep in thought.

"Are you well?" she asked her mother-in-law and saw her jump slightly.

"Oh, Alessandra, I did not hear you enter. Yes, child, I am well. Come. Sit with me," she said, moving along the bench to make room.

After Alessandra had sat down, Edward's mother continued. "How are you feeling? Physically, I mean."

"I feel as well as I did before I learned I am carrying a child. I do not notice any difference yet."

"Alessandra, I understand you were tentative about announcing because you are aware that I was told long ago that I could not have any more children."

Alessandra nodded.

"You must forget such thinking. My time for children is gone, and even if it wasn't - even if I were a young woman in my youth and wanting to start a family - this is nothing you should hide. It is joyous and something to celebrate. Edward's father and I look forward to seeing our son become a father, and us being able to meet our
~~~~~

grandchildren. It is something that brings us happiness."

"Thank you. I shall try to not do anything that might … harm … the baby," Alessandra replied.

For a long while, the two of them then sat quietly in contemplation.

"We have a good physician in Bath, who you may see as you wish to. If you would prefer, you are welcome to find another one. You might also like to find a midwife who can help you when your time is near."

"I do not know how to find such people," Alessandra replied.

"Worry not. We are all here to support you, and I will put the word out for a midwife. Someone will know of one who has been used recently and is spoken highly of."

"Thank you."

~~~~~~

That evening, in the quiet of their bedroom, Edward and Alessandra stood in front of the fire. They held each other and kissed deeply while slowly undressing each other. Being in the privacy of their room again, Edward felt more at ease in making love to his wife. He took great care and joy in removing her clothing at a pace that seemed almost unbearable to Alessandra, who found herself wanting him more and more, and with greater urgency.

Finally naked, she lay back on the seat by the fire and rejoiced in the feeling of Edward pleasuring her with his mouth.

"I am still going to keep doing this to you, even after the time passes where we cannot join, Alessandra," he said.

Alessandra did not say anything. Instead, she focused on the delicious feelings he invoked in her. Soon she was tipped over the edge in a moment of blissful release.

As he came up to her level, she kissed him passionately and enticed him to enter her, hearing him
~~~~~~

groan deeply. No matter how often they joined, that first moment of entry always felt like something that had never been felt before.

After Edward climaxed inside of her, he clung to her. He felt the depth of how much he had come to truly love her, despite how rocky things had looked when they had first met.

Alessandra held him, reading his emotion and rejoicing in their suitability in marriage and physical love. She encouraged him to stand up so they could both move into the bed. As they stood up Edward looked closer at his wife and touched her belly softly.

"You are starting to grow now," he said, smiling at her as his hand moved over the very slight bump that had started to form. "You become more beautiful every day."

CHAPTER 32

"What do we need to do today, Father?" Edward asked at the breakfast table one morning, three weeks later. The response he got back was a broad smile from his father and his mother, who looked as if they had done something underhand.

"Today you shall take your lovely wife into Bath," he started. Alessandra raised her head in surprise. Since arriving on the estate, she hadn't ventured to any of the nearby towns. She felt a familiar excitement grow inside of her at hearing the words. "Your mother and I have agreed that you and Alessandra - should you wish to - shall take some time off from your duties around the estate. Go and enjoy some time together before Alessandra is too large with child. The weather is fine now and the roads are clear as we move into spring. We have arranged for you to stay at The Railway Manor for the next four nights."

Edward and Alessandra looked at each other with an equal look of surprise, then excitement, and then joy.

"Father! Mother! Thank you!"

"Shall I assume that you both would like to do this, and arrange the carriage for you?"

Edward looked enquiringly at his wife, excited but concerned about her journeying.

"It is up to you, Alessandra. Do you feel up to some travel and exploration?" he asked her.

Alessandra smiled broadly and nodded with great enthusiasm. Three hours later she sat beside her husband in a carriage, heading off to a new town that she'd greatly heard about but had never visited. As they travelled, she placed her hand on her belly, silently telling her unborn child all about it.

~~~~~

After they checked into their accommodation, Edward and Alessandra stood at the window of their room. It was a glorious view, looking out over the view of the township.

"Oh, Edward, your mother and father are so kind to me," Alessandra said, feeling emotional.

"Alessandra, they love you, as do I," he said, placing his hand over her belly once again. "When this little one comes we may not have as much time together alone like this, so let us enjoy it."

Edward kissed her, as a gesture with the thinking that they would then walk out and start exploring. He soon realised that his wife had other plans. It wasn't long before he found himself taken into the world of pleasure once again.

"Do you think other married couples spend as much time like this, as we do?" he asked her after they were sated once more, the thought having crossed his mind curiously.

"No. It is my understanding from what other people have told me, that some couples very much do not spend time like this together. It seems some do not, in fact, even enjoy it. It is difficult for me to understand. I think I could spend all day every single day of my life like this, with you," Alessandra said with a serious tone. Edward laughed at her, making her laugh softly also.

"My beautiful wife," he said, kissing her again. "How different you are now, from the shy, timid little thing that came into my home and was too afraid to speak."

Alessandra smiled at him indulgently. "That is your doing, Edward," she started to say and saw a look of surprise on his face. "Every single day you make me feel like I am beautiful."
~~~~~

CHAPTER 33

The young couple spent their first day in Bath in their room, eating, drinking, making love and talking. Always they seemed to find it so easy to talk to one another about so many things, continuing to learn new things about one another.

The following morning, Alessandra looked out the window and let her excitement take over.

"Oh, let us go out and walk around the town, Edward," she said. "It looks so beautiful."

Edward came up behind her and kissed the back of her neck, making her temporarily wonder if she did want to leave their room. "You look so beautiful, my lovely wife."

Alessandra pulled away from him as she smiled. "Come, Edward. There are things for us to see and do," she said with mock sternness.

Edward laughed before putting on his coat and starting to follow her.

~~~~~

As they walked through the streets, Alessandra found herself wide-eyed in looking at the many people around. Everyone she saw seemed to have come from a much higher place in society than she had ever seen. She found herself looking at gowns, jewels, and the elaborate ways the women wore their hair. If she had been of another kind of nature, the experience might have made her feel ugly and not of a class high enough to be among such people. With her exuberance and keen eagerness for learning, she walked among them like a scholar in a
~~~~~

university.

Edward watched his wife much more so than he looked at anyone else. Her facial expressions were a constant source of allurement to him. He knew that even he, with the standing his family had in the land due to the size of his family's estate, would never be regarded as high in society as many of the people around them were. Despite that, he at least had grown up around such people through his parents' entertaining at the estate. To now know and fully understand where his wife had come from, made him even more in awe of her for so easily walking among such people without any indication of unease at all.

~~~~~~

From a distance, another pair of eyes found their way to Alessandra and were now watching the way that she and her husband looked at each other. As Tom Missinger stared at the couple, he felt a deep regret once again for not having insisted to his parents that she was the one he wanted to marry. He also recognised that he had a deep longing for her. He needed to be looked at the way that Alessandra looked at the man beside her.

While continuing to watch her discretely, he took a moment to think about his own marriage and look at his wife beside him. Of course, their marriage had seemed an acceptable idea at the time. With his intended bride, he would be able to add much land to Missinger Estate, his family property. It had been easy when he had first met his intended as he'd been truly struck by her immense physical beauty. That hadn't wavered since they'd wed, but now he looked at Alessandra and even though she was no beauty - and had never been - the level of happiness and contentment on her face transformed her into someone with a very attractive quality about her indeed.

"Are you well, Tom?" he heard his wife ask.

He smiled sadly at her. "Of course, Katherine."
~~~~~~

That was all it took for her to be reassured and turn her attention elsewhere. Even though they had been married for so long, she still seemed to him to be just an accessory to him. Equally, Tom felt like he was just an accessory to her. She had never seemed to have any desire for them to have true intimacy. She treated the marital act like it was a necessary unpleasant thing that had to be done, but should be done as quickly as possible and then forgotten. Even in that, there was still no child. That had left tom wondering what the point of all that land would be if there was never going to be any heir to inherit it.

Looking at his previous beau and her beloved, Tom could tell that they had an entirely different type of marriage. It was evident that Alessandra's husband was sharing with her all the things that Tom had always wished for. The thought made him feel unbelievably sad. He was still processing that thought, looking at Alessandra, when he came back to the present and realised that she was looking straight back at him.

Without any thought of his wife, Tom Missinger moved forward.

~~~~~~

Alessandra and her husband enjoyed exploring and looking at many things. They were just about to head back to their lodgings when Edward saw Alessandra's face change from joy to surprise, and then to intense thoughtfulness. When he followed her gaze he was unhappy to see heading toward them the same handsome man he'd seen her with in her home town. Thinking quickly, this time he made sure to be in the picture that this man saw of Alessandra. Edward remained close to her, holding her hand.

"What a delightful surprise, seeing you here," Tom said directly to Alessandra and not at all giving Edward any acknowledgement.

Alessandra curtseyed but avoided his eye contact.
~~~~~~

"Tom, what are you doing?" Tom heard his wife ask as she approached them. Alessandra saw his face cringe.

"Katherine, please allow me to introduce an old friend, Alessandra, and her husband," he said, trying to seem normal even though his nerves were frayed. "This is my wife, Katherine."

"It is a pleasure to meet you, Mrs Missinger," Alessandra said to the woman. She couldn't help but see the icy cold look being returned to her. "It is good to see you, Tom. Please excuse us as we cannot stop," she said and walked away quickly, holding Edward's hand tightly.

Once they were a suitable distance away, Edward stopped their walking. "Alessandra, take a deep breath. I can see you are wound up. What is upsetting you so much?" Edward asked her.

She gave him a look that almost made him reel. "I do not feel comfortable being around a man I once thought I had feelings for. It makes me feel … ill at ease."

Edward looked at his wife and did not want to say anything more that might upset her. He decided to divert her instead, moving forward to her, putting his arms around her and kissing her. It was not a done thing to do in such an open and public place, but Alessandra reacted quickly. As she put her arms around him and held him, she let her mind be taken to another place - a far more pleasurable place.

She looked at him demurely and whispered close to his ear, "Could we please go back to our room?"

Edward smiled at her and she could see - and feel - his reaction. It was strong.

"Yes, of course my love, but I do need a minute to think about the weather," he said, smiling shyly, and causing her to giggle in her more relaxed state.

~~~~~

Across the road, the same eyes were still on the two of them. Tom watched as the two of them embraced. He
~~~~~

watched as Alessandra's husband kissed her, and saw how eagerly she responded. What hurt even more was the way her husband said something to her, and she laughed so freely and easily, with true happiness on her face. What it must be like to have a wife look at me like that, he thought to himself. He watched Alessandra and Edward walk off, hand in hand. Even as they moved further away, Tom could still see them looking at each other with a message of desire broadcast openly on their faces.

~~~~~

In their room, Edward felt Alessandra undress him and then walk him backward to the bed, pushing him down so that he was lying on his back. He lay still as he watched her undress before him, and then climb up to lie down on top of him. As aroused as he was, he kissed her as she moved over him in a way that enabled her to rub against him. To Edward it was exciting, to have his wife moving in her own way when usually he was on top.

Alessandra felt confident and highly aroused, taking control of the movements between them. She moved down on him, experimenting with how it felt. Both of them groaned at their joining.

"Oh, Alessandra," Edward breathed out, enjoying these new feelings while watching his wife move on him. "Oh, my love … what you do to me," he continued, moaning in pleasure while alternating between kissing her and watching her. It wasn't long before Alessandra saw, heard and felt his release.

She relaxed on him, content to just be with the man she loved so deeply now. They kissed softly, immersed in emotion, both knowing that nothing needed to be said.
~~~~~

CHAPTER 34

The following day Edward took Alessandra to the Pump Room at her request, providing her desired freedom to watch all the people there. It wasn't an amusement he gained joy from, but he was happy enough watching her watch everyone else.

Once settled in a comfortable spot, Edward left her to go and get her a refreshment. Almost immediately after he'd walked off in one direction, Alessandra found herself approached by Tom.

"Alessandra," he said quietly.

As she turned she was surprised to see Tom Missinger looking around guiltily.

"Tom, you seem to be appearing everywhere," she said to him, not unkindly but certainly not in a friendly manner. Upon seeing him she realised that every tiny bit of feeling she had ever had for him had now disintegrated.

"Alessandra, I cannot stop thinking about you," he said, blushing furiously. His words surprised Alessandra as he had always seemed to be the confident one of the two of them. "I wish…"

He stopped talking mid-sentence but in her curiosity, Alessandra didn't let it end there.

"You wish … what? That you and I were married?" she asked.

"Yes … no … oh, I do not know what I want. All I know is that you are on my mind all the time. Please…"

"Please, what?" Alessandra asked him, wondering why he was showering all this attention on her now when so much time had passed.

"Please … I would like to spend some time with you," he blurted out, not even knowing himself what he meant by such a declaration.

Alessandra looked at him closely. He was a handsome man and yet when she looked at him now, she did not see attractiveness. She knew that she was now incredibly happy that he'd taken himself off when he did to get married. Edward was ten times the man that Tom was.

"Tom, you are married and I am married. Not only am I happy in my marriage but I am also expecting a child. I am living a life that I love. Please do not talk to me anymore. It makes me uncomfortable, given what my feelings for you were before, and I am doing what I can to remain calm, for the sake of my baby," she said as plainly as she could. She saw him look at her belly.

"You are with child?" he asked, with an incredulous tone in his voice. He could not believe that so much that he wanted in a wife appeared to be standing right in front of him.

Behind Tom, Alessandra saw Katherine approaching so nodded in response to his question and informed him quietly.

"Tom, your wife is nearing us," she said. She saw recognition in his eyes before he turned and started walking away, meeting his wife in the process and avoiding her coming face to face with Alessandra again.

Just as Tom walked away, Edward came up behind Alessandra, startling her.

"Are you alright?" he asked, not giving any indication if he had seen Tom or not.

She smiled at him, appreciating yet again what a good, loving man he was.

"Yes," she said. "Tom just approached me again but I have told him not to do so anymore."

Edward had no response except to hand her the

refreshment she had wanted. Both of them then determined to put Tom Missinger out of their minds for good.

CHAPTER 35

After waking and breakfasting the next day, Alessandra looked at Edward across the dining table and spoke, breaking him out of deep thoughts.

"Edward, if this is to be the last day you and I have completely alone for a long while, would you be upset at the idea of us not going anywhere today? I would very much like to just be with you, without any restrictions or plans," she said tentatively.

He looked closely at her before responding. "Are you alright, Alessandra? You do look pale."

"Oh, yes, I am well but I do not feel like being around people today. I just want to be with you."

He nodded, took her hand in his and stood up to leave.

"Come then, my lovely wife. Let us return to our room and relax," he said quietly in an effort to keep her calm.

"Relax?" she asked in her teasing manner, making him laugh at her attempt to get him heated again.

~~~~~

Through the day they lay around on the bed and had meals delivered to their room when they desired to eat. For the whole day, Alessandra felt like they were in their own little universe that no-one else could touch.

As she lay back on the bed on her back, even though there was no large physical bump yet to indicate her being pregnant, Edward gently caressed her belly. It was a small movement but soothing to her. She giggled as he started to talk to the little life inside of her.
~~~~~

"There is no harm in telling him early on about the world, my love," he said with a humorous tone to his voice.

"Him? Oh, I see you already know that this is a boy," she teased him back.

"No," Edward said. "I know people always say boys are more important as heirs, but all I want is for you to be safe and well, no matter whether we have a daughter or a son."

They both lay quiet, thinking about life to come.

CHAPTER 36

On their journey back to the estate the next day, Edward and Alessandra were both quiet, wrapped up in their individual thoughts.

In Edward's mind, he still had a pressing reminder about the man who had kept turning up and approaching Alessandra - Tom. He knew there was no reason to give Missinger any more consideration, and yet now and then a thought would enter his head and cause him concern. Not that he would voice that concern to Alessandra of course. His main job in the coming months, as far as he was concerned, was to keep her calm and happy in the hope that she would be able to carry their child to full term. Even in that, he didn't have any real reason to worry. It was mainly the limited success of his and Alessandra's parents to easily have children that inspired him to think about that possibility being passed down to the expected little one also. He knew that all he could do was try and do what he could to provide his wife with as happy a life as he could and let nature decide whether he would become a father or not.

Beside him, Alessandra felt him squeeze her hand firmly. When she looked at him she could see he was deep in contemplation, under the guise of looking out over the scenery passing them by. She was hopeful that whatever was worrying him, he would talk about when he felt the time was right.

Even though their four nights away had been welcome and enjoyable, Alessandra found herself looking forward to getting home. She had particularly enjoyed the day before, not having to see anyone except Edward all day long. She suspected he carried concern for her and the baby growing inside of her, so she was determined to not give him any real reason to worry. But she did look forward to the months passing and them knowing one way or another if they were to be parents or not.

~~~~~

Upon arrival at the manor house, Edward's mother once again ran out to greet them, throwing her arms around them in a loving embrace.

"Oh, my children! Did you see and do many exciting things?" she asked excitedly as she ushered them inside and into the drawing room.

Edward looked tired and not receptive to his mother's enthusiasm so Alessandra laughed quietly at his mother and responded.

"It was lovely to be able to spend so much time together alone," she said. The openness of the comment seemed to stun Edward's mother into silence.

Edward must have heard her response in the background of whatever he was thinking. Alessandra saw him turn and give her a shy yet sad smile.

"Mother, we are going to get settled. We shall return shortly," he said, leading Alessandra out of the room and upstairs to their bedroom.

When the door closed, he pulled her into his arms and held her tightly. He didn't speak or kiss her. Alessandra allowed him to engulf her while she held him close to her. She remained silent, allowing him whatever time he needed.

Finally, he pulled far enough away so that he could look into her eyes and kiss her softly on the lips. When she looked at him she saw he was trying to not let tears appear in his eyes. She pulled him close again, waiting for him to speak, but he did not.

"Edward, what is making you so upset?" she asked
~~~~~

quietly, trying once more to look into his eyes.

"I love you so much, Alessandra. I cannot even consider the thought of not having you here with me," he said, wiping a tear away from his eye.

"But why should you think I am not going to be here with you?" she asked. "I have no desire to be anywhere else."

He hugged her tightly again. "I know. I am sorry. My emotions are overpowering me today. I have never felt love like this before and sometimes it is overwhelming."

Alessandra pulled away completely and took his hand to lead him to the bed, where she bid him to lie down. There she lay down beside him, holding him against her.

"Are you certain there is nothing in particular worrying you, Edward?" she asked quietly.

In response, Edward moved even closer into her arms. "No, my love. I just want a few minutes here with you, like this, and then I shall go downstairs and see my mother and father."

~~~~~

When the two of them ventured into the drawing room once again, they stumbled into a conversation neither of them had thought about yet.

"We will need to find a nanny and open up the nursery once more," Edward's mother was saying.

The comment surprised Alessandra. She hadn't considered anyone other than her and Edward raising her child. She remained quiet with the determination to voice her thoughts on the matter at a much later date. She was still only around ten weeks into her pregnancy, by the reckoning of her and Margaret. She didn't want to invest too much thought or planning into the baby just yet.

Upon hearing Alessandra and Edward come into the room, his mother quietened, having received a stern look from her husband to do so.

"Thank you both once again for arranging our time
~~~~~

away," Alessandra said quietly to them. It was her attempt to change the subject whilst not indicating she'd heard their words at all.

Highly out of character, Edward's father came forward and hugged her. "You are most welcome, Alessandra. I am glad you enjoyed it."

He then turned to Edward. "Edward, I would like you to accompany me on a visit to see John Homer, who is having some problems with the sheep he is tending. Can you spare yourself today?" he asked.

Edward nodded. "Of course, Father. I can come with you now if you need me to," he replied before kissing Alessandra fondly and walking out.

~~~~~

Alessandra walked to the drawing room window and watched out as her husband and his father mounted their horses. As if sensing her watching, Edward turned to look at her and wave before he rode off slowly beside his father.

When Alessandra turned to her mother-in-law, she caught her watching her thoughtfully.

"Is there anything you would like me to do today?" she asked, seeming to break Edward's mother out of her gaze and thought.

"Yes! Spring is upon us so you and I must start planning our annual spring cleaning of the house. In the steward's room are lists that we can go through them together," she said eagerly.

Alessandra nodded and followed her mentor to the steward's room. Together they sat down at the large wooden desk and looked through the pages of details that seemed to go on forever.

"As you can see, Alessandra, this list is extensive as it has been formulated over many decades. I have found that it works well to ensure that every room and surface is cleaned to the standard needed after winter. The weather is starting to fine up now so soon we shall be
~~~~~

able to open up the rooms that remain closed over winter. Every summer we hold hunts here, with a great many guests to stay. All bedrooms get used then and the rooms, beds and linen need to all be aired out in preparation for that."

"It will be a busy time for us then," Alessandra said, feeling overwhelmed all of a sudden.

"Do not worry about the work itself, Alessandra. We hire additional service staff during the height of the spring cleaning, and our regular household staff will do the rest. The part you and I play is working through these lists to make sure everything is planned to be done, and everyone knows what their job is and when it has to be done by."

Alessandra took a deep breath and determined to remain calm.

CHAPTER 37

Over the following four weeks, Alessandra was introduced to directing staff and checking the standard of their work. She found it exciting to be slowly discovering new areas of the house as the weather warmed and more rooms could be opened up for attention. She found it hard to see how Edward's mother could be right in saying that all the rooms would be used for their upcoming hunts. The rooms seemed to go on forever around the complex formation of corridors and stairways.

In the estate responsibilities, slowly she learned more and more. Each day she became increasingly confident in her ability to identify and relate to the service staff and recognise who was responsible for what.

Coming into her fourth month of pregnancy all appeared well but she could see that the further along she was, the more stressed Edward was in his concern for her. Lying in bed at night, he would fondly caress the bump that was now forming. It was an action that Alessandra never tired of, but she worried that Edward always seemed preoccupied.

"Edward," she said, forcing him to look at her directly. "I am worried about you. Please tell me what is on your mind."

"My love, you only need to concentrate on yourself and this little one," he said quietly.

Alessandra would not let that lie. "No, that is not true. You are my husband. I love you, and I am very worried that something is wrong with you. If you do not want me to be worried, please share with me whatever is hurting you so much."

Edward looked at her and knew that by trying to not cause stress in her, he was doing the exact opposite. Finally, he decided to speak.

"Alessandra, I love you and I trust you," he started to say, alarming Alessandra in his choice of words. "Letters have been arriving for you … and I have been preventing them from reaching you."

Alessandra's first thoughts were that she had not heard from her mother, but as she looked at her husband she could not believe that he would have stopped her correspondence.

"You have kept my mother's letters from me?" she asked with an incredulous look on her face. In return, she saw a look of horror on Edward's.

"No! Of course not! Alessandra I would never want to stop you having contact with your mother or anyone else in your family!"

His comment left Alessandra confused. She had never shared written correspondence with anyone else.

"I do not understand. No-one else writes to me," she said.

Edward took a deep breath, not wanting to admit what he had been doing. He equally didn't want to cause her more stress, especially with her having made it almost halfway through her term.

"They are all from Tom Missinger," he finally revealed.

"What?" Alessandra asked. "And when you say 'all', how many do you mean?"

Alessandra saw Edward's face go redder and redder as she saw guilt and remorse on his face.

"Over the past two months he has written to you six times," Edward replied. He paused before continuing, watching his wife process the information he'd provided. Feeling tears come to his eyes, he could no longer hold back how deceitful he'd felt each time he had taken the letters and hidden them. "I am so sorry, Alessandra. I do not know what came over me. I just could not face you being in contact with him."

Alessandra watched her husband, not with anger but with huge relief at finally knowing what had been eating him up inside.

"Edward, I do not care about letters that Tom Missinger has written to me. I would like to read them as I am worried I have not heard from my mother, and he is from my village originally. In case he has some news of my parents, the letters should be read if you still have them."

Edward nodded and retrieved the letters from one of his drawers before coming back to the bed and handing them to her.

"All I want to know is if there is anything about my family in these," Alessandra said. "Come and lie with me. You can read them with me so your mind is at rest about whatever is in them."

She began opening up the letters with the hope of finding any reference to her mother or father. As soon as she started reading the first one, she and Edward both realised that they weren't letters of just a childhood friend. They were love letters.

Edward moved to get up. "I should not read these," he said.

Alessandra put her hand on his and restrained him.

"Stop, Edward. These letters are only one-sided. If you run away you will keep torturing yourself inwardly, wondering what they say. No, let us both face this together and then we can forget it," she said.

Edward agreed with her logic and sat down again, even though he knew it was going to cause him pain.

Alessandra opened, held up and let the two of them read page after page but it was all the same. Tom Missinger was obsessed with thinking about her. He wanted to see her and to be with her. He would leave his wife for her, and he would raise her child as his own once it was born.

Alessandra read the pages like they were a novel and she was a student, learning about human behaviour. She felt no attachment or romantic notion about the words that had been addressed to her. At most, she was relieved that nothing in the letters pointed to something bad having happened to anyone in her family.

After she finished them all she handed them to Edward.

"Put them in the fire, Edward," she said and watched as he did so. "All this time you have been worrying internally and I have seen your stress because of it, but you never had anything to be concerned about."

"He is trying to make love to you, to lure you away from me," Edward replied, looking at her to try and read her true feelings. There was nothing on her face to suggest deceit or even any particular interest in the man from her past.

"There is only one man who will ever make love to me and he is here with me right now. Edward, you are truly the most beautiful man I know…"

"But I am ugly, and he is…"

"He is a handsome shell with no respect for my marriage or my feelings," she said before pulling Edward close to kiss him deeply. "You are no ugly man. You are my husband. I love you, and only you, and you are going to be a wonderful father to our child. Please hear and believe me when I tell you that I do not care who sends me letters, or what they say. I only want to be with you."

Edward kissed her, immediately feeling a blend of relief but also pain at not having trusted how strong she was. He should have believed that she would be able to read the letters and not be seduced by them.

"Now, please, whatever else is bothering you, let us

talk of it now so we can start tomorrow refreshed and relaxed again," she said.

He smiled shyly at her. "That was all that concerned me. There is nothing else."

Alessandra let out a deep breath and kissed him but then he could sense stress in her again.

"Edward, I have not heard from my mother in over a month. She has not replied to my last two letters. Can anything be done to find out if she is well?"

"I will talk to Father tomorrow and check if he has heard something and perhaps forgotten to pass it on to us. If he has heard nothing I can ride to your home and see your mother and father if you wish."

Alessandra didn't want him to leave her alone, but the concern for her mother was too great.

"Thank you. I do not want to be apart from you, but Edward I am very worried about her."

~~~~~

The next morning Edward's father and mother both confirmed they had not heard anything from Alessandra's parents. Edward resolved to go and find out what was happening at her family home.

"It is a long journey, Edward," his mother said, looking worried. "It will take you at least four days to get there and back."

Edward nodded but smiled. "Mother, Beauty has not had a good run through winter. It will be good for him, and it will put Alessandra's mind at rest," he said as he looked at his wife and saw her smile gratefully at him.

~~~~~

"Please be safe. I shall miss you very much but I thank you for doing this for me," Alessandra said quietly to him as he prepared to leave the manor.

Edward kissed her lovingly and saw only love shining back at him from her.

"As soon as I get there I shall send word to you of what I find, and I shall be back soon. Please remain calm and relax, and keep this little one safe."

Edward's mother watched with pride at seeing her son reach down and kiss the belly of his wife. They may have married for money, but even she could not deny the success of their union and their love.

As he set off, Edward felt sad at leaving his wife, but as he and Beauty began to gain speed he also rejoiced at the feeling of freedom as he rode. Winter was always restrictive in his riding, but now that spring had arrived, he needed to get out and run Beauty more. There was nothing quite like the feeling of the two of them when they could travel with speed.

CHAPTER 38

Unwilling to stop at all in his riding, Edward rode through the day and night and arrived at Alessandra's family home the next morning. After securing Beauty, he knocked on the door. At first he thought that no-one was there. Then an older woman who he had never seen before opened the door.

"I am looking for..."

"Oh, you are Miss Alessandra's husband! Has something terrible happened to her?" she asked, with a look of terror on her face.

"Oh, no. Sorry ... you are?"

"Oh, Mister Edward, sorry. I am June, the housekeeper. Sorry, we were not introduced when you were here before."

"Alessandra has been worried she has not heard from her mother so I have come to see if everything is alright," he said, still wondering what was going on.

"The mistress and master are well, Mister Edward. Come inside and sit down. They are not quite up for breakfast yet, but the food is ready. If you are hungry, you are welcome to sit at the dining table and I can bring in some food for you."

Edward entered the house, reminded again of how small it was. He thanked the housekeeper in her offer to have breakfast, having not stopped for a meal along his journey.

Just as he was finishing his meal, he was joined by Alessandra's mother and father.

"Edward! What brings you here? Oh no! Something

has happened to Alessandra?"

"No, Sir. Alessandra was worried that something had happened to you, as she had not had any reply to her last two letters. I want to keep her calm so I thought I could just ride here and see that you are both alright," Edward replied.

Alessandra's mother looked confused but sat down and took his hand.

"We are both well, but I have written to Alessandra twice in the past month, Edward. Why would she not be receiving my letters? Are you having problems receiving post at your home?" she asked.

Edward laughed quietly to himself, remembering the painful letters that most definitely had been arriving.

"No, there has been post most days. Perhaps it is a problem at this end?" he asked.

"I do not think so. Other letters I have sent have been replied to. An old friend of Alessandra's, Tom, has been kindly bringing our mail to us and sending away our outgoing correspondence."

Alessandra's father watched as he saw horror and then anger come over his son-in-law's face. It was a level of emotion he had never seen on Edward before.

"Tom ... Missinger?" Edward asked, trying desperately to maintain calm.

"Yes, do you know him?"

Edward rubbed his eyes and both parents looked at him in confusion.

"Is there some problem, Edward?" he heard Alessandra's father ask. Edward felt uncertain about whether to speak to them or not.

"Is there any possibility that Tom Missinger has prevented your letters from getting to Alessandra?" Edward asked. "Could it be that he never sent them?"

"Why should he do that?" Isabella asked.

Edward took a deep breath and then spoke.

"When Alessandra and I were in Bath not too long

ago, he was there. He made a declaration to her, which she rejected. Since then he has been writing to her, persisting in declaring his love for her. He has written of his desire to leave his wife and make a new life with Alessandra and the baby," he said.

The anticipated shock appeared on both of Alessandra's parents' faces.

"Oh, but Tom is a nice boy. What would he gain from doing this?" Alessandra's mother asked, remembering that Tom had been particularly attentive to them in recent weeks.

"I do not know…"

At that moment they heard a knock on the front door. Shortly afterward the person in question walked into the drawing room. Upon sight of Edward, Tom's face changed from the charming smile that had entered the room, to surprise, and then a surprising degree of eagerness.

"You!" Edward said, standing up and walking closer to him. Alessandra's parents watched on nervously.

Tom maintained his composure long enough to ask, "Is Alessandra here?"

Edward breathed out a sigh of realisation. "That is why you have been stopping letters from her mother reaching her? Because you thought it would bring her home, and you could see her?"

Tom quickly realised that he had miscalculated something in his plan. Now, without Alessandra to witness, he took the opportunity to speak plainly.

"You need to let her go, you ugly, horrible man," Tom said. "She deserves better than you, and she and I are meant to be together."

Edward took a moment to maintain composure for the sake of Alessandra's mother and father, who watched on with confusion on their faces. It was evident they were now realising they'd been charmed by a man who was all the time having plans of ruining their daughter's marriage. Edward remembered how Alessandra had described Tom the night before - only a beautiful shell. That was all she considered him to be.

Before Edward could speak, Alessandra's father came forward and placed himself between Edward and Tom.

"Tom, you have brought unnecessary concern on my daughter, and particularly so in the state she is currently in. That is something I could never forgive you for. Please leave our house and do not return. You are no longer welcome in our home," Edward watched Alessandra's father say, with the strength and fortitude of someone twice his size.

Tom ignored him, now needing him no more in his quest. He turned to face Edward once more.

"You do not deserve her, and I will have her," he said with a more menacing tone to his voice than anyone in the room had heard from him previously. After his declaration, he stormed out.

Edward and Alessandra's parents all looked at each other, perplexed as to what just happened.

"I cannot believe it. Was he making us like him, to win us over so that he could take our daughter away from you, Edward?" Alessandra's mother asked.

Edward nodded. "I had not thought he was quite so serious but yes, it does appear so," he said quietly.

"Edward, what will you do now? You are welcome to stay here for the night, before returning home," Alessandra's father said.

Edward weighed up options. He was tired, as Beauty must be also … Beauty! He quickly remembered that the township seemed to be largely horse-free so immediately worried.

"Thank you. I do need to think about letting Beauty rest and feed…"

"All taken care of, Mr Edward," the housekeeper said as she entered, catching the end of the conversation. "My John has taken him around back and is letting him enjoy some fresh grass and a little bit of hay. Worry not, John has been a horse lover all his life. He will look after him alright."

"Thank you. I do need to let Alessandra know you are all well, as she has been fretting somewhat. Is there some way for me to do that from here?"

"I can do that for you, Mr Edward. If you write a quick note, I can arrange its delivery when I go into the village shortly for supplies," June replied.

Alessandra's father leaped up to get writing supplies. Edward wrote as quickly as he could that her mother and father were well. He then faced the dilemma of what else he should disclose to her.

"I do not know whether to tell her about Mr Missinger or not. I would not like to alarm her," he said out loud. Immediately he was glad he did as both of his in-laws offered their view on the subject.

"Oh Edward, I do not know," Isabella said. "If she is already fragile, would it do any good to tell her?"

"Do you think there is any chance he will go to her now?" her father said, putting Edward in a further panic.

"Oh, I should get back to her..." he started to say as his worry intensified.

"No! Edward, you have been riding all night and you will need to rest. Just send her word that we are alright. If you want to alert anyone to the issue of Tom, perhaps you could send a second note privately addressed to your father, just so that someone there is aware of how this young man has been acting."

He thought about that and agreed.

"Yes, you are right. I shall stay tonight if you are sure I am not inconveniencing you. Tomorrow I shall set out first thing. Thank you."

Edward wrote the two notes and gave them to the housekeeper, who assured him they would be sent off later that afternoon.

"I have also put some hot water up in your room, Mr

Edward, for you to wash with if you wish," she said.

Edward was appreciative of her kindness. "Thank you," he responded.

When all was done he considered that he was alone in Alessandra's family home, with her family but without her. It did seem an odd situation to have gotten himself into.

~~~~~

Edward spent the afternoon partly in the company of Alessandra's father, then partly just with her mother, and at times with both. He found himself enjoying their company very much. In particular, hearing her mother talk about Italy was exciting for Edward.

"Alessandra has never been to my homeland," Isabella said. "I always hoped we would one day go there so I could show her some of her heritage, but it never happened. As your family grows, Edward, you must not forget that there will be some very special Italian blood in your children."

Later in the evening, lying in bed alone for the first time since he had wed, Edward kept thinking about the images of Italy he'd had put into his head during the day. He filed those thoughts away in the 'one day' section of his mind, to talk to Alessandra about at a later date. Lying back on the bed, the image of his beautiful wife came to mind. In exhaustion he was almost instantly asleep, a smile settled on his face.
~~~~~

CHAPTER 39

"Edward!" Alessandra called out as she saw him approaching the manor two mornings later.

Being the confident horseman he was, Edward seemed to fly down off Beauty before he cast the reins at the groom and rushed into his wife's arms. The young couple kissed as if they had been apart for much longer than only three nights.

Breaking apart, breathless, Alessandra looked at him. She had missed him desperately and felt the need to be closer to him. Her desire made her feel shy around him all of a sudden.

Edward looked at her face and smiled in the knowledge of just how much his wife had grown to love him. No matter how handsome his adversary was, it was he - Edward - who held her love.

"My beautiful wife, how I have missed you," he said before kissing her again.

Upon realising they had an audience, he laughed softly. "Father, Mother," he greeted his parents.

"Edward, it is good to have you home. Come and see us when you have given your wife the attention she deserves," his father said, walking his wife away and leaving the lovers to go to their room and have some privacy.

~~~~~

Once in their room, they were immediately in each other's arms, making Edward laugh at her enthusiasm.

"Wait, Alessandra. First, tell me if you did get the message about your mother and father being well,"
~~~~~

Edward said.

Alessandra nodded and smiled. "Yes. Oh, Edward, it was so kind of you to go and check on them for me. It is a relief for me to know they are well. Were they good to you, without me there?" she asked, curious since she'd spent the previous three nights in the company of just his parents also, and had found that not uncomfortable but very strange.

"Yes, of course. They were very kind, and I learned much about your family background, which was good to know since that will be part of our children's heritage," he said as he led her to the seat by the fireplace. "Speaking of which, how is our little one?"

As he asked, Edward placed his hand on her belly, caressing it softly. Alessandra rested her hand over his, having missed his touch.

"All is well, Edward. I am happy to have you back with me. It was not the same being in bed without you," she said, looking at him with a look that fuelled him instantly.

"Oh, how you invigorate me, Alessandra, even when I should be feeling so tired," Edward said.

He looked at her fondly, trying to back away from the desire he was feeling. As she leaned in to kiss him, he found himself eager to please her. He gently guided her back so she was reclining on the seat. There he let his hand move up her leg, inside her gown, and felt her legs part as her breathing deepened.

After moving all of the fabric up and aside so that he could kiss her there, he heard her moan with the pleasure he was providing her, and very quickly reach that peak that she loved. When he pulled away from her and rearranged her dress, he smiled at her, seeing how much more relaxed she was now.

Alessandra made to move toward him but he held himself back from her reach.

"Later, my lovely wife. I must find my father and talk

to him. Come down with me," he said to her with teasing in his voice. As he held out his hands to help her up, she tried to kiss him again.

"Do not try and tempt me any further, Alessandra!" he laughed at her as he led her out the door.

~~~~~

"I was disturbed in reading your note, Edward. Who is this man and why do you believe he might come here?" Edward's father asked when the two of them were alone in the steward's room.

"He is a man Alessandra had feelings for before we met her. He has appeared several times now. Since she told him in Bath that she did not want to see or talk to him, he has been writing love letters to her, trying to tempt her away from me," Edward said. He immediately saw distaste on his father's face. "He was the cause of Alessandra not receiving her mother's correspondence. He had been pretending to send them but instead was not. It was his hope that Alessandra would get so worried that she would go back to her village, and he would be able to see her."

"It is a shocking business, my son. But do you truly believe that he would dare come here?"

"I do not know. I hope not, but he did seem particularly determined in his quest, when he spoke to me," Edward quietly said to his father, who had a look of increasing concern on his face.

"Very well. You and I will begin visiting tenants tomorrow and make sure everyone is vigilant across the estate. In the meantime, do you agree it is best to keep this from Alessandra and your mother?"

Edward nodded. "I do, Father. I do not think any good could come from either of them being worried about this."

His father nodded. "Very well then. Let us not speak of it. Perhaps this man may not know where you are living and all this worry will be for nothing." Edward
~~~~~

remained silent to the fact that of course Tom must know where they lived if he'd intercepted the letters. He saw his father pause and look at him. "I am very proud of you Edward. I hope you know that."

Edward was taken aback at such a declaration. They had always had a sound father and son relationship but Charles Chisholm was not generally one to talk about his feelings.

"I am glad you convinced me to take heed of your mother's wishes about Alessandra as a choice for you," Charles continued. "I do not think we could ask for a better daughter."

The expression in his father's voice worried Edward. "Father, are you alright? Why are you speaking like this?"

His father smiled sadly. "Yes, I am well, Edward. I must now do some paperwork. You are free to return to your wife. She missed you terribly when you were away."

"I can help you with the paperwork…" Edward began to offer.

"No, thank you. Leave me now," his father said. "Tomorrow we shall resume regular duties around our visits to the estate tenants."

Edward knew he was dismissed. He left the room and started to head toward the drawing room. As he walked, he passed view of the glass room and saw Alessandra sitting peacefully and alone. For several minutes he stood and watched her before he entered quietly but with enough sound to make sure she wasn't startled.

As he moved into the room he saw her turn to him and smile. He approached and sat beside her on what now seemed to have become her own little bench on the property. Taking her hand in his, he looked into her eyes. They smiled at each other before she laid her head on his shoulder. Edward sat quietly, waiting to see if she wished to speak, but she sat silent.

"You are very quiet," he whispered. "What is on your mind, my lovely wife?"

Alessandra took a deep breath before seeming to find the words to answer.

"The weather is warm most days now. I would like to be outside more, but I do not want to risk riding Misty in case something happens. I am scared that I may fall or do some damage to our little one," she said, instinctively placing a hand on her belly.

Edward sensed her impatience at sitting still. "I agree that it might not be good for you to ride, but what about just walking?"

Alessandra looked up in surprise. She had not even considered going for a long walk. "But where could I walk to?"

"Oh well, I would not wish you to walk anywhere, well, not alone anyway. However, I know of a very nice path that sneaks around behind the manor and leads to a magical place indeed. I would be very happy for us to walk there if you like," he replied, making it all sound like a dream. "It is quite a walk to get to the destination, but very flat. If you feel up to it, we could begin walking there and come back whenever you feel tired."

Instantly Alessandra brightened and gave Edward a magnificent smile.

"Do you mean it?" she asked and saw Edward nod, his smile broad. "Oh, but do you have to help your father today?"

"No," Edward replied. "Tomorrow I am going to spend the day out with him, visiting tenants. For the remainder of today I am all yours," he replied indulgently. He was tired from his journey but considered that a long walk might be just what he needed himself to stay awake for the rest of the afternoon. "Let us go and visit Cook, and see what food we can pack up in a small bag to take with us and then we shall head off."

~~~~~

Half an hour later Alessandra found herself being led through one of the back gardens behind the manor, and then on to another garden behind that one. Having not seen the second garden before, she was already surprised and thought that perhaps that was their destination, but still Edward walked. They made their way through the rear wall gate of the second garden before entering in a bushy area with tall trees and shade.

"Oh!" Alessandra exclaimed as she realised she was visiting an entirely new area of the estate. "How pretty, Edward!"

He smiled at her, letting memories of his childhood flow over him. He remembered the days when he would run around the estate in complete freedom. At times he'd explored the area for hours on end while his childhood tutor had tried to keep watch over him from not far away.

"Are you alright to keep walking?" he asked.

Alessandra nodded. "Yes, I feel fine."

"We do not have to go the full distance today. If you tire, let me know immediately and we can turn back and come back another day."

Alessandra held his hand tightly. She felt more alive than she had in weeks. She relished the feeling it inspired in her.

"I did not know that you ever walked anywhere," she said, surprised at seeing a different side of her husband.

Edward laughed softly. "I do not tend to walk anywhere now but when I was young I spent many hours exploring out here. I must be honest and tell you that I had forgotten about it until you spoke earlier about getting out in the fresh air."

"I know nothing about your childhood, Edward. Tell me about it," Alessandra said.

For the next half an hour, as they slowly trekked forward through the bush and forest area. For the
~~~~~

duration, Edward shared with her story after story of different things that had happened. He enjoyed reminiscing over such fond memories.

Alessandra was so caught up in his conversation and the pictures it promoted in her head, that when he stopped talking she almost didn't notice.

Edward quietened as he knew they were close to where he wanted to take her. He began to watch her face so he could see her expression as he walked her a little bit further. As they moved closer the sound of water could be heard and began appearing louder. Finally, Alessandra seemed to hear it.

"What is that?" she asked with the look Edward had seen on her face so often, being that of a scholar on a journey of learning.

Edward led her further still. Their eyes adjusted to the light as they slowly emerged from the darkness of the forest. Ahead of her, Alessandra could see a grassy area with sunshine streaming onto it. Off to the right side of that, a small body of water sat with a tall waterfall flowing into it.

Edward watched her face, mesmerised. On it, he saw what he'd hoped to - the sense of having been transformed from such darkness of the forest area, into a small but beautiful piece of paradise bathed in sunshine.

Alessandra looked at him and smiled broadly before letting go of his hand and walking forward. She moved until she was standing in the middle of the grass area with sun rays shining directly onto her. As she held her face up to the light and closed her eyes, she listened to the water flowing behind her. She felt like she'd woken up from sleep in a new dream.

Edward gained joy from watching her. He waited before he approached her, letting her enjoy her pleasure. When he saw her open her eyes and look at him again, he moved forward and gladly accepted the hand held out to him as an indication for him to join her. Quietly he put his arms around her to hold her. Instantly he felt her cling to him as though they were going to be apart again. When he pulled away from her, he could see she had started to silently cry.

"Is this making you sad?" he asked, curious.

She smiled through the tears. "No, I am just so very happy, Edward. I love you so much."

As she kissed him passionately he indulged in it, this time welcoming it.

~~~~~

Edward pulled a blanket out of the satchel and laid it down on the grass, encouraging Alessandra to sit down and rest. She did so gladly and lay back on her back to let the sunshine flow over her. As Edward sat beside her and contently looked down at her, he loved seeing the happiness on her face.

After a few minutes of watching her lie down with her eyes shut, he saw her look up at him and reach out her hand to touch his face, guiding him down to kiss her. Edward lay down fully beside her. They kissed for a long time, with no move toward anything more.

"Can we make love here?" she asked, making him laugh as he once again remembered how shy she had been when she'd first come to the estate.

"Perhaps, but not today, Alessandra. I do not want to risk you getting a chill, and the weather is not as warm yet as it will get," he said stroking her cheek softly. "In summer perhaps."

Alessandra made a face like a child might make at being told they could not have pudding after their meal. "In summer I shall be too large to make love."

Edward smiled at her indulgently. "Then after this child is born, we shall take our time and plan the timing of conception a little better so that you are not with child in summer. Let us declare that to be our baby-making time from now on, rather than baby carrying time."

She laughed at him. "You are so wise, Edward," she
~~~~~

said with humour in her voice before becoming serious. "But Edward, will you want us to have children straight after each other?"

"Do you mean will I want you to become with child again as soon as a child is born?" he asked and saw her nod in reply. "No! I would like you to have a proper amount of time to rest and enjoy what you want to. We shall have a new child in our lives. Let us take time to enjoy getting to know them."

"But when I am closer to giving birth than this we will not be able to..." she started to say but then felt incredibly shy all of a sudden. "You will be ... hungry ... by the time the child is born."

He laughed at her wording but kissed her to reassure her. "You and I are happy even without joining, are we not? We will still share pleasure, just not always like that."

"How then?" she asked, attempting to deliver a look of innocence.

Edward laughed out loud. He knew she was working her magic on making him heated. "You know," he said, grinning at her.

"You may need to show me, so I can be sure," Alessandra said.

Edward swallowed hard and kissed her before moving so he could tentatively touch inside her dress and run his fingers up her leg. As he watched her face, she stared back at him as he moved his finger to that place she had discovered with him on their first night as husband and wife. He didn't move for anything else, just moved his finger over her, pleasuring her as he kissed her, until he felt and heard her release.

Alessandra felt the climax and indulged in it. No matter how far through the pregnancy she was, her desire for him felt like it kept growing, not lessening. She looked at him as he removed his hand and gently put her skirt back the way it had been. Aware that it was twice he had pleasured her since arriving home, she felt eager to return the feeling. She kissed him passionately until he groaned in his arousal from it. As she touched him through his clothing, she heard his groan change and become deeper. She tried to rearrange him so she could access him.

"Alessandra, what..." he started to ask before she succeeded in subtly positioning the two of them, gaining full access to him. She touched him with her hand and then her mouth. "Oh, my love..."

Edward did not try to argue with her anymore. Instead, he concentrated on the intense feelings he was having. It wasn't long before he was in his climax also. Immediately afterward he relished the feelings going through his body. He remained like that for several minutes before turning his attention to Alessandra. Seeing the smile on her face, he returned the smile with a slight laugh in his voice.

"I see you now know how we shall survive quite nicely even without joining," he teased her. They laughed together as he made himself presentable once again. "I think I had better get our food out so that you have the energy to return home."

She laughed loudly at him. "I have not done anything active, Edward!"

They sat up, close to one another, both appreciating what a special moment it was. Their laughter and conversation continued as they ate.

They did not know that nearby in the dark of the forest, two eyes were on them.

~~~~~

Having seen Alessandra and Edward from a distance as they had embarked through the bushy area, Tom had taken the opportunity to follow them and watch them. He hated the way they walked together, hand in hand, and laughed together. It was painful to see the way Alessandra looked up into her husband's eyes, and the
~~~~~

way he looked back at her. Tom had seen them lie down together, and the things they did to each other. The level of pleasure they both seemed to get from that, even without intercourse, invoked feelings in him that he found confusing. He knew that everything that Edward had with Alessandra, he wanted. He wanted her love, yes, but he wanted mostly her appreciation for sexual pleasure and her body.

As he watched them from his current position, he saw them continue to smile and laugh together, even after they had done those things to each other. It was nothing like what he had with his wife. Katherine did not welcome his touch. She did not like to be kissed. The only time she laughed was when someone said something cruel about someone else.

At some level, Tom knew that what he was doing - following them and watching them - was not right. Regardless, he could no longer help it. Alessandra was his object of affection. He would have her.

~~~~~

"Come, my beautiful wife," Edward said, standing and helping Alessandra up. "We should head back to the manor as it will start to get colder soon. This area only has sunshine like this at the peak of the day when the sun is high, and only in spring and summer. All other times it is not so pretty. It can get very cold, being so close to the waterfall and forest."

"Can we come back?" she asked and he gained great joy from her enthusiasm.

"Of course," Edward replied. "For the next few days, however, I need to spend time around the estate with Father. As much as I would certainly like to only spend time with you like this, you and I must know everything we need to when the estate passes to us."

Alessandra nodded, understanding the seriousness of what he was saying. He was right in subtly suggesting that the two of them did not work as much as they
~~~~~

should. She vowed to herself that she, too, would start making working with Edward's mother a priority. The estate was, after all, something that would be passed to their children, and their children's children. It certainly deserved their love and respect.

They packed up and started their slow walk back through the forest and gardens, completely unaware that they had not had any privacy at all on their journey out.

CHAPTER 40

When Edward finally felt it was a polite time to remove himself from the company of his parents and go to bed, he was pleased that Alessandra appeared to want an early night also. He didn't expect anything of traditional pleasure, but even as tired as he was, he took his time enjoying undressing her and climbing into bed with her.

Alessandra was mindful of how much Edward had done to please her since coming home earlier that day, even though he'd not slept the whole night before. She happily cuddled into him and remained still and quiet as she sensed him finally find the sleep that his body needed. She was joyous simply to have him next to her once again, finding comfort in his warmth beside her.

~~~~~

The next morning Edward woke to find Alessandra lying beside him still but awake. She was watching him with a smile on her face.

"What a beautiful sight," he said to her, smiling in a way that turned her heart before he moved closer and pulled her tightly to him. "And what a lovely thing to feel," he continued with joy in his eyes as he touched her ever-increasing belly.

Once again Alessandra cuddled into him, not eager to get on with the day.

"So quiet first thing in the morning, my love?" Edward asked her, wondering what joyous journeys were happening in his wife's mind. "What are you thinking?"

As Alessandra continued to remain quiet, he pulled
~~~~~

away from her to look at her closely. Initially alarmed at her silence, he relaxed as he saw she only had a look of contentment on her face.

"I am well, Edward," Alessandra said. "I am just happy to have you here with me."

He kissed her deeply but then remembered his responsibilities.

"I must get up and go and see Father," Edward said. "We must travel around the estate today, talking to our tenants. That will take most of the day. Are you sure you are alright?"

Alessandra nodded and kissed him. "Yes. I must get up and spend some more time with your mother, learning."

Edward climbed out of bed and started to dress while looking at her. "Well, do not overdo it, my love. Mother does not expect you to be doing a lot right now."

Alessandra got up and began to dress also, enjoying having Edward help her in doing so. She heard the sound of surprise when he tried to secure the back of her dress.

"My love, you need some new clothes to get you through the coming months. Has Mother talked to you about that?" he asked.

Alessandra shook her head. "No, I did not want to ask."

"I shall mention it at breakfast," Edward said. "Do not worry. You do not need to ask, but you cannot wear clothes this tight. It cannot be good for you or the baby."

They headed down to breakfast, where Edward was true to his word.

"Father, Mother, Alessandra needs looser garments to wear as she is getting larger with child," he said.

"Oh, Alessandra, I am so sorry! I did not even think," Edward's mother said. "Yes, let us organise that today. What a good idea, Edward."

Alessandra felt relieved. She understood why all of her family's money had been given to the Chisholm family, but there were times when she felt awkward in having to rely on them for money.

"Thank you," she said shyly and gave her husband a grateful smile, only to receive one of his smiles of high amusement at her shyness.

CHAPTER 41

Edward and his father rode around the estate throughout the whole day, visiting almost every tenant on the large property. Over and over they told the same story of a man who might venture onto the estate with the intention of causing harm. Each tenant was asked to be vigilant and report to the main house details of anyone they had not seen before.

"Do you think he will venture this far, Father? It is a long way from where he lives, I believe."

"Hopefully not, Edward, but I will not have my family threatened. We must do what we can to help Alessandra remain calm and relaxed, although I think she shall carry to full term now, given how far along she is."

Edward did not talk to his father anymore on the journey home. In his mind, he was letting himself think of different scenarios of things that could happen or go wrong and had to make a conscious effort to stop his mind from venturing into those spaces.

~~~~~

Back in the manor, Alessandra was fitted for new day to day outfits of varying sizes to get her through to the birth.

"These will be ready no earlier than next week, however I brought with me a gown that was ordered but then cancelled by a young lady who is of a similar size and stage. I would not normally suggest you wear something made for someone else but your mother-in-law has said you have no clothes that are loose enough.
~~~~~

If you would like to try it on, I have it here, and it can be yours. The person it was made for paid for it but just did not want it in the end," the dressmaker said quietly to Alessandra, not wanting to offend in any way but wanting to help the young woman to be more comfortable while she waited for her new clothing to be prepared.

"Thank you. I should like to try it if you think it might be of a close size," Alessandra said shyly. She watched as the dressmaker pulled out a gown of luxury. "Oh! This is not a dress for wearing at home, I do not think," she said, running her hands over the beautiful item in her arms. "Oh, but it is so beautiful!"

"Try it on and see if it fits you," the dressmaker said as she smiled. "After you have it on and can see how it fits, you can decide if you would like me to leave it here for you."

Alessandra allowed herself to be fitted into the gown. Instantly she felt the difference in the looseness of the garment compared to her own clothes.

"Oh, Miss! It fits you perfectly. And the colour becomes you greatly. What do you think?"

Alessandra was quiet as she experienced for the first time what it felt like to wear such an item. It was of the calibre that she had seen the women wear in Bath. She felt like she imagined a queen must feel like each and every day.

"I do not know what to say," she said quietly.

"Do you like it?"

"Oh, yes, it is beautiful," Alessandra replied. "It feels so luxurious … too luxurious for me…"

"Oh, Miss, no! You look like the beautiful woman that you are."

Alessandra looked the dressmaker in the eye, needing some kind of reassurance of what was acceptable and what wasn't.

"Will I cause any offence to anyone by accepting a

gown that was made and paid for by someone else? I do not know what is right."

The dressmaker smiled warmly at the young woman before her. She'd already sensed that Alessandra was from a lesser class than she was presently living, but not a young woman who had purposely aimed so high. She seemed to have fallen into the place she was in. She had no arrogance about her at all, or any desire to cause upset in anyone.

"If acceptable to you, I shall bring your mother-in-law up here and the two of you can discuss it privately before you make a decision," the dressmaker said.

Alessandra was uncertain about that. Her mother-in-law was the exact person she didn't want to offend. Regardless, she consented and the dressmaker returned shortly with Edward's mother beside her.

"Oh, Alessandra! You look so beautiful. What a lovely gown, and that colour on you shows your Italian colouring so well."

The dressmaker took a moment to explain to Edward's mother the situation so Alessandra could see how the situation presented looked to her.

"Oh, I see, but Alessandra, your new dresses will not be ready for a while yet. Why should you not be comfortable in the meantime? I think it is a very generous offer being made," Edward's mother said quietly, appreciating the modesty and frugal nature of her new daughter. That could only be good for the estate when it passed hands to the younger generation. "I have no doubt at all that Edward will love to see you in this," she added on with a look of knowing in her eye as she looked at Alessandra, who smiled shyly in return.

"Alright. If you are sure, then I shall be very happy to accept this gown from you. Thank you so much," she said.

The dressmaker was pleased, knowing she had secured a young woman who in years to come would require a great many dresses. Smiling, she excused herself as Edward's mother also moved toward the door.

"Keep it on, Alessandra, and wear it to dinner. You deserve it," she said before closing the door.

~~~~~~

As Edward and his father came into the house and walked toward the drawing room, expecting both women to be there, Edward heard his mother's voice calling out down the staircase.

"Go and see your wife, Edward," she said simply, with a look that he had not seen on his mother before. "She is in your bedchamber." Edward initially looked alarmed, worried something had happened. "Do not stress. She is well, but I am sure she would like to see you immediately."

Edward raced up the stairs, full of concern. When he entered the bedchamber, the sight before him stopped him.

Alessandra was standing at the window, looking out as if deep in thought. She turned to him as she heard him come in. She gave no thought to the gown she had on. All she could focus on was seeing Edward. She did not know why he was looking so strangely at her.

Edward moved forward toward her, awestruck at the sight of his wife. He touched the rich fabric and looked at how the colour made her eyes look. With the neckline so low, he could not stop himself from leaning in and kissing her on the neck. His lips followed the line of the neckline, delivering small kisses everywhere, making her want to melt. When he had covered every piece of skin revealed to him, he kissed her deeply on the mouth and heard her moan.

"You look so beautiful, Alessandra. I did not think you could look any more beautiful."

As she looked at him with her unique blend of shyness and desire, Edward felt heavily aroused.

"Do you like it?"
~~~~~~

"Yes, but Alessandra, seeing you in this fuels me greatly," Edward replied.

"Undress me," she replied, feeling her arousal too great to not be satisfied.

It had been too long since they had joined, they both found themselves thinking in the comfort of their own minds. In each other's eyes, they knew it was what they both wanted more than anything.

Edward took his time, removing the gown as slowly as he could, kissing every new piece of skin that became visible. Once his wife stood naked before him, he guided her to the bed and undressed quickly before kissing her all over. No part of her body did he neglect, taking his time teasing her before encouraging her to climax.

He held her and kissed her, uncertain whether he could join with her still or not. Alessandra knew what she wanted and she did not allow him to have doubt. She pushed him down on the bed so that he was lying down, and positioned herself above him. Before she took him in, he held her back and looked at her closely.

"Are you sure this is still alright?"

"Yes, let me move slowly so I can feel if anything is uncomfortable," she said.

Edward nodded, kissed her fully, and felt her edge her way down onto him. He closed his eyes, feeling the sensation. It was extraordinary. Her determination to move slowly brought about new feelings in him that overwhelmed him greatly. He could hear her enjoying the sensations being cast on her also. When he opened his eyes and saw her face, he knew he would not last much longer.

Alessandra stopped suddenly and leaned forward to kiss him deeply again, momentarily stopping his increased level of excitement before moving again, looking into his eyes.

"Oh, Alessandra ... I ... ohh ..." Alessandra heard him try to say before she felt him convulse inside of her.

He lay still with his eyes closed, enjoying fully the waves of pleasure flowing over him. When he opened his eyes again he saw her hovering over him, her face covered in a beaming smile.

Edward smiled back at her and pulled her down for further kisses before remembering her state of pregnancy.

"Are you sure you are alright?" he asked, showing his concern.

"I am. I just … needed you so much," Alessandra replied as she rested down on him fully.

"Oh, my darling, how I do love you."

CHAPTER 42

Two weeks later, with the weather starting to warm up, Edward suggested once again that he take Alessandra for a slow walk to the waterfall.

"Only if you feel up to it," he said as they sat with his parents at breakfast.

"Really?" she asked, hiding no part of her excitement. Edward's mother and father both looked at the interaction between the two young people. It inspired them to remember how it had been for them in their first year of marriage.

Edward smiled indulgently at his wife. "Yes! We shall set out immediately after breakfast so that we do not need to rush. We can walk as slowly as you need to."

Alessandra laughed loudly. "Oh, Edward, I can still walk!"

~~~~~

A short time later they were making their way through the gardens and the forest slowly. Once again they reached the quiet and sunny grassed area where they lay down the blanket and sat down, listening to the waterfall.

"Thank you for this, Edward."

He looked closely at her. "Time with you means everything to me," he said before lifting her hand to his lips.

The two of them sat and lay down together. Talking, laughing and eating, they each felt true joy at just being able to spend so much time together for the whole day without either of them having to rush off to do
~~~~~

something else.

"Edward, do you think we would be too presumptive to start assuming that our child will be born healthy?" Alessandra asked, surprising Edward with the question.

"Oh, my love, why do you ask that?"

"I find myself wondering about names," she said.

Edward breathed a sigh of relief. "Oh, I see. And what are your thoughts?"

"Do you have any preferences?" Alessandra asked.

"No. I only wish for you to remain healthy and happy," Edward said and kissed her softly.

Suddenly both of them heard crackling from the forest behind them. They looked up, frozen and silent as if to check if there was anyone there. Hearing nothing more, they relaxed once again.

"The weather is warmer now," Alessandra said, out of context with the conversation they were having.

Edward laughed at her. "Warmer than when, my love?" he teased her, knowing exactly what she was thinking.

"Than when we were last here," she responded, openly smiling and teasing him back in knowing that he knew what she was thinking.

He laughed openly at her and tried to control the level of arousal she was inducing in him so easily. "My beautiful wife, there is nothing more that I would like right now than to make love to you, but…"

Alessandra put her lips on his, stopping him from continuing his sentence. She kissed him passionately, pushing him to forget his argument while she coaxed him until they were both naked. When she lay on top of him, both were aware of a small person lying between them.

Edward looked up at his wife, taken away in the vision of her moving on him. She sat upright due to her belly being larger. He felt like he could not live a moment without her. He would never want to live a moment without her.

Alessandra revelled in the feelings, taking her time to concentrate on her own body and ensure all was well.

Once again it did not occur to either of them that they could be being watched from a distance.

~~~~~~

Tom Missinger remained still as he watched the scene before him. He had seen them walking, sitting, talking and laughing. When he had seen them moving toward marital relations, he had wanted to run in and stop it to keep Edward's hands off his Alessandra. What they did together - the way they moved together - was something he craved. He couldn't stop thinking about her, and the joy she could bring to him if he could just get her to consent to be his wife. He'd completely forgotten about his own wife, Katherine. He'd had no qualms whatsoever about walking out the door of his home on either that first occasion or the present one. He didn't believe Katherine cared at all about where he was going or what he was doing.

He felt a mix of excitement, greed and hatred as he watched Alessandra on top of her husband. Seeing her naked body, as much as it fuelled his desire, also reminded him that she was noticeably with child. What he considered to be love for her prevented him from the possibility of startling her in that condition. As much as he wanted to run in, break the two of them apart, and beg her to come away with him, he wasn't so heartless that he would risk causing her pain by losing her child.

With the realisation that he could not approach or seduce her while she was with child, Tom decided he couldn't watch any more of their lovemaking. He slowly turned and started to walk through the forest, to head toward his home.

~~~~~~

Edward watched his wife moving on top of him. Seeing her body and facial expressions during lovemaking was intoxicating. He listened to her moaning in her pleasure as he caressed her in the spot she loved to be touched. Immediately after she climaxed on him, he couldn't hold back any longer. The two of them were silent for minutes, together engulfed in the feeling of release.

Alessandra pulled off him and lay down beside him as he repositioned and turned to face her, loving the smile she had on her face. He kissed her softly.

"What were we saying about baby names?" she asked, making him heavily laugh out loud.

"Oh, how I do love you, Alessandra!"

CHAPTER 43

"Oh!" Edward heard his wife say as they sat at breakfast. Immediately he jumped up in concern, seeing her hands go to her belly.

"Alessandra, what is it?" his mother asked, also moving closer to her.

"Oh … it feels like … fluttering," Alessandra replied, showing her face to be in her scholar mode as she tried to find the right words to explain the new feeling she was experiencing.

Edward saw his mother smile at his wife.

"You are not in pain?" she asked.

Alessandra shook her head. "No! It feels … odd … but nice."

Edward's mother asked for permission to touch Alessandra's belly. After receiving it, she placed her hand on her daughter-in-law.

"Your baby is moving, Alessandra … inside of you. Edward, come and feel your child," she said. Edward rushed around the table to put his hand on the belly of his wife.

"Oh, Alessandra, how wonderful," he said as he knelt beside her. After she adjusted her chair slightly, he held himself against her, his emotions overwhelming him. On his face, she could see that he was feeling the same wonder that she was. She leaned down to deliver a kiss, which he accepted eagerly.

Edward's mother and father exchanged a knowing look, both happy to see their son enjoying his marriage so much. With their daughter-in-law now more than halfway through her term, they held much hope that they would see the successful delivery of a child - the first child that had been born in their home since the day Edward had been born.

~~~~~

Later that day Edward's father received a letter from Alessandra's father, which, concerned about why her father might be writing to him directly, he put aside until he could be alone to read it. Once in the steward's room, he opened the letter and was stunned by its content.

"I write to you with urgency after having been informed that a known acquaintance of Alessandra's, Mr Tom Missinger, who I understand has been trying to secure her affection for some time, has been reported as missing for the past two weeks. Please be vigilant in case he has travelled to your location. I beg you to keep my daughter and our grandchild safe."

Edward's father sat alone for some time, thinking about the situation. He had not laid eyes on Missinger so wouldn't be able to identify him even if he did see him, and yet he could not sit and do nothing either.

Walking around the manor, he finally found his son in the glass room, sitting quietly with Alessandra. He was reluctant to disturb them, and adamant that his daughter-in-law must not know of the possible threat. He also knew that Edward had met the man and might be the only person able to know if he crossed their paths.

Considering the option to disturb the young people or not, Edward's father moved away and decided to let them have their time together. In the meantime, he would go and spend time with his own wife. He didn't know to what extent this 'Missinger' desired to claim Alessandra, nor how far he would go to try and win her. The thought resulted in a shudder passing through Edward's father. He had never had conflict in his life and was too old for it to come his way now. Regardless, he was determined that he would protect his wife, his son,
~~~~~

his daughter-in-law and grandchild with whatever means he would have to.

CHAPTER 44

"I do not understand, Father," Edward exclaimed in horror after receiving the news of the letter. He stood in the steward's room with his father, holding the letter and forcing himself to read it again and again. He needed to make sure he understood it. "Tom Missinger has not been seen for two weeks? And people think he might have been coming here, to see Alessandra?"

Edward's father looked at his son and nodded. Edward paced the room, overwhelmed with fear for his wife and child.

"But why would this news come now? So late?" he asked and saw his father shake his head with unknowing.

"Perhaps his wife did not report him as missing immediately, or perhaps the news reached Alessandra's father at a later date. We do not know that, Edward, nor does it matter. What does matter is that you and I go around the estate and make sure everyone watches out for him. You are the only person, other than Alessandra, who knows what this man looks like, so you must describe him to everyone." He watched his son pace more and saw his face become increasingly agitated. "Edward, you must calm down..."

"Calm down! My wife and child are at risk of being ... I do not know what ... by some man who has unhealthy intentions ... and you think I should calm down?"

His father walked up to him and placed his hands on his son's shoulders.

"Yes! Edward, your wife must not be distressed by

this. She is perceptive. She will know something is seriously wrong if you do not find a way to not have this in the forefront of your mind when you are with her. I am also not going to tell your mother, as she will not be able to contain the knowledge without worrying Alessandra either," he said before becoming quiet for a moment. "It is not a good situation, I know, but there is a chance that he has not ventured to this part of the country at all. Worrying Alessandra and your mother would be fruitless."

Edward took a deep breath and sat on one of the seats in the room, understanding what his father was saying and knowing his advice to be wise. There was nothing he would do to contribute to stress in his wife. If Alessandra became concerned, it could affect the health of their child. With a mother who had been told she must never get pregnant after his birth, and Alessandra's mother also having had so many miscarriages when she was younger, Edward and Alessandra both had an awareness of how difficult it could be for some people to have children. Neither wanted to take any risks at all.

No, he thought to himself, the only option was to alert the tenants around the property and make as best an effort as possible to try and not let Alessandra know anything was wrong.

"Alright, Father. Let us begin talking to the tenants again. There is still enough time today for us to begin, is there not?" he asked and his father nodded.

"We can at least visit Old John and his family, then head over to see Mrs Howard. She is living alone. I do think it most urgent that we see she is alright."

Edward nodded and they left, both full of concern over what situation might present itself in the weeks to come.

CHAPTER 45

Edward jumped down from Beauty as Old John came out of his house to greet him and his father. He wasn't a man who ever smiled but as a tenant, he was hard working and reliable. He'd always been a distant figure in Edward's life since he was very young, and had watched the 'Young Master' grow into the man he was now.

"Old John," Edward heard his father say in greeting as he shook his hand respectfully. "We might have a problem on the estate. There is a man who could be headed here to cause distress. Have you seen anyone lately who you had not seen before?"

"No, Master," Old John replied. "It has been a long while since I seen anyone new around these paddocks, but tell me what this person looks like. I'll keep watch for him and pass the word to others."

Edward came forward and gave a physical description of Tom, all the while shuddering inwardly at the thought of the man who had so openly declared he would 'have' Alessandra.

Old John nodded when Edward had given his description. "What shall I do if I see him, Sir? Report it to the manor?"

"Yes, but we do not wish for the Mistress or Edward's wife, Alessandra, to know about this. Edward is soon to be a father…" he said, cut off by the older man coming forward to Edward and shaking his hand.

"Oh, Young Master! Congratulations," he said, smiling for the very first time Edward had seen him do so. Edward thanked him and accepted the handshake.

"We do not want Alessandra to be distressed in any way, so if you do see this man - or anyone you have not seen before - can you please let me know directly, Old John? If you come to the manor, tell my man that you wish for him to tell me, and only me, that you are there."

Old John nodded. "Very good, Master."

Edward and his father mounted their horses and prepared to leave.

"And please be careful yourself. We do not know if this man is dangerous, but it would be best that we expect that he is, until he is found."

Edward saw Old John nod again and wave before Edward's father started to ride away with Edward behind.

~~~~~

As they pulled up to the tiny cottage of Mrs Howard, something immediately looked amiss. Although she was a woman of the land, leaving the front door as wide open as it was, was never something that either man had known her to do.

Edward saw his father jump down with impressive speed to get inside as quickly as possible. At his father's instruction, Edward walked around the outside of the house to see if he could see her.

On entering the house, Edward's father let out a cry of distress.

Edward ran to see what his father had found. It was quite a scene to observe. The woman was lying on the floor, secured to a chair with her feet bound, her mouth gagged, and her hands tied behind her.

"Oh, Master!" said the elderly woman inside, expressing utter relief at seeing a face she knew as Edward untied the ties covering her mouth. "A man was here and he did this to me," she continued, starting to shed tears.

"Who did this, Mrs Howard?" Edward asked as he
~~~~~

continued to untie her hands and feet and helped her to stand up.

The woman struggled to find her balance and her voice, but then mustered the determination to speak.

"I did not know him. He was a young man, about the Young Master's age. He came here and tied me up, and then he was sleeping there," she said, starting to cry desperately as she nodded to the bed in the corner of the room.

"Last night?" Edward's father asked, uneasy at developments unfolding.

"No! He came here nights ago."

"You have been tied up here all this time?" Edward asked. He was horrified at the thought that an elderly woman had been left alone without anyone to check on her. He made a mental note that he must start visiting tenants more often, given how isolated some of them lived.

Now she was crying visibly, as she nodded. "He came here to sleep every night for a week, but then did not come back again. He has not been here for, I think, four nights now, but I do not feel quite right at the moment, Master, so my reckoning could be wrong."

"Of course you feel unwell, Mrs Howard. When did you last eat?"

She looked timid and weak as the tears began once more. "I know not. He did give me a little food and water when he was here, but I do not know when that was."

"Right, food first then," Edward said as he looked around the tiny cottage, desperate to find something he could give to her.

"Thank you, Young Master, but he took everything with him."

Edward found himself perplexed at the horror of the situation. "Father, I think I should ride up to the manor..."

"No, Edward. Mrs Howard has had a terrible ordeal. I do not want to leave her here alone," Edward's father started to say and the elderly woman started to object.

"Mrs Howard, I understand you prefer to live alone but for this night at least, you will come with us and stay at the manor. Do not refuse, I beg you, as you desperately need sustenance and I will not sleep if I think of you alone here with a madman on the loose. When you are at the manor I can also summon the doctor to come and check your health."

Edward looked on, admiring his father for his generosity, although also seeing in his eyes a real fear now, which flowed on to him also.

"Yes, Master," the elderly woman said, her head hung low in shame of having found herself in the situation.

"Come, Mrs Howard, you can ride on Beauty. I will walk alongside you so you have nothing to fear from him. He is large, but he is gentle and good-natured," Edward said with a soothing voice.

After securing the little house they made their way slowly to the manor, where Margaret came out to meet them. Edward pulled her aside.

"Mrs Howard here has suffered a horrible ordeal and will stay here for the night. Can you please set her up in a guest room and ensure she gets some food? She has not eaten for at least a few days, as far as I can tell, so tell Cook to prepare only small amounts of food suitable, and make sure she also has plenty to drink," Edward said to Margaret and she nodded. Before Margaret turned to the elderly woman, he added, "Please do not tell my wife or my mother about this. I do not want either to be worried or stressed."

Margaret looked at the young master and could see the level of seriousness on his face. She nodded, appreciating the love for his wife that he so easily displayed to everyone he talked to. Quietly she guided the elderly woman away and toward the guest wing of the manor to set Mrs Howard up with food and a warm fire.

"Now Edward," his father said with a real depth of concern in his voice. "It is starting to get dark so we will not go any further tonight but early tomorrow you and I shall set out and visit the remaining tenants."

Edward nodded, remaining close to his father but feeling particularly desperate to get to his wife.

"Go and get ready for dinner and then we shall dine. And not one word of any of this to Alessandra or your mother."

Edward bounded into the drawing room to check if Alessandra was there. Seeing no-one in the room, he ran up the regal staircase and to their bedchamber.

As he made his way to her he considered the timeframe that Mrs Howard had said. Her calculations may have been completely wrong but she'd indicated that over the past few nights the man had not been back. Edward calculated that the last time Tim Missinger was there, was the day Edward had walked with Alessandra to the waterfall. Fear descended upon him as he remembered the moment they had thought they had heard something in the forest behind them.

Before opening the bedchamber door, Edward stopped and took deep breaths until he was sure he looked calm and could put a smile on his face once more.

Alessandra heard the door open and turned to see Edward enter, making her smile. It had been two weeks since they had been intimate. It was the longest they had ever been withdrawn from each other. When she looked at him she was reminded of how much she had come to love her husband and the way that he looked.

She watched as he walked in calmly but with a smile on his face that said exactly how he felt about her. She walked toward him to receive an embrace, which they both indulged in for a long time before pulling apart.

As Edward started to wash and change for dinner, Alessandra watched him. "Is all well, husband?" she asked.

Edward smiled at her. He loathed having to lie but wouldn't risk the shock she might feel if she knew the truth.

"Yes, my lovely wife. It has been a long day, but I am fine," he said, dressed and moving toward her for another embrace. "Come, let us go eat and you can tell me all about your day."

CHAPTER 46

Despite the chatter that passed between the household staff, the news of Mrs Howard's ordeal was contained from the ladies of the household, much to the relief of Edward and his father.

At breakfast, conversation was much the same as usual before Edward's father spoke up with a stern sound in his voice.

"Come, Edward. We have much to do around the estate today, so we will be out all day," he said.

Immediately Edward rose at the summons, eager himself to get out and try to do something to ensure there was no danger to his family. He gave his wife a particularly long farewell kiss before removing himself to leave. Inwardly he felt dread at the thought of something awful possibly happening in the near future that was going to result in her unhappiness.

Once on the road again, Edward and his father did not say anything to each other. They were each in their individual thoughts about what the man in question was willing to do to get to Alessandra.

One cottage after another they visited, stopping to talk to the tenants. Edward explained what Tom looked like and asked the tenants to immediately notify the master at the manor if they saw anyone suspicious or unknown in the area.

"But Master, is that enough? We can round up men from the nearby farms and do a proper search for this man. For him to do what he did to Mrs Howard is just not right."

Edward looked at the man before him, agreeing silently in his head that actively searching for Tom was a good idea, but not wanting to argue with his father, who always seemed to know best.

Finally, the evening rolled in and Edward was pleased they had spoken to every tenant on the estate. No-one else had seen anyone new on the estate. That relieved Edward's worry a little but also made him fearful that Tom could be hiding anywhere, ready to strike whenever he was ready.

When they arrived back at the manor, Edward went to find Margaret. "How is Mrs Howard?" he asked her quietly when he had found her.

"She is very weak, Sir, but she has been eating somewhat, and drinking some wine. She is looking better but I do think it may be several days at least before she is strong again," Margaret said.

Edward nodded at her and smiled kindly. "Very well. Keep tending to her and do not let her leave until you believe she has the strength to. She is to be well looked after and kept warm at all times," he said quietly before walking off. Mrs Howard was one of the many tenants he had known all of his life. Although she was of a much lower position in life than he, as with all the tenants he had been taught to respect and love everyone around the estate.

~~~~~

That night in bed Edward held his wife tightly and kissed her softly. He could feel her wanting him to yield and make love to her, but he was steadfast in adhering to the agreement they had made to each other after the day at the waterfall. He wanted her - oh, how he wanted her - but he would not risk endangering her or the child. It wasn't easy. She knew how to please him and make him yearn for her. He counteracted that with laughter toward her.

"Alessandra, stop being wicked toward me," he
~~~~~

teased her.

She laughed back at him, appreciating how eager he was to keep her safe and well. "What do you mean, Edward?" she teased him back with an innocent look on her face. "Whatever can you mean? I am only showing my affection."

They laughed together. "My innocent wife. I love you, and you know how easily you enflame me."

"Oh!" she said unexpectedly.

Edward was alarmed for a moment before he saw her smile at him, completely distracted from her previous attentions.

Alessandra revelled in the feeling she had started to get used to now - that of a small person inside of her, moving around. She took Edward's hand and placed it on her belly once again. Immediately she saw him smile and display the same look of wonder that he always did when he felt the baby move.

"He is hearty, isn't he, my love?" Edward said, smiling.

"Oh, you still are thinking this is a boy, then?" Alessandra asked, teasing him further.

"I shall be pleased with a boy or a girl, Alessandra," he replied and kissed her deeply. "But I think you must agree, he is active enough to be a boy."

CHAPTER 47

Over the following week, nothing more was said or heard about Tom Missinger. But the next week, as Alessandra moved into her sixth month of pregnancy, Edward and his father received notification in the steward's room that Old John had come to the manor and was waiting in the stable to see them. Edward and his father looked at each other before walking quickly to see the man waiting for them.

"Oh, Master!" he said, removing his hat and bowing his head slightly at the two men as they got closer to him.

"What is it? What has happened?" Edward's father asked, trying not to sound as desperate as he felt inside.

"Oh, Master, we have found a body and we did not know what to do…"

Edward felt a sinking feeling of dread inside of him, with the thought of anyone being dead and having been found on the estate.

"Where?"

"Out by the waterfall, Master. It looks like it has been there for at least two weeks, but I do not know the man. I thought he could be the man you spoke of as it is not too far from Mrs Howard's cottage," Old John said, pushing Edward's feeling of despair even lower still. The last time that he had taken Alessandra there, they had thought they heard someone in the forest. As Old John spoke, Edward felt another level of horror inside, at the thought that perhaps whoever was there might have seen his wife's body.

"Alright. We must notify the constable at once. Edward, you might have to see the body to check if it is Missinger," Edward's father said to him. He could see his son was in shock but he needed Edward to do what he must. It was the only way they could all know if they would now be safe and in peace once again.

Old John nodded. "I can ride into Bath now, Master, if you need me to."

Edward's father nodded at him. "Yes, thank you," he said. He then remembered his manners, which he had always been desperate to hold onto where all of his tenants were concerned. "Before you go, come into the kitchen and Cook will give you some food and wine."

Edward saw Old John look horrified and appreciative at the same time, torn between his obvious hunger but also feeling it was not right for him to go into the manor.

"Come with me," Edward said, stepping forward to try and put the older man in front of him at ease. "I believe Cook has some rabbit pie left over from last night, which I can greatly recommend. I will ask you, though, to please not talk about the issue of the body. We have worked hard to keep the concern about Missinger from my mother and my wife. The fewer people who know, the better."

Old John nodded in response. "Of course, Young Master."

~~~~~

When the constable came to the manor to question Edward's father later that evening, Alessandra suspected something serious had happened but equally felt like whatever it was, she was not to know about it. The way Edward had avoided her most of the day even though he was in the manor with his father, and the way his father looked at his mother, all gave clues that something of great concern had happened and somehow the manor was involved.

The men escorted the constable to the steward's
~~~~~

room, where conversation began.

"We have removed the body but I do have to ask you questions about it," the constable began. Edward and his father nodded. "Do you know the man who was found?"

Edward's father was surprised by the question. "We have not seen the body so we cannot know for sure…"

"But?" the constable pushed.

Edward came forward, sensing some frustration inside of his father.

"We received notification about a week ago that a man who had known my wife when they were younger, had gone missing from his home, and he might have been on his way to this area."

The constable looked at him and wrote notes in his notebook.

"So he knew your wife. Should I be questioning her then?"

"No!" Edward and his father both exclaimed simultaneously, causing the constable to raise his head sharply.

"No," Edward continued more quietly. "My wife is presently with child and I would not cause her any stress if we can help it. Please, I can tell you whatever you need to know." He paused before continuing, seeing the constable nod in recognition of what he was saying. "A short time ago we had a problem with letters from my wife's mother not reaching us, so I rode to see my in-laws to check they were alright. When I was there it was revealed that the man in question had been stopping that particular post from coming, as a way to worry my wife and encourage her to go there, to her parents' home. This man had earlier written to my wife, declaring his love for her. I believe he planned to see her if he could get her to return to her family home. When she did not go there - when I went there instead - he confronted me and told me he was determined to win her. His plan was to encourage her to leave me and go live with him."

The constable wrote carefully but quickly in his notebook. "And this man's name is?"

"Tom Missinger."

"And you say he was reported missing?"

Edward nodded. "That is what we were told, yes."

The constable wrote what he seemed to need to and then stopped and looked at Edward. "Do you know the man, then?"

"I would not say that I know him…"

"Could you identify him?"

Edward nodded, dreading the thought. "Yes."

"Right then. I shall leave you now, but tomorrow you will need to come to see me, and see if the body we have is this Mr Tom Missinger."

"Of course, Sir. I shall come in the morning," Edward replied. He had never seen a dead body before. It wasn't something that he particularly wanted to do, but knew he had to.

The constable excused himself, leaving Edward and his father looking at one another with shock on each of their faces.

"If nothing else, Edward, at least we will know for sure if it is him or not," his father said. Edward nodded before they both left the room to see their wives, hoping neither of them revealed the great deal of concern both felt.

~~~~~

"What are you keeping from me, Edward?" Alessandra asked later, in their bed.

For Edward, the worst part of the entire business was not being able to be completely honest and open with her, as he always had been about everything so far.

"Alessandra, there is something I am not telling you right now, but please trust that when I can tell you, I will," he said softly.

Alessandra knew him well enough to respect when he needed to keep quiet and think about things before he
~~~~~

spoke. She lay quietly, cuddling into his chest and pushing all things from her mind so that she would not be sleepless. Soon she was deep asleep while he held her, thankful he had a wife who did not pressure him into revealing words he did not want to say.

CHAPTER 48

Edward stood over the body, dealing with all the conflicting emotions flowing over him. He felt horror at the realisation of the situation, sadness for the wife of the man in front of him, uncertainty at how he would tell his wife the news … but also relief that now there would be no more threat or worry from this man.

"It is him?" the constable asked.

Edward nodded. "Yes, that is Tom Missinger."

"And you think he came all this way to try and take your wife away?"

Edward felt perplexed at the question.

"All I know is what he told me at Alessandra's parents' home - that he was determined to have her. Only he could know to what extent he meant those words," Edward replied.

"Very well. Thank you for coming. I may have more questions for you after I speak to the deceased's wife," the constable said.

"Of course," Edward nodded at him before realising his curiosity had not yet been completely fulfilled. "How did he die?"

The constable looked at him thoughtfully before replying.

"From the position of the body, we believe he slipped down a sharp drop in the forest and hit his head on a tree trunk. We do not believe there was any foul play involved. He was simply in the wrong place at the wrong time," the constable said.

"Thank you," Edward replied, finding himself

saddened although also relieved at the news. For a moment he could see how he could have been viewed as a potential suspect if it had looked like Tom's death was not an accident.

He walked away from the constable with a new dilemma. Should he tell Alessandra, or keep the news to himself for the moment? She was now six months into her pregnancy. She was two-thirds of the way there. Was she at a time that would still be safe if she received a shock?

Before riding home he took a detour to the office of the family physician.

"Edward," the older man before him said happily as he held out his hand to shake Edward's. "What can I do for you? Are you unwell?"

"Oh no, Sir, I am here about my wife, Alessandra."

"Ahh yes, Alessandra. Is she still with child?" he asked.

Edward nodded. "Yes, all appears to be going well, but I have some bad news to give to her. I am not sure what such a shock may do..."

The physician sat down behind his desk and watched Edward's face to see if he would continue. When he did not, the doctor sat forward.

"Alessandra must be ... six months along?" he asked and Edward nodded.

"Edward, the most dangerous time has passed and your wife seems a strong young lady. If you need to tell her something that could shock her, by all means try and do so gently, but I think she will be fine."

Edward tried to absorb the advice being given to him but it conflicted with thoughts that had always been in his head.

"I know that you have grown up knowing the limitations on your mother to have more children," the physician continued and Edward nodded. "I do understand why you would have a natural concern for your wife when she is with child. But there are no indications that anything will happen, or that she cannot see this pregnancy through and deliver a healthy child when it is time."

They talked some more and then Edward left with the determination to immediately stop avoiding breaking the news to Alessandra.

~~~~~

When he returned to the manor he was instantly pulled aside by his father.

"Well?"

"It is him, Father," Edward replied. He watched as his father looked more and more morose.

"What will you do, Edward?"

"I must tell Alessandra. She knew him and would want to know…" Edward said.

"Are you sure that is wise?"

Edward found doubt entering his mind about what was the right thing to do.

"Yes, Father, I think I need to tell her. Even if they were not current friends, she should still know what has happened to him," Edward said, thinking about the possibility that had crossed his mind when he had first heard the news that the body had been found - that Tom might have been watching Edward and Alessandra when they were last at the waterfall. That thought made him shudder. Thinking about that man - or anyone - watching them as they made love, was detestable. That was something that he did not want to disclose to his wife, but to leave that suspicion out would mean that he would not be able to tell her where exactly on the estate Tom had been found. "I must go and tell her. Excuse me, Father."

~~~~~

Edward went straight to where he knew to be Alessandra's favourite place of peace - 'the glass jungle room', she had now fondly named it. When he entered quietly, she turned and a smile immediately graced her face as she saw him.

Straight away Alessandra could tell her husband had something of serious importance on his mind. She moved over on her favourite stone bench so that he could sit down beside her. She waited as he gathered his words, seeming to want to say something but then not say it.

"Edward, what is it?" she asked him quietly, encouraging him in whatever it was that he had to reveal to her.

Edward sat quietly, still uncertain what the probability was that telling her this particular news could upset her to the point where something serious happened to the health of her or their child. Remembering the words of the doctor, he decided to put trust in the physician and the strength of his wife. He formulated the words in the best way possible so that the shock might be lessened.

"Tom," he started, and immediately saw the surprise on his wife's face.

"Tom Missinger?" Alessandra asked, wondering what Edward could be going to say about the man who had courted her so long ago and had written letters to her more recently.

"Yes," Edward continued, once again feeling such dread inside of him. He also felt a sliver of guilt because even though he had not done anything to contribute to Tom's death, he certainly had wished silently that Tom would go away and leave Alessandra alone. It made no logical sense to feel guilty but it was in his nature to do so, given how strongly he had felt about the man who had threatened to pursue his wife.

Alessandra saw distress on Edward's face and put her hand over his to hold it tightly.

"Edward, whatever you have to say, it is alright. Please relax and tell me."

Edward took a deep breath and held her hand tightly.

"Alessandra, there has been news of Tom," he said, still trying to formulate words for what he had to say. "He ... died."

Alessandra heard the news and felt shocked. What she'd just heard could not possibly be true. She had not welcomed the attentions Tom had put on her since her marriage, but for a fleeting moment she cast her mind back to the time before she had met Edward. It was a time when she thought all it would take for her to be happy was to be married to Tom Missinger. Now that she was in her marriage with Edward she could, of course, see that she would never have been happy with Tom, but for a moment she let herself feel the feelings that naturally came from the news.

"Dead?" she asked faintly, as if not believing it. Edward sat quietly, giving her space and time to fully comprehend the news. Silently he hoped she might not ask questions so he could spare her any details, but of course she would. One of the things he loved about her was her ongoing curiosity about things that made her question so much. "How?"

Edward breathed out slowly and deeply, desperate to let only one piece of information leak out at any one time. "I do not know. His ... he ... was found, already dead."

He saw confusion cross the face of his wife and knew that over time to come, she would ask all relevant questions to get the full story. This same trait in her that had always delighted him, was now feeling like the source of heartbreak.

"Where?"

Alessandra felt like her head was racing, with so many questions in it that she felt like she had to breathe deeply to slow it all down. Now, as she asked this particular question, she looked right into Edward's eyes and suddenly became aware of how difficult it was for him as the deliverer of such bad news. She saw him look away and then slowly return his gaze to hers once more.

"Here. On the estate," he said as if the words came out only one at a time. He didn't expand on the explanation, watching as yet another level of knowledge sunk into her.

Alessandra looked at him with disbelief on her face.

"He was here?" she asked and saw Edward nod in confirmation. "But why?"

Edward kept quiet as she processed information being fed to her, and could make sense of it.

"He was here to see me?" she asked and he waited further. "He died, coming here to see me?"

Alessandra became aware that her husband had stopped speaking and knew there must have been more to the situation.

"Tell me all, Edward," she said "Whatever you need to say, I am prepared for. Please do not hold it inside."

Edward waited a few minutes before moving on in his conversation.

"Just over a week ago, when Father and I were visiting tenants, we found Mrs Howard tied up. Upon questioning her she told us that a man had done that to her, and had left her like that while he used her cottage as a place to stay for several nights."

"And you thought it might be Tom?" Alessandra asked. Edward nodded. "But why would you think that? He lives a long way from here."

"Before we saw Mrs Howard like that, we had received news that Tom was missing. It was suspected that he might come here to see you."

Suddenly all the moments in recent weeks that Alessandra had noticed her husband's quietness, became clear and obvious to her.

"You have been worried about telling me what was going on," she said and watched Edward nod whilst avoiding her gaze. "Oh, Edward, this news of Tom's death is heartbreaking. He had no right to think of me as he did after he was married, and after I was married, but he was someone I knew and had great regard for when we knew each other. I find this very sad."

She placed her hand under his chin and raised his face gently so he was looking at her again.

"I understand why you have kept all of this from me, and I am not going to ask any more now, but in time - after our baby's birth - you will share with me all the details you know about this," she said. Edward nodded before kissing her gently.

Alessandra welcomed the kiss, determined to put all thoughts about Tom from her mind. The sadness she knew could come from that knowledge, she wanted desperately to put on a shelf and forget for the moment. She only had another 10 weeks or so to get through before her baby would be born so it was important for her to remain calm in the meantime. Even she recognised that importance and would not do anything that might cause harm to her baby ... or herself.

CHAPTER 49

Four weeks later Edward and Alessandra began spending time together outside more. They enjoyed the simplicity of walking around the gardens as summer established and the days grew warmer.

"When would you like your mother to come and stay, my love?" Edward asked her, noticing her tiredness as she became larger with the life growing inside of her. "We can send for her at any time."

Alessandra looked at her husband and was once again thankful for having been wed to a man who was so considerate and seemingly not at all afraid of his in-laws. In response to his question she nodded and smiled at him.

"It would be nice to see my mother and father, Edward," she said. "As soon as it is possible, I would like them to be invited. They can then decide when is most suitable, if you are in agreement with that."

Edward nodded at her. "Of course. Write to them and let them know they are welcome whenever they are ready to come. I will arrange their travel here," he said quietly.

Alessandra looked at him. Although a month had passed, she knew that he still clung to something about Tom's death but was determined to not talk to her about it. She respected that and did not push him, but it made the length of her pregnancy seem to go on even longer, knowing that something was between them that was not being spoken of. Silently she wished time would pass more quickly so that their child could be brought into the world, and she and Edward would not have to be so careful anymore.

She clung tighter to his arm as they walked. He looked at her face, also feeling a void between them that he too knew was due to the censoring of conversation they now had between them, at least temporarily. Even though they were together every day, still the lack of desire to speak freely in case he caused her stress, contributed to a slight feeling of loneliness sometimes in each of them. He knew that Alessandra would welcome the conversation but would not pressure him to provide further details about Tom's death. If he was honest with himself, Edward could not pinpoint which aspect of the matter he most wanted to avoid telling her. Still in his mind was the haunting possibility of Tom having been in the forest, watching Alessandra and Edward making love. He knew it made no sense to think about it as Tom was now dead so it did not matter what he had seen. It still felt like a violation of Alessandra's privacy, and the love Edward and his wife shared, knowing that another man might have seen her body.

Suddenly feeling weighed down by the undesired quietness between them, Alessandra stopped walking and forced him to turn and look at her.

"Alessandra," Edward said with a slight sound of alarm in his voice. "Are you alright?"

She moved up to him, her large belly settling between them, and put her hands up to either side of his face before leaning in and kissing him. Although Edward tried to hold back, this time she did not let him. She held him there, kissing him as passionately as she could, with all the love she had for him. She desperately wanted him to let go of whatever was inside of him that was keeping him from being with her fully.

Edward felt overwhelmed. His wife knew how to capture him and make him forget things, making him breathless and dismissive of responsibility. As she kissed him in the first truly passionate exchange they'd had in weeks, he fought in his resolve to do the right thing by her. She persisted in forcing him to acknowledge that they should be intimate. It was how the two of them were meant to be. Regardless of them agreeing to not join again until after the baby was born, the void between them had overflowed into their intimacy when it hadn't needed to.

Alessandra heard Edward moan as his passion deepened in the kiss. Finally, she felt his resolve start to fall away as he put his arms around her and held her firmly, kissing her back with overdue fervour.

They stood like that for a long time, not touching in any other way and yet heavily fuelled in their passion. Edward argued with himself that he should keep away from such passion with her. At the same time, he conceded that he needed it - he needed her. He wanted to be away from her, to let her be relaxed until after the child was born, but she had initiated the kiss. He knew she wanted him, just as she had always wanted him. He still could not understand why that was when he was who he was, and he looked like he did, but he could not deny that she always wanted him. Neither her pregnancy nor news of Tom's death had changed that. The only person who had changed was him. As he continued to enjoy the feeling of her lips eagerly devouring his, he was angry at himself for having acted so rashly in trying to control everything between them, instead of letting things happen as they were meant to happen.

Alessandra indulged in the blissful feelings rushing through her entire body. She knew that Edward had been right to hold back from the two of them joining in recent weeks. Even without any consideration of the baby itself, she acknowledged inwardly to herself that she had become so large that it was no longer comfortable to be with him in that way. The feelings that occurred between them, even from their passionate kissing, seemed so exciting and so natural. A part of her did not want to stop. They continued until eventually, they both eased off and away from each other enough to be able to look into each other's eyes.

"I miss you," Alessandra said quietly. She spoke with great passion in her voice, determined to make him understand that the decision he'd made to not talk to her as he always had done before - openly, about everything - was affecting their relationship.

Edward looked closely at her with great conflict. Everything seemed right and yet everything seemed wrong. Being so close to her, he took time to look deeply into her eyes, and down to her lips. He realised that despite them having spent normal time together every single day, he had been missing her too.

He said nothing. Instead, he took her hand and led her as he started to walk.

Alessandra sighed to herself, accepting he was not reachable yet. As she became mindful of where they were walking, she realised he was leading her to their bedchamber.

Inside the room, Edward began to kiss her passionately again. He knew that she needed the closeness as much as he did and felt her lean firmly against him as their lips and tongues entwined. As he kissed her neck, he heard her moan. It was a sound he'd missed. It seemed far too long since he'd last heard it.

He took his time alternating between kissing her lips and undressing her slowly, until she stood naked before him. With the time that had passed since they had last lain together, he saw how much her belly had grown. It fuelled and increased his love for her. He led her to the bed and guided her to lie down before removing all of his clothing and joining her under the blankets.

Kneeling near her, he kissed her from head to toe. Alessandra lay back and let him take things at his own pace, understanding he was forcing the start of a healing process over whatever had been haunting him. She watched him as he looked at every piece of her, lowering his hands and his lips at different spots while returning his gaze to her eyes intermittently. She did not try and touch him, knowing that if he wanted her to, he would encourage her to.

She watched as he kissed all over her belly. The depth of her love for him surged through her. At that moment she didn't care about anything to do with Tom's death. Yes, it had saddened her to hear that he was dead, but whatever Tom had done, or whatever aspect of his death had Edward consumed, Alessandra knew she wouldn't care about it. It was nothing compared to the emotion that she felt with and for Edward. If only she could get him to understand that, and just let go of whatever worried him.

Edward kissed and caressed her over and over before lying down beside her, pulling her to him as they faced each other. Still he continued to kiss her, this time gently and with love more than passion.

Alessandra indulged in the loving kisses and waited for him to get to the place she knew he would, where he would open up and talk to her once again.

Edward felt himself relax. He didn't need sexual release at all. What he needed most of all was to just be close to her, without holding back. He continued to kiss her lips, enjoying the taste of her and the sound of her deep breaths. It was like meditation for him. He finally felt his body relax and his mind quieten after weeks of internal stress.

Alessandra felt him pull away from her. When she opened her eyes, she saw him looking at her.

"I have missed you too," he whispered as he held her close but could still look into her eyes.

Alessandra waited patiently, looking at him without any pressure being placed on him.

Finally, he spoke. "I love you so much, Alessandra,

and I worry that anything I say…"

"Edward, you need not worry as much as you do. I am well and our child is healthy. What is causing you so much concern?" she asked and waited. Edward continued to look conflicted. She forced him to look at her as she continued to speak. "Whatever is worrying you, is flowing through to affect us. That is far more heartbreaking to me than whatever you are thinking about, I am certain. Please, Edward, let it out so that we can be as we were before this happened."

Edward looked at her and felt desire for her but pushed that away. Instead, he focused on his words.

"The letters that you were missing from your mother … that were not reaching us…" he started and she nodded, encouraging him to continue. "They were being intercepted by Tom so they would not reach you."

Alessandra felt and looked confused. "That makes no sense. Why would he do something like that? And how did he do that?"

"He returned to your home and befriended your mother and father so he could offer to send the letters on their behalf, but instead of posting them, he held onto them and did not."

Edward watched his wife's face as she tried to make sense of what she was being told.

"Alessandra, do you remember how worried you were about your mother when you had not heard from her?" he asked and saw her nod. "That was his plan. He wanted you to worry so that you would go home to see your mother. He had not considered that with you being with child, it might be me who rode to check on your parents, rather than you."

Alessandra heard and analysed the revelation as Edward studied her face.

"Did you see Tom when you went there?" she asked

Edward nodded. "Yes."

"What happened?"

"When I was with your parents he walked in. Initially, he appeared surprised to see me there. He then went on to tell me that he was going to do whatever it would take to get you back because in his mind the two of you were supposed to be together."

Alessandra pictured the scene in her head.

"Were my parents there?" she asked and saw Edward nod. "They saw this interaction between you and Tom?"

"They did. I think they only then realised they had been fooled by him - used by him for the purpose of causing grief in our life together."

Edward saw Alessandra's face intensify with concern. It made him question whether he had done the right thing, starting the conversation. Still she asked more questions, leaving him no choice but to keep moving forward.

"But that is not what has been bothering you, is it? Yes, I am sure it must have been horrible for you and my parents to discover Tom's intent and his true nature, but what are you still not telling me, Edward?"

"Tom's body was found on the estate," he said and paused before finding the strength to continue. "He was found not far from the waterfall, and the estimation of how long he had been there…"

Alessandra finally understood the conflict in the man before her - the man she loved so deeply.

"You think that Tom was watching us, that last day that we were there," she said and saw him nod slightly as a tear appeared. "You are worried that he saw us make love."

Edward looked up at her, the horrific thought crossing his mind again and resulting in his eyes clouding over with tears. He knew it was not something to cry over, and yet something about the violation of their privacy did deeply affect him.

Alessandra kissed him softly, summoning her strength to put him at ease.

"Edward, even if he was there that day, and even if he did see us, it does not matter. Why does this upset you so?"

"He would have seen you..."

"Oh, my love. My body is yours alone and I do not wish for anyone else to see it - ever - but if he watched us, then that is done. If he was found nearby he did not have any opportunity to share anything he saw, even if he had intended to, which I doubt he would have. I love you for wanting to protect me so much, but Tom is dead. He will not be able to hurt us, and I am not hurt by thinking that he might have seen me with you like that. If he saw us together then all he would have seen was how much I love you and how much we share as husband and wife."

"To me, it feels like he violated you..." Edward started to say Alessandra pulled him closer and soothed him.

"Yes, I can see how much it affects you, but, Edward, I have not been violated. Even with this news, I do not feel it. Tom does not matter to me. All I care about is you, and our child, and my parents, and your parents. Whatever Tom was intending, and whatever he did, he is gone and he will never hurt us. He could never have hurt us because I love you so much. There was never any way he could have changed that."

Edward looked into her eyes and felt himself start to relax. She had such inner strength that sometimes he found himself in awe of her. Suddenly he thought back to when she had arrived at the manor, and how incredibly timid she had been. He smiled at the memory.

"What makes you smile so?" Alessandra asked him, hoping his worries might finally be at peace.

Edward gave her the most incredible smile. It made her blush softly.

"I was remembering how you were when you first came here - those first few days. I never would have guessed at that time, just how strong you are," Edward said and relaxed into himself for a further moment, formulating words in his head. "I am blessed to have you, Alessandra, and I do love you so much."

Alessandra saw tears once again return to her husband's eyes. She kissed him softly before speaking.

"I love you too, Edward, but please, if there is anything else bothering or worrying you, speak now. Let me put your mind at ease. It has not been the same with you so concerned about Tom. You are far more important to me than anything you can be worrying about."

Edward kissed her in reply and pulled her closer to him.

"All is well, my lovely wife. It has been just this horrible business about Tom that has been consuming my mind. Are you sure you are alright with what I have told you today?"

Alessandra kissed him once more, pulling him into a passionate embrace and reassuring him through her actions that she was not giving Tom Missinger another thought.

CHAPTER 50

Edward looked up at the sound of his wife crying out in pain and gripping his arm tightly as she sat beside him in the drawing room. Immediately he felt panicked.

"Alessandra! What is it?" he asked as he heard her moan again.

"Oh, Edward. I think this might be it. It is starting," Alessandra whispered before taking another deep breath in an attempt to sway the feelings beginning inside of her.

Edward looked around him, perplexed as to what to do, before one of the service staff came in, having heard the cry.

"Get the mistress at once!" he commanded and watched the staff member begin to leave the room quickly. "And my wife's mother!"

He watched Alessandra's face as she realised she was going into labour. She had been patient in past months. With the support of Edward, his parents and her parents, who were now both installed in the manor house in preparation for the birth, she had done all she felt she could do to remain calm and do whatever she could to bring her child into the world safely.

"Alessandra, come. Stand up. You know the midwife said that would help when the pains started," he said to her as he finally found peace in his mind and could focus on what they had both been told in preparation for the birth.

Edward stood and held out his hands to her. As Alessandra accepted his help to stand up, she almost immediately doubled over. It was the most difficult thing for Edward to watch as he felt completely helpless. He feared that something would not go right either for the child or his wife, whilst also feeling happy and hopeful that soon he would meet his child. He also felt the deepest love for the woman who had entered his world and changed it so much.

When the drawing room door opened, Alessandra's mother, Isabella, rushed in. She was followed by the remaining three parents, all with worried looks on their faces.

"Oh my daughter, how are you feeling?" Alessandra heard her mother's voice ask. At that moment Alessandra felt another spike of pain pass through her. It was like nothing she had ever felt before.

"Oh my, I think it is time we ready the birth room," Edward heard his mother say. He watched her leave the room hurriedly, call out for staff to help and then return. "Edward, help Alessandra up the stairs so we can get her settled into the birthing bed."

~~~~~

After much fuss by everyone around her, finally Alessandra was made comfortable in a large bed in a room she had not even seen before. Despite it now being summer, the fire was lit so the room would not get cold. That, combined with the room receiving the late afternoon sun, allowed Alessandra to bask in the warmth streaming in the window.

Over the next 14 hours, she continued to feel the pains, over and over. Although both mothers insisted it was not right for Edward to be in the room, he stayed with her and held her hand. The only times he let go were when he had to eat, or would help her to eat. Watching her go through the contractions made him almost cry. Deep inside he was terrified that he was going to lose her in childbirth.

Finally, after some manipulation and final
~~~~~

encouragement by the midwife, a baby girl was delivered. Alessandra immediately fell into a deep sleep, not even aware of all the happenings now going on around her. She was oblivious to being cleaned and changed into another nightgown. That was something Edward insisted he be the only person allowed to do.

Only after he had attended to his wife, ensuring she was clean, comfortable and sleeping soundly, did he leave the room to find the other family members and accept the small being that was placed into his arms. As soon as he found the confidence to hold her and look at her, he knew he was in love all over again. He didn't try to stop the tears.

Alessandra's mother looked at Edward's and smiled a knowing mother smile.

"We will need to find a wet nurse for her immediately, Edward," he heard his mother say.

Edward stood firm in his resolve as he answered her.

"Alessandra will decide what is best for her and our daughter, Mother. I will talk to her about it when she is rested," he said and saw his mother start to protest. "Mother, I love you and I respect you but Alessandra and I will make decisions about our children, together and on our own."

Charles Chisholm saw his wife start to speak. He immediately held her hand and squeezed it to silence her before she could upset what was the happiest day the estate had seen in so long.

Edward continued to look fondly at the small bundle in his arms and was reluctant to let her go to anyone else even though he was the only person present who had never held a baby before.

"Take her to your wife, Sir," the midwife said cheerfully to him. "The little one will need to feed and if you do not have a wet nurse here, the mother will have to do it."

Edward nodded and walked carefully back to the

chamber where his wife lay. He opened the door softly and crept in. When he reached the chair by the side of the bed, he saw that Alessandra was already awake again.

"Edward," she said quietly as if still waking from a deep sleep. She looked at him, desperate to focus. Seeing he had something in his arms made her jolt awake and sit up. "Is that…?"

Edward laughed at her in her sleepy but still curious state.

"Yes, my love. This is our daughter, and she is beautiful," he said, making Alessandra cry with the joy she felt in seeing her husband and her baby together. "Will you hold her?"

Alessandra smiled and sat right up before reaching out, nodding as Edward placed the small bundle in her arms, and sat on the bed beside them.

Alessandra looked down into the small face in wonder and let the small fingers tighten around her little finger. Edward looked at them both and saw tears come to his wife's eyes.

"She is so beautiful, Edward … and she is part of you and me. We made her," she said, with the usual wonder of her voice.

"The midwife said that she has to feed, Alessandra. Can you?" he asked her. Alessandra felt embarrassed and shy all of a sudden, but finding her resolve to do the right thing, and to learn, she responded positively.

"I must try," she said and shyly opened her nightgown and encouraged her nipple to the lips of her daughter.

Alessandra leaned back and adjusted to the new feeling. As she held the baby in one arm, she reached out for Edward with her other hand and saw the look on his face. He was looking at her in awe, as if she had done something no other person in the world had ever done before. She smiled at him.

"Kiss me," she whispered.

Taking care not to put any pressure on the bundle between them, Edward moved closer and obliged. When he moved back, he smiled at her while continuing to hold her hand.

"Mother has offered to find a wet nurse to feed her..." he started to say. Alessandra immediately cut him off.

"No! If one is needed, then yes, we can find one, but Edward, look at her. She seems fine. Can we please just try this, this way, first?"

Edward looked at her, pleased at her decision even though it may vex his parents.

"Yes, of course, my love. I told Mother that you and I will be making all the decisions regarding our child. If need be, I will remind her and Father of that if and when I need to. You must not worry about anything, but do not be afraid to ask for any help you need."

Alessandra felt a lessening in the suckling on her breast. When she looked down she realised the baby had gone to sleep.

"Will you take her, Edward, and put her down in her bed there?" she asked.

She watched as he carefully lifted the small life and placed her carefully within the bassinet set up near the bed. They smiled at each other as he moved back to his wife, who reached out with both arms and pulled him close to her. Already she was thinking about the aspect of their marriage that they had both missed in recent months. She held him tight and pulled him into a passionate kiss and embrace, from which he eventually pulled himself away, laughing quietly.

"Oh, Alessandra," he said with amusement in his face.

"I have missed being close to you," she said quietly, looking down with a slight blush on her face.

"As have I," Edward replied. "It will not be long, but

not yet, my beautiful wife. For now, you must concentrate on letting your body recover."

They looked at each other intently, both aware of times to come. Inflamed by the thoughts, they heard a knock on the bedroom door. Immediately Edward moved away and stood up, refocusing his mind quickly before opening the door.

Seeing four grandparents eager to see their granddaughter again, he stood aside and welcomed them all in and let them take turns at looking at the baby and chatting to Alessandra. After he moved to the other side of the bed and sat on it, his back to the bed head as Alessandra's was, he gladly took her hand in his, finding great contentment in simply being close to her.

"What name shall you give her?" they both heard Edward's father ask. Edward and Alessandra looked at each other in realisation they had not even decided upon any potential names yet.

"I should like something from Mother's family line," Alessandra said, looking at her mother, who took her hand and held it, smiling. "And something from Edward's also."

She reached out and took Edward's mother's hand and smiled at her. "What is a good name that has held importance to you?" she asked and saw a tear come to his mother's eyes.

"I always thought Elizabeth was a strong name in my family, and Edward's father's family…"

Alessandra looked at Edward, who gave a nod and a smile, knowing this was a way to make his mother happy once again.

"Elizabeth it is then. And Mother, what name from your family?"

"Gabriella, Alessandra. That was the name of my mother, who you never met, but was a strong-willed woman," Isabella said.

"Elizabeth Gabriella … hmm … I do like that. What

do you think, husband?" Alessandra asked Edward, seeing a thoughtful expression on his face.

"Elizabeth Gabriella Chisholm. I like that very much. Let it be so," he said and Alessandra reached across for him to kiss her happily.

"Now then everyone," they all heard the midwife say from behind their happy gathering. "I shall be leaving soon but I would like some time alone with the young mistress, if you please, to make sure all is as well as it seems."

Edward ushered both sets of grandparents out of the room and followed them himself, leaving his wife to the care of the brash but likeable woman who had helped deliver his daughter into the world. Once the door was closed, the midwife moved closer to Alessandra and sat down beside her quietly.

"How are you feeling, lass? It is not an easy thing, birth, but you seem like you are not suffering from it."

Alessandra shook her head. "I feel well, only very tired."

The midwife nodded at her. "That is only to be expected after being in labour for so many hours. I would like to give you a small check-up of an intimate nature, to make sure you have not torn anything. Are you comfortable with that?" she asked and received consent.

Alessandra relaxed as she felt herself bared and touched lightly and then covered up again.

"There does not seem to be any damage, which is good. Do you have any questions for me, before I leave?"

"I fed her from my breast," Alessandra said and the midwife nodded. "Can I keep doing that?"

"Oh yes, of course you can! As long as there is milk, you can feed her. Sometimes it does dry up. If that happens you must not put pride ahead of her need for food. You may not wish to have a wet nurse but if your child needs to be fed..." she said and Alessandra agreed with her, before starting to blush profusely.

"And with my husband…?" she tentatively asked and the midwife smiled softly but knowingly.

"I would recommend you wait at least a month before resuming marital relations. Some women have to wait longer - six to eight weeks - but I do not think you will need to wait that long as you do not appear to have any tears at all. But certainly a month," she said and readied herself to leave.

"Thank you so much for being here for me," Alessandra said to her. The midwife smiled at her graciously before nodding, curtseying and quietly leaving the room.

Finally having quiet, Alessandra let her head rest down on the pillow just for a moment … and then was sound asleep once again.

CHAPTER 51

Downstairs in the drawing room, the midwife said her farewell to the rest of the family and left the five of them sitting silently with their individual thoughts.

"She will need someone to help her, at least, Edward. Who does she trust to help her with the baby?"

Edward looked up, suddenly realising he was not certain who Alessandra even interacted with on the household staff. But remembering how trustworthy Margaret had been when he and his father had brought Mrs Howard to the manor, her name was the first one that entered his mind.

"I think Margaret might be the person she would prefer, at least initially," he said, standing up. "I shall locate her and talk to her."

~~~~~

Walking around the rooms in an attempt to find the right staff member, Edward found himself cursing the size of the manor. With it being summer, it was even worse as everything was cleaned and set up for the upcoming hunt his father had arranged, when a great number of people would be staying with them.

Finally, he found Margaret in one of the guest rooms, preparing it for the arrival of a guest.

"Margaret," he said and she looked up, surprised to see the young master seeking her out.

"Yes, Sir?"

"You are aware that my wife has safely delivered our child," he started and saw her nod in acknowledgement. "I would like her to have someone with her to help as
~~~~~

she requires it, and to give her support, particularly when I am not nearby. It will require some help with my daughter..." he said tentatively, not even sure if Margaret knew anything about children or babies.

Margaret smiled at him. "Sir, I have nursed babies and raised children. I would be happy to provide help to the young mistress if that is what you are asking."

"Yes, thank you," Edward said. "Will you pass this work to someone else go to her now?"

Margaret nodded, curtseyed and walked off to find Alessandra, a smile on her face as she had come to consider the young mistress a very likeable and affable young lady who she would take pleasure in assisting.

Before leaving the room, Edward took a moment to go to the window of the presently unused bedroom, and just looked out, enjoying the view. From there he could see the hill he and Alessandra had both come to love riding up to the summit of. He felt himself grow excited at the thought of things such as horse riding, which she had not been able to enjoy in recent months.

He thought back to their conversation at the waterfall, where she had expressed her desire to not be with child again in summer. He resolved that he would do whatever he had to, to make sure that did not happen. But even in thinking about how to not get her pregnant, he felt his arousal come on strong, due to his anticipation of their intimacy soon being able to resume again. Even just thinking about her like that was enough to create deep feelings of passion for her. He realised then, standing at the window, how much his body had missed hers after all.

CHAPTER 52

In the following weeks, Alessandra's mother and father returned to their home. From Margaret, Alessandra learned how to do things that she knew her mother-in-law did not approve of her doing herself - bathing Elizabeth and changing her clothing and nappies. Even Edward was eager to assist with aspects of his daughter's care, and at the end of every day made sure he had his turn to let the little life nestle into his arms and fall asleep there before being put into her bed by her father.

Margaret was well set up to support Alessandra but at the young parents' request, she did not work nights and left the care of the young one in their care completely.

After putting Elizabeth into her bed for the night - by now she was sleeping more and more of the night with each passing day - Edward climbed into bed with Alessandra to hold her close.

"Can we move back into our own room soon, Edward? I do not think we need to stay in here any longer," Alessandra asked, letting her mind wander back to pre-birth times.

"Of course. We can do that tomorrow," he replied, bringing up his hand to touch her cheek and run his fingers over her lips.

So far they had not moved toward anything physical, both being aware of the advised four weeks before resuming intimacy. Often when he was near her, his arousal was overpowering. He yearned for her greatly.

"Can everything return to normal tomorrow, Edward?" she asked.

Edward laughed at her, knowing precisely what she was asking. "I have not forgotten your desire to not be with heavy with child in summer, my love."

Alessandra thought about that, doing mathematics in her head.

"But it is only the start of autumn now. If we do not start trying to make a baby until summertime, that will be many months before we are joined again!" she exclaimed unhappily. "No, Edward … no!"

He smiled at her. "Well, we can still be close, Alessandra," he said as he lowered his hand to that private part of her and felt her legs part to grant his hand access. Alessandra kept as quiet as she could, mindful of the little person sleeping nearby, but at the same time relished the delicious feelings that she had missed.

Edward felt his arousal reach another level as he became aware of the way her body was moving in her arousal, and the quiet but noticeable sounds she was making. He kissed her neck in the spot he knew she loved and kept moving his finger on her. It was a short time before he felt her climax and release.

Alessandra took a few minutes before she opened her eyes and looked at him. When she did, Edward saw her fire. She leaned in and kissed him passionately and started to pleasure him, also with her hand, and once more it was a short time before he also released.

Their kissing took another turn, both fuelled greatly by their passion for one another, and much time passed before they eased off slowly.

"I know you are right. We can pleasure each other without joining. That is all we did when we first married. It just seems so long to wait!" Alessandra said, secure in his arms.

"We only have to align it right once, my lovely wife. We can work on the baby-making mid-spring, allowing you to be out in the sunshine more over summer, and then you could be giving birth near the middle of winter," he explained softly to her, although silently thinking to himself that it did seem like a long while until he would be able to move as one with her once more. "What say you to that?"

She cuddled closer into him, letting him take on the role of stronger partner, and agreed.

"I would very much like for us to be able to ride at least up to the summit more together in the warm weather, Edward," she said and paused before continuing. "And walk to the waterfall."

He laughed at her, purposely not letting his mind wander to other memories relating to that area. Moving so he could look into her eyes once more, he kissed her softly.

"Then let us remember that in the middle of spring … hmmm … but until then I shall do what I can to keep you distracted from such thoughts."

Alessandra suddenly realised he had not finished his pleasuring of her yet. She felt his lips move down her body until his lips and tongue found that point once more, and again she was taken away in wondering why she was thinking so much about their physical joining at all.

CHAPTER 53

Once Alessandra was fully recovered and felt completely back to her normal self she found herself appreciating Margaret more and more, letting her take on the role of Elizabeth's nanny. While Edward and Alessandra both indulged in spending time with their daughter, while the weather was still warm enough they started finally to get out for walks and horse rides together, reclaiming their simple enjoyment of each other's company.

Lying down together at the top of the summit, looking down over the estate, Edward heard Alessandra sigh. He looked down at her from his higher position as he leaned on one elbow beside her.

"What is that sigh for, my beautiful wife?"

She looked up at him and moved her hand to the side of his face.

"I am blessed in this life with you, Edward. I am thankful to you for giving me Elizabeth, and for loving me…" she started to say, but cut short her words as she felt tears come to her eyes.

He kissed her softly for a long time.

"And I look forward to spring," she added, making him laugh once again at her suggestiveness.

He pulled away from her and stood up, holding out his hand to her.

"Come, Alessandra. We need to start moving back to the manor," he said and they stood together, relishing a standing hug for a long time. "We both need to start doing our share of the work around the estate again."

"I know," Alessandra replied, nodding. "I do feel like

I have been letting your mother down."

"No, you haven't, but we do need to resume our duties. Mother and Father will hand the estate over to us in the future and we need to be skilled in managing it completely by ourselves."

Alessandra pushed her lips onto his and kissed him passionately while they enjoyed the last few alone moments. In response, Edward gently placed his hands on her shoulders and eased away from her, shaking his head whilst smiling what she thought was the most beautiful smile ever.

~~~~~~

As they approached the manor and dismounted from their horses, they both sensed that something was amiss inside. With the first thought for both of them being that something had happened to their daughter, they ran inside and prepared to move upstairs to where she would be with Margaret. As they approached the base of the main staircase, the drawing room door opened and Edward's father came out to them, closing the door quietly behind him.

"Father, what is it?" Edward asked with desperation showing in his face and his voice.

"Is it Elizabeth?" Alessandra asked at the same time.

"No, little Elizabeth is well. There is nothing to worry about there, but we have been surprised by a visitor, and a most unwelcome one at that," Charles said. "I did not want to ask her to leave until I had spoken to you both."

Edward and Alessandra both waited patiently for further details and when they said nothing, Edward's father resumed his news.

"In the drawing room with your mother, is Mrs Missinger."

Alessandra felt the warmth and colour drain from her face as she processed the news that was presented to her.

"Katherine is here?" she asked her father-in-law, who
~~~~~~

nodded at her. "I do not understand. Why would she be here?"

"She says she needs to see you, Alessandra," Charles said.

Edward moved closer to his wife, feeling a desperate need to protect her all of a sudden, even though he knew the great depth of her inner strength in every situation she was presented with.

"You do not need to go in there, Alessandra. We can have her removed from the manor," he started to say.

Alessandra shook her head whilst taking his hand. "No, Edward. She has come all this way. Please, come in with me if you wish, but I have to see her. No matter what Tom did to us, he was her husband and he is now dead."

Edward nodded to her and the three of them made there way reluctantly through the drawing room door. Almost immediately upon sight of her, Tom's wife moved to stand directly in front of Alessandra, her face contorted in anger.

"You! I knew it was you that they were talking about - the way you threw yourself at my husband in Bath. I did not realise the length then that you would go to, to ruin things for me and Tom."

Alessandra looked at Katherine, surprised and shocked at the words being thrown at her. She held Edward back forcefully by his hand when she felt him start to move forward out of protection.

"Edward, all is well," she said quietly to her husband, her eyes never leaving those of the woman in front of her. "Mrs Missinger and I need to talk alone."

She was not sure how the woman would react to her words, but Alessandra saw something of a slight melting in her eyes as Edward and his father both started to object.

"Please, Edward, go with your parents and wait outside of this door so you are close enough if I need you, but do leave us alone for a few minutes please."

Edward looked at both of his parents and they all left the room quietly, silenced by the power of Alessandra's request. When the room was vacant except for the two young women, Alessandra gathered her strength and moved to a sofa near the fireplace.

"Please, sit with me and tell me what has driven you to come here and confront me."

Slowly Katherine approached and sat, the anger draining further from her face and demeanour, as she seemed to find the words to speak. When she looked up and directly at Alessandra, there was a blend of sadness and frustration in her eyes.

"You were the one he wanted," Tom's wife said simply.

Alessandra hoped that Katherine would continue to explain what she meant. When she did not, Alessandra finally spoke. "If that were true, I would have been the one he married, do you not think?" Alessandra asked. She could see the woman considering that in her head, but she did not say anything in response. "Why are you here? Please tell me directly so I know what you are angered about."

"He left everything to you," Katherine said finally, the words flowing out of her like air deflating.

Alessandra assumed she must have misinterpreted what had just been said. "I am sorry. I do not understand what you are saying," she said.

"I think you do, Mrs Chisholm. My husband loved you - and only you. His direction for when he died was that everything he owned - his land and his fortune - would all be left to you."

Alessandra sat in shock, not wanting this news to be real.

"No! That cannot be true. You are his wife."

"Did you love him?" Katherine asked, a sad tone underlying in her voice.

Alessandra looked at the poor woman who had gone through so much.

"At one time, yes, I thought I was in love with him. It was only a childish crush from before I met my husband, and before you and Tom married."

"But he always loved you," Katherine said.

"No, I do not think he did - not ever. At any time when we were getting to know each other, he could have told me he was betrothed to you. He could have told his parents that he wanted to marry me. He did neither, and the only reason that could be was because he did not feel that way about me … and he wanted to marry you."

"When he introduced me to you in Bath, I could see how you were with your husband and I believe he - Tom - wished for that. We were never like that. He always had such a wall up around him. I believed when I saw you in Bath, and the way that Tom looked at you, that you were the reason for that."

Alessandra looked closely at Tom's wife. Her first impression of Katherine in Bath had been that she lacked empathy or true feeling for anyone but herself. Something about her countenance now made Alessandra believe that perhaps she had loved Tom after all. What good would it do to confirm his widow's beliefs by telling her about the love letters Tom had written to her, or the actions he had taken to see her?

"I cannot say how your husband felt about me, but he married you, and you are his wife…"

"Was!" Katherine exclaimed passionately. "I was his wife. Now he is dead, I am his widow, and because of his love for you I have nothing."

"Why do you think this?" Alessandra asked.

"His will states it," Katherine said abruptly as if that was the end of the matter.

"But when was the will made up? Surely after he married you…"

Alessandra saw the frustration on the woman's face.

"He changed his will after he saw you in Bath!" Katherine exclaimed.

Both women sat silently as their minds flowed over memories of their respective interactions with Tom Missinger.

"Katherine," Alessandra said quietly, trying to calm the woman before her. "I do not know why Tom did such a thing with his will but I promise you that I have no desire to receive anything that was his - that now should be yours. I know nothing of the law but I am sure that with good advice we can together put this right so that you have all that was his."

Katherine looked up at Alessandra - her adversary - with surprise. She had not expected such a reaction to the news at all.

"You would do that? Even if it goes against what Tom wanted?"

"If Tom wanted to leave everything to me instead of you, then perhaps he was not thinking properly at that time, because for him to do so, makes no sound sense. Let me bring in my father-in-law. He will know who we can talk to about this, and what can be done," Alessandra said, seeing Tom's widow relax more as she nodded.

Alessandra brought Charles in, followed by Edward and his mother, who sat quietly off to the side, curious about what had been happening.

"Mrs Missinger and I require some legal advice and I am hoping that you might be able to at least provide us with an idea of where to start," Alessandra said to Edward's father directly.

"Of course, Alessandra. But what is this about?" Charles asked.

Alessandra took a deep breath before continuing, knowing that she could be about to cause her husband pain in her revelation.

"Mrs Missinger has been informed that everything that her husband owned, he left in a will … not to her …

but instead to … me."

She took her time getting through the sentence. At the end of it, she saw Edward stand up in hurt and anger. She cut him off with a stern and pleading look in his direction before he could say anything that she knew could hurt the widow in the room.

"I do not welcome this news and would like to work with her in any way I can, to make sure that everything in question rightfully gets transferred to her, and not to me," Alessandra continued.

Edward's father sighed and rubbed his eyes, trying desperately to separate feelings about how the dead man had acted in his final weeks, from how he must project his feelings as being, in front of the dead man's wife.

"Mrs Missinger, this does seem a complex issue that is indeed unfair to you. Please give me all the details you have about the lawyer who is processing the will. I will instruct my legal man to make contact and get this sorted," Charles said.

Katherine looked from one person to the next. Overcome with emotions she had not expected to have in the Chisholm household, she felt the tears start to flow.

"Thank you. I did not expect…"

"Katherine, you must return to your home and talk again to the lawyer. Ask them to write to me directly here. You have nothing to fear from me. I will help to put this right. Please believe me," Alessandra said.

Katherine nodded, feeling drained. "Very well," she said, standing up. "I will take my leave of you now. I am sorry for coming here unannounced."

"I will walk you out," Alessandra said to distance them from the other family members.

As she approached her carriage, Katherine turned to Alessandra once more.

"I know that he did love you and that when he died he was in this area, hoping to find you … but I also believe that you did not know the depth of his feeling or intention toward you."

Katherine climbed into the carriage and moved away from the manor, leaving Alessandra at the front entrance with much on her mind.

She felt hands move around her from behind, and she leaned back against Edward for support. He said nothing, just held her like that, pushing aside his ongoing infuriation at Tom Missinger yet again invading their marriage - even now, from his grave.

~~~~~

That night in bed alone together, Alessandra felt Edward holding her particularly tightly to him.

"It will all get sorted, Edward. Stop thinking about him," she said and he sighed.

"It just felt like he was delivering yet another attempt to drive us apart from one another, even though he is no longer in this world."

"Perhaps that is why he did it," she replied, making his head come up and look at her deeply. One thing Edward he had not considered was it being simply another attempt of Tom's to cause friction between Alessandra and Edward. "And that is exactly why we are not going to let it affect us, Edward. You do not wish for me to lay claim to the land and fortune he has left, do you?"

"No! For him to not leave everything - anything - to his wife or any other family members, is despicable. No, you are right, Alessandra, it must be put right for her sake," Edward replied.

Alessandra pushed him back so he was lying on his back and kissed him deeply.

"Good. Now stop thinking about such unpleasurable things," she said before kissing her way down his body.
~~~~~

CHAPTER 54

Alessandra sat in the lawyer's office, angry at what had been said to her. Silently she wished she had not told Edward he had to wait outside.

"I do not understand," she said once more to the short, balding man in front of her. "You seem to be saying there is no alternative but for me to accept all of the land that has been in Mr Missinger's family for generations. And the dowry he obtained from his wife's family!"

Mr Hogelby maintained his patience in determination to not upset the wife and daughter-in-law of one of his most prestigious client families.

"That is correct, Mrs Chisholm. The will is iron clad and there is no deviating from it. Mr Missinger's mother was his last remaining family member but passed away shortly after she received news of her son's death. There is no other living relative that has been found. I will also point out to you that it was Mr Missinger's specific instruction that you - and only you - will be recipient to this fortune. By that, I mean that he has made sure that your husband and his family can have no access to it. You - and you alone - will inherit a considerable amount of land and money."

"But his wife?" Alessandra asked, not believing what was being told to her.

"He left very specific instructions not only that you should get everything, but that she should get nothing. You cannot contest that, I am afraid, as that aspect of the will does not concern you. She can contest it, however as yet she has not."

Now Alessandra's confusion reached a new level. "I do not understand. Katherine has not tried to claim … anything? She did not come back to see you again and ask that this be put right?"

She saw the lawyer shake his head. "No. As yet she has not appeared to be bothered by the will at all."

"Then why did she come to see me? What was the purpose of her visit?" she wondered quietly.

"Mrs Chisholm, you have to understand that Mrs Missinger was already very wealthy before she married her husband, and she held onto much of that wealth through their wedding contract. Her family is one of the wealthiest in the region. She will still inherit a great deal of land and fortune from her parents, so it is possible that she simply does not need to claim for her husband's wealth."

Mr Hogelby watched the young woman before him and certainly understood her dilemma. Although he had been a lawyer all of his working life, it was the first time he had met someone who not only was not demanding a higher inheritance than had been left them but in fact would prefer to not receive it at all.

"Very well, Mr Hogelby, what do I need to do now?" Alessandra asked, resigned to what she could only accept and not change.

For the remainder of their meeting papers were read through and signed. Alessandra walked out with the realisation that now she was a very wealthy woman in her own right, without any input or expense from her parents, her husband or Chisholm Manor Estate.

Seeing Edward waiting for her, she walked into his arms.

"I cannot talk about this at present, Edward. We will discuss all of this at a later time, when I have had time to think," she said quietly.

Edward nodded and walked her out, his curiosity

persistent in his thoughts.

~~~~~

When they arrived back at the manor, Alessandra immediately ran up to the nursery to visit Elizabeth. She was greeted by Margaret with her usual cheerful manner, who stood back as Alessandra lifted her daughter and held her tight against her.

Margaret watched the interaction, feeling pride in how the young mistress had grown since her initial awkward arrival at the manor a year earlier.

"Margaret, I think my milk is drying up. What shall I do?" she asked shyly but was only greeted with a smile.

"Miss, I believe the young lady is old enough now to go onto cow milk."

Alessandra showed her surprise but was also relieved. She was glad that perhaps a wet nurse would not be required. That was something she did not want to do willingly, as she could not enjoy the thought of someone else sharing such intimacy with her child.

"She is?"

"Yes, Miss. It is quite normal by this time for the change to be in place. While you are still producing some milk, it is a good time to introduce a small amount of cow milk each day. This will ensure she goes through the changeover slowly."

Alessandra considered the information she was being given and nodded.

"Very well, let us work toward that."

"I will give her a little tomorrow morning after you have given her a little of your milk. That will give us the whole day to monitor her and make sure there are no problems."

Alessandra nodded and settled herself into the nursing chair in the nursery, willing her milk to last another few days. Mother and daughter looked at each other quietly as Elizabeth suckled.

The door to the nursery opened and Edward walked
~~~~~

in quietly, smiling at Margaret and taking in the view before him.

"What a beautiful sight," he said quietly, leaning over and kissing his wife. Looking down at his daughter, he saw her pull away from her milk source and look up at him. As had become usual routine, he reached down and scooped up Elizabeth into a close cuddle to allow Alessandra to discretely restore her gown tidily.

Edward walked around the room, never letting his eyes leave his daughter's face until he saw her eyes close as she drifted into her post-feed sleep. Gently he placed her in her bassinet and tucked her in, before turning back to his wife and leading her out the door as they headed together down to lunch.

"I need to go with Father to visit some tenants after we eat, so I may not see you until supper time," he said. Curiosity of the morning's visit to the lawyer was still in his mind but he would not invade his wife's privacy, or pressure her to speak.

Alessandra stopped short of the dining room door and turned to him, moving forward and providing him with a full standing hug, before kissing him lovingly. She did not say anything, and Edward felt the fullness of the depth of love exuding from her before he kissed her back.

CHAPTER 55

"What do you mean, she's not told you what is happening with that man's will, Edward?" Charles Chisholm demanded as he and his son rode on horseback around the estate.

Edward felt conflicted, torn between respect for his father and respect for his wife.

"She has not mentioned it, Father, and I will not pressure her to do so. If she wishes to speak to me about it, she will," he said.

"But if she has been left anything, it is lawfully yours," his father said.

Edward took a deep breath, wondering if he should speak his thoughts about the very subject they were embarking on. He did believe that in doing so he might upset or anger his father. Finally, he found the courage to express his views.

"No, Father, if she has accepted Missinger's fortune, it can remain her own," Edward said.

"What?!" Charles exclaimed in disbelief. "What is this madness, Edward? What has made you think that is acceptable..."

"What has made me rethink this 'system' of everything going to a woman's husband, is the fact that my child is a daughter, not a son," Edward said, cutting his father's words short. "Father, take a moment to think - as Elizabeth grows and eventually marries, would you want all of this to be taken from her and placed in the hands of her husband? No! It shall not be! This land has been passed down through your family for generations and I intend to make sure that it stays in our family, not whoever my daughter marries."

Edward looked at his father and saw his face relax in understanding of what his son was saying. It was different for Charles as he had been the oldest son in his generation. Edward had the only son in his. Edward saw things differently, being father to a daughter.

"You may yet have a son," his father said quietly, not wanting to argue too hard with his son, given how much little Elizabeth had begun to charm him also.

"Perhaps we shall," Edward said. "Alessandra and I will discuss what is to happen in that event. For now, however, please respect whatever is happening with Missinger's will, as far as my wife is concerned. The estate is fine for now, is it not?"

"Yes, my son," Charles said as he nodded. "With the money that was injected from Alessandra's dowry, the estate is in good condition and will be so for some time yet. You are right. For now, we do not need to worry about any other income. I will not say another word about it."

"Thank you," Edward said softly to his father, knowing that the way that he and his wife were doing things was different from the way his father had done things. Even Alessandra and Edward spending so much time with their daughter was different to how Edward's parents had raised him.

~~~~~

In the 'glass jungle room', Alessandra sat quietly and thought about all that had been told to her by the lawyer that morning. Soon she would go and see her daughter once again. After that, she planned to seek out her mother-in-law to see how she could be of help to her. For the current moment, however, she needed to be alone to think.

Everything was being signed over to her and while it was not what she had wanted, she was determined that
~~~~~

she would make good decisions about what to do with it. In addition to the financial gain she would have for herself, she was inheriting an estate that incorporated the Missinger family home and associated land. The lawyer had offered to look after everything for her but had also advised that she try and get to the property when she could, to decide if she would want to keep it or sell it.

The property was not anywhere near the estate she now lived on, so she was not in a situation where she could add it to Chisholm Manor Estate. It was closer to her parents' home, which provided some options, she supposed. The lawyer had said there were staff on the property who would be eager to know what was happening to them and deserved to meet their new mistress and receive instruction from her.

For the monetary side of things, she had talked to the lawyer about options for investment. She had agreed with him that she would like to receive a regular payment to herself as money just for her spending. That was something she'd never had. She couldn't help but feel excited at the prospect of being able to purchase something if she wished to, without it being billed to the estate and Edward's parents and adding to their expenditure.

The most pressing issue about it all was what to do as far as Edward and his family were concerned. Alessandra knew she had to tell them that she was inheriting land and fortune, but would they be offended by her wanting to keep it separate from their estate?

Standing up, she resolved to put legal and financial decisions aside in her mind. Instead, she would go and see her little Elizabeth, determined today, as every day, to make her a priority over other less important aspects of her life.

CHAPTER 56

After giving Elizabeth her final feed for the evening, Alessandra and Edward left the nursery and walked quietly back to their bedchamber. Alessandra wondered what she could tell him about her meeting with the lawyer, without causing him pain. In turn, Edward wondered what he could ask her.

Upon entering the room, Alessandra moved to stand in front of the fireplace, letting the warmth from it seep into her. Edward watched her, uncertain from the day's events what she would want from him. Should he approach and ask, or should he stand back and avoid questions?

As if hearing the question in his head, Alessandra reached back with her hand and pulled him so that he was standing behind her. With both of his hands wrapped around her, together they watched the flames in the fireplace.

"Kiss my neck," she whispered to him. Edward obliged, enjoying the way she moved her head to allow him access, and the sound of her breathing deepening and the quiet moan that escaped her lips.

Feeling not only highly aroused, but also completely empowered, Alessandra moved one of his hands upward onto her breast and immediately felt him start to caress her nipple through the layers of fabric. Even through their clothing, she could feel him grow hard against her. She reached back with one hand and touched him, driving him to groan against her neck.

They stayed that way for some time, both enjoying

giving and receiving the pleasure, until Alessandra turned around and faced him, wrapping both arms around him and kissing him passionately. In doing so she pushed him to another level of arousal that Edward knew he would have to satisfy. He turned her away from him again and with slowness and patience, undid and removed each article of her clothing, one piece at a time, kissing the skin before him as it became visible.

When she was naked, he hurriedly removed all of his clothing. They stood together, naked in front of the fire, holding one another tightly and kissing. Everything about her was intoxicating to him. Even in seeing how her body had changed since having a baby, Edward still yearned for her, hard and extended in desperation to be much closer to her.

Alessandra revelled in the high degree of arousal she felt. Holding him close, hip to hip, she felt him nestle between her thighs - not inside of her but still enclosed by the tops of her legs. They stood like that, kissing each other while in no hurry to move from that spot.

Finally, eager to pleasure her husband, Alessandra edged Edward back onto the sofa and knelt before him, taking her time to tease him with her hand and her mouth, doing what she could to not drive him to climax too soon.

"Oh, Alessandra, what you do to me!" he exclaimed as she worked to draw the pleasure out for him. The feelings she felt when knowing he was so aroused made her want to please him. She no longer cared that she knew women were not meant to enjoy marital relations. To her, it was a beautiful thing that she shared only with Edward. She would not feel bad about that.

"Oh my darling, I'm going to..." she heard him say before he convulsed before her, making her giddy in delight and arousal herself at his climaxing. She knelt before him, watching his face as he relaxed back in recovery, and waited until he opened his eyes and looked down at her.

Edward leaned forward and kissed her passionately, wanting to give her everything in the world in that moment, as full of love as he was for her. He pushed her back on the rug on the floor in front of the fire and knelt between her legs to pleasure her in return. Leaning over her he kissed her all over - her lips, her nipples and down over her belly. Finally, he came to rest as she placed her hands on his head and guided him. As aroused as she was, it took only minutes before she felt the release, and all stress that had been inside of her, flow out.

He pulled away and lay down on top of her, nestled between her legs on the rug, enjoying the flames beside them. He took his time kissing her lips over and over, in between the two of them looking at each other and saying nothing.

Alessandra looked at the face of the man she had come to love so deeply. She felt the heaviness of having not immediately talked to him about the matter of Tom's will and suddenly felt the need to make sure there was nothing unsaid between them.

As if sensing the change in her, Edward pulled away and held out his hand to help her up.

"Come and get into bed, my love," he said quietly, coaxing her but letting her lead.

They settled themselves under the covers and lay facing each other quietly.

"Edward," Alessandra started, then found herself uncertain how to go on.

He touched her cheek and ran his fingers lightly over the side of her neck and onto her shoulder, in an attempt to relax her.

"What is it, Alessandra? I can see that you have something consuming you."

"Tom's will..." she started again and paused until Edward prompted her to keep going. "Mr Hogelby informed me today that the will has been set up in such a way that I must accept what is being gifted to me. Not only did Tom state that I was to become the owner of everything he left behind, but also expressly that his wife was to not have anything."

Edward listened and Alessandra saw his face change in disgust about what she'd said.

"But his family…"

Alessandra shook her head. "There are none. His mother was the last remaining relative in their line and she died shortly after his death."

Edward let the information process in his mind, focusing on not letting his anger toward the man who had tried to ruin his marriage, affect anything that Alessandra had to say. Aware that she was waiting patiently, as if to reveal more to him, he encouraged her to keep talking.

"There is more…" he said and she nodded, with a slight blush forming on her face.

"I … he …" she stuttered, trying desperately to muster more confidence in her words. "The will states that everything left to me is to only come to me - to be only mine."

"Yes, you said he did not leave his wife anything…"

"No, Edward, you do not understand. Everything is to come to me, and it is not to come to you."

Edward let out a sigh.

"Oh, Alessandra, is that what you have been worried about all day? That I might want to make some claim on whatever he has left to you?" he asked and saw her silently acknowledge just that. "Oh my love, no. When you came into this marriage your parents gave everything they had to my parents for the sake of the estate. I have been aware from our wedding day that it is difficult with you not having any money of your own. I know it has been hard for you, always having to rely on my parents for things like your dresses or things for

Elizabeth," he said and paused in silence for a moment before continuing his words. "As much as I despised the man, if he has left you a small income for you to enjoy, I want you to enjoy it."

Alessandra revelled in the words she was hearing, wondering why she had thought Edward of all people would want to take anything from her.

"It is not a small income he has left me, Edward," she said timidly, looking into his eyes so she could gauge his reaction. "He left me a considerable fortune, which I have asked the lawyer to pay me a small allowance out of, but there is much, much more. I have asked the lawyer to invest it for the moment, until I know for certain what I want to do with it."

Edward thought about what he was being told - that his wife was now wealthy - and found himself slightly insecure. He endeavoured to keep the feeling as well hidden as he could.

"Is there more?" he asked, sensing she still had not finished her news.

"His entire family estate has been left to me also, Edward. I have an estate property not far from my parents' home. In that, I do want us to make choices together. I need to explore whether to keep the property, with the income that it produces, or sell it. I would like that to be a decision we both make because I want us to think about it in terms of the future of Elizabeth, and any other children we might have."

Edward was silent for some time, letting his mind flow through a myriad of thoughts about all that he had been told, but he could not think what to say in response.

Surprised at how silent he was, Alessandra kissed him softly.

"We do not need to make any decisions now, but I would like us to travel to the estate and deal with things that have to be done there. Staff are there, uncertain what is happening…"

"Yes, of course," Edward responding, understanding fully the importance of staff and tenants on a large estate. "And the property is near your parents' home, you say?" he asked and saw his wife nod. "Then we shall go, if you wish. We will need to bring Margaret with us, to help with Elizabeth - or would you prefer they stay here?"

"No! Oh no, Edward, they must come also, so my parents can spend time with Elizabeth. Perhaps the four of us could travel to my parents' home, and from there you and I could go alone to the estate for one night to assess things," Alessandra said.

"But Elizabeth's feeding…" Edward started to say.

"No," Alessandra responded. "She is weaning off my milk and on to cow milk so Margaret will be able to feed her."

"Very well. Winter is not far off though, my love. Should we go soon, or on the other side of that?"

Their conversation continued far into the night, discussing different options and deciding to leave as soon as Elizabeth was fully weaned. Eventually, they fell asleep in each other's arms, both feeling much better that once again nothing was being hidden between them.

CHAPTER 57

With an approaching chill of winter in the air, a carriage pulled up outside the family home of Alessandra's parents. She eagerly jumped out, seeing her mother running toward her.

"Oh, Alessandra!" she heard before being enveloped into the familiar, loving arms.

Edward looked on over the loving reunion and shook hands with Alessandra's father before both grandparents noticed Margaret, with Elizabeth in her arms.

"There is my granddaughter," Isabella exclaimed as she gathered the small bundle up into her arms. "Oh, how she has grown since I last saw her! Come inside quickly. It is starting to be too cold to be outside for long now," she continued, ushering everyone inside the small home.

Margaret appreciated further her young mistress upon seeing the home that she grew up in. She had suspected since first meeting her that Alessandra had not come from money. Seeing how well she fitted back into the little home - how much it meant to her - confirmed it.

After general talk about their long journey and the progress of Elizabeth in her growth, Margaret was shown to the room that she would share with Elizabeth. Alessandra and Edward were left to finally speak in confidence to Alessandra's parents.

"Now, my child, you did not say much in your letter, apart from you and Edward needing to visit a property near here," Alessandra's father began, making both young people nervous about mentioning Tom to the people before them.

"Yes, Father, I have … inherited … a vast property not far from here. If agreeable to you, Edward and I would like to leave Margaret and Elizabeth here with you for one night so we can go and visit the property. We wish to meet the staff there, so we can decide what to do with it."

Edward saw both of her parents look at her in surprise at the news.

"But who has left such a gift to you, daughter? I know of no family members who have passed recently."

Alessandra blushed and looked down before summoning strength and looking both of her parents in the eye.

"I was left it … by … Tom Missinger."

"Oh, dear, but he was married, Alessandra. How could you possibly have been left his property?" her father questioned, not at all understanding what could have brought about such a situation.

"I know, Father. It appears that in his will he named me as the full recipient of his wealth, including land and money."

"But what of his wife?" her mother asked, confused. "Will she receive nothing?"

"No, it seems he expressly put in his will that she was to receive nothing from him. Furthermore, the lawyer has said that she has not come forward to make any claim at all on the will. It appears that she wants nothing from what Tom owned - not even the money and land that he received from her family when she married him."

Everyone was quiet as they thought about the situation that had presented itself.

"So you now own land near here?" Isabella asked and saw Alessandra nod in acknowledgement. "Will you move here then?"

Edward looked at his wife, not having even considered the possible allurement of her wanting to live closer to her parents. As he watched her face, Alessandra turned to him and smiled, taking his hand in hers to reassure him.

"No, Mother, we will remain living where we are. However, we do need to see the property and assess what is to be done with it. That is why we are here. Are you agreeable to our plan?"

"Yes, of course. We will take good care of little Elizabeth, and Margaret too. Take as long as you need to visit the property," Isabella replied.

"Thank you, Mother. We will stay here tonight and travel on tomorrow morning for just one night," she said and turned to her father. "But Father, after we visit the land, I would welcome your thoughts and advice on options for it."

Edward saw Alessandra's father nod and smile softly. "Of course."

~~~~~

Once settled in bed that evening, Edward held Alessandra close. The question of living location still lingered in his mind.

"Is there a part of you that would like to live closer to your mother and father, Alessandra?"

"No, Edward," she replied. "I thank you for asking, but your home is now my home and I love living there with you and your parents."

"But you would be able to see your mother and father more often…"

"I will very shortly be receiving my own income. That will enable me to come here when I need to," she said, moving closer still to him and kissing him. "We already have a home, and I am happy there. I have no need or desire to live anywhere else."

~~~~~

The next morning the two of them set out toward a home and land that neither of them had ever seen before. Of most concern was the expectation that the staff and tenants on the land would not be welcoming of them, given the circumstance through which Alessandra had obtained it. In both of their minds that would be understandable since the property had largely been in the Missinger family for generations.

As they approached the property they were immediately confronted by the size of the main house. It was not as large as the estate manor of Edward's family, and yet somehow it held a presence that was commanding, as though it were a great person, famous for its strength and power.

When they approached the front door they saw Mr Hogelby walk out. His presence surprised Alessandra.

"Mr Hogelby! I did not expect to see you here," she said happily.

"Mrs Chisholm, Mr Chisholm," he started, bowing whilst smiling at them both. "When I learned that you were intending to visit, I wished to ensure that I was here, in case any explanations were required. I have already taken the liberty of speaking to the staff and many of the tenants. They are all understanding of how the property has now changed hands, and they are eager to meet you both."

The lawyer ushered them inside and Edward found himself in awe of the design of the house. Perhaps being not as old as his own family home, it had aspects to it that made sense to him in a way that he had not even considered before.

"It is a fine home, is it not? This house was constructed only fifty years ago after the original home burned down. It has every modern convenience, and is very handsome indeed," Mr Hogelby said. "Ahh, here are your service staff."

One by one, Edward and Alessandra were introduced to everyone lined up to meet them. Overall, Alessandra found they were cheerful and eager to make their acquaintance, and not at all resentful as she had thought they might be. Soon afterward the two of them were given a tour of the home, walking from room to room in a daze while wondering again what was the best thing to do with the home.

Mr Hogelby moved to excuse himself but found himself invited to sit in the drawing room and talk more to Alessandra and Edward. He took his time, answering all of their questions about options for keeping the estate running and earning, or selling it. Eventually he dismissed himself, saying he would be ready to move forward with anything they wished for, whenever they needed him to.

When he left it was mid-afternoon and Alessandra made her way to the kitchen to speak to the cook, and on to all the individual household staff members, Meanwhile, Edward ventured out to the stables to inspect the staff, the horses, and the way things were run out there.

Over an intimate dinner that had been lavishly prepared in their honour, the two of them compared notes of their separate investigations, both feeling excited about various aspects of the property.

"How are you feeling about everything, my love?" Edward asked tentatively, still not sure if perhaps she might be lured to live in that part of the land after all.

"It is a fine home, Edward. I think I need to keep it, at least for the moment, rather than sell it. Mr Hogelby is certain that the financial side of the estate is profitable, and we can use that profit to keep it maintained and running well. I do think we would need to find someone to live in it. I have no reason to think it cannot run without direction as the staff all seem very established in their roles. It would seem a waste, leaving it with no-one to enjoy it."

They spent the evening talking about all the different options they could think of, before settling into a bedchamber which they found to also be similarly modern and comfortable. The newness of it all - even down to the fireplace which somehow seemed to generate and project much more heat than the ones they were used to in Edward's home - provided a new source of excitement. That, in turn, overflowed into the realisation that they were once again alone without any parents in the house with them. While they missed their daughter, once these feelings started flowing, even she was dismissed from their active thoughts.

CHAPTER 58

The following morning Edward and Alessandra rose early, greeted by a sumptuous breakfast when they made their way into the dining room.

"Are you up for a ride, my love? There are fine horses in the stables and one that I think will be particularly suited to you," Edward asked, excited by the prospect of riding out with his wife more before winter set in.

Alessandra looked up at him, surprised as she had not considered the possibility.

"Yes, I think I would greatly enjoy that, Edward. We should ride around the estate, in any case, to visit some tenants I suppose."

He laughed at her. "My wife, the estate manager! I was thinking more of an easy ride at a slow pace, purely for pleasure and exploration."

As Alessandra looked at him she saw him emphasise the last few words and blushed in response. Her blush made him laugh hard at her sudden shyness. Always she surprised him with her ability to sometimes be bold and courageous, but at other times equally young and timid.

She smiled at him, knowing he was attempting to make her face go the same beetroot red colour that it had done so often when they had first met. As she watched his face, she felt only fondness for the man in front of her.

"You tease me, my wonderful husband, but I shall accept your offer to take me out on the horses. I have not yet seen the stables. But I will have to change into my riding habit first."

"Let us be off then," Edward said, standing and holding his hand out to her to help her up, before putting both of his arms around her and kissing her softly.

From a distance, two dining room staff members glanced at each other and smiled discretely. It had been a long time since they had seen in the home such love as they could clearly see between the new owners.

~~~~~

At first glance at the new mistress, John, the head groom, was surprised and enamoured. He had met the new master the previous day and thought him an intelligent, friendly and likeable gentleman, even though he was not at all handsome. John had found himself wondering what kind of woman would be married to such a man. Looking at Alessandra as they were introduced, John saw that she also would not be considered any great beauty, and yet there was something about her that made her easy to look at and talk to. She was a far cry from the previous mistress, he thought to himself. She wouldn't even look at him, let alone talk to him as a human being.

"I am very pleased to meet you, John. I must inform you that I am quite new to horse riding so still in the learning stages," she started to say before anticipating Edward was going to cut her off and disagree. Looking at her husband with a degree of love that John had never seen on the estate for as long as he had worked there, Alessandra laughed and continued. "See how my husband begins to argue my point, but do not listen to him, John. Please tell me honestly, do you have a quiet horse that is suited to someone still quite unfamiliar to horse riding?"

John smiled at her, mesmerised by her friendly and joyful outlook. "I do indeed, Mistress. Come this way and meet my little Clover. She is a gentle soul and will not bolt."
~~~~~

Alessandra and Edward both approached the pony and immediately sensed her goodness and obedience.

"Oh, she is beautiful. Yes, please, John," Alessandra exclaimed. "Can you saddle her for me? And provide the master and I both with some directions so we can venture out to start visiting tenants on the land?" she asked, smiling greatly.

John obliged, gladly.

~~~~~

Staying within the borders of where they had been told the estate began and ended, Edward and Alessandra rode slowly. They visited people and talked endlessly about all that they could see, and what would need to be fixed or changed.

When they came to a border ridge that overlooked a valley below, both were silenced by the beauty before them.

"Alessandra, this is a phenomenal property," Edward said in awe of what was now under the ownership of his wife. "Everything about it - the house, this land..."

Alessandra looked at her husband's face, pleased that he was finally finding some pleasure in the exaggerated gesture of a gift from her previous beau of long ago. She watched Edward for some time before he felt her looking.

Feeling her eyes upon him, Edward turned to look at her in return. On her face, he saw great passion and desire. Instantly he felt a longing to be even more alone with her, but then realised the area they were in.

Alessandra heard him groan. "Oh my love, do not look at me like that! We do not know this area. We do not know where is private," he said, his face revealing everything that he was feeling at that moment.

Alessandra pulled back her desire and smiled shyly at him. "You are right, husband. It would not do to reveal quite so much of ourselves to our tenants!" she said, laughing with him so that the moment was not forgotten,
~~~~~

but put away until a more suitable time.

~~~~~~

As they rode back into the stables, John, the head groom, took time to consider why the previous master had left his estate to the new mistress and not Mrs Missinger. On Alessandra's face, he saw something he had not often seen on a woman. The way she looked at her husband was so far removed from how the previous mistress had looked at her husband - the previous master - that he could completely see how this woman would have made an impact on Mr Missinger.

"Thank you, John. Your recommendation was perfect. Clover was wonderful," Alessandra said to the groom before she and Edward rushed away in perfect sync, with only one thing on each of their minds.

Under the guise of Alessandra having to change out of her riding habit, they immediately went to their bedchamber. Once the door was closed, Edward eased her up against it and kissed her deeply.

Alessandra held back from being forward, letting the feelings rush over her as she allowed Edward to set the pace with whatever he wanted to do. Taking care with the unending patience he seemed to have, he undressed her only enough to gain access to that part of her where he knew he could satisfy her. With her still leaning up against the door, he took pleasure in tasting her, groaning at how aroused he could tell she already was. The effect of standing - something that felt so new to her - was almost instantaneous. Alessandra felt her knees buckle slightly as the familiar feeling flowed through her.

Edward restored her misplaced clothing and stood up to kiss her once more before she led him backwards to the bed, undressing both herself and him completely and not hurrying at all to bring him to sweet climax.
~~~~~~

CHAPTER 59

"We must start heading back to your parents' home so we arrive before it gets dark," Edward said as they took a moment to lie together naked before getting dressed to leave the house.

Alessandra lifted her head and looked into his eyes, well satisfied with their visit to the estate, in so many ways.

"This has been wonderful, Edward. Thank you for coming here with me. I know you always have so much to do at home," she said quietly.

Edward kissed her fully. "This is wonderful for me also, Alessandra. I never would have not come here with you," he said, pausing a moment before continuing. "A part of me would like to stay longer."

Alessandra sighed. "I know, but I am eager to see Elizabeth. And we can come back here if we wish to. We could bring my parents and Margaret and Elizabeth here."

"Yes!" Edward exclaimed, not having considered it before. "Yes, let us do that, Alessandra. We shall return and stay at your parents' home tonight and if they are willing to, we shall bring them back here tomorrow or the day after."

~~~~~~

"Oh, the house is so grand, Mother, and the staff so friendly and well organised. I would very much like for you, Father, Margaret and Elizabeth, to all come with us tomorrow for a visit. We can all stay there. It is a very large house," Alessandra said excitedly, her youthful
~~~~~~

exuberance visible.

"I am not sure," her mother said quietly and thoughtful. "What do you think, Edward? Is it too far for us to travel?"

"Oh, no! It is not too far from here, and what Alessandra says is true. There is plenty of room for everyone. It would be good for you to know what Alessandra is talking about with regard to different things if you could see them, I believe, Sir," Edward responded, largely to Alessandra's father. "Winter is not far off, now, so it would be best to go soon, if you wish to see it, rather than in a few months."

Alessandra's father weighed the option over in his mind, thinking about things that had to be done in his home. The happiness in the voice of his daughter overruled any doubt he had. He nodded and smiled at her.

"As you wish, my daughter. Let us all have a good night's sleep tonight and see how we feel tomorrow morning. If we need to, we can wait one day before we go over."

~~~~~

In bed, Edward could sense Alessandra's excitement, and he smiled in the dark.

"Do you think the walls in the other house are thick?" she asked innocently, causing him to laugh out loud, which in turn made her giggle. "Oh well, it is not long till spring," she continued, referring to their agreement to not physically join again until that time.

"Oh, my lovely wife, how I do love you!"
~~~~~

CHAPTER 60

"It is a fine house, indeed," Alessandra's father exclaimed as he approached the front door. He couldn't help but be pleased with how well his daughter had settled into a secure life. As a father, it gave him joy and relief.

As they entered, the service staff greeted the family, taking joy in meeting Alessandra's parents, little Elizabeth, and even Margaret. Almost immediately the family was ushered into the drawing room and a lavish tea served with various dainties.

After eating and talking, a grand tour was given and Edward took his father to meet the outside staff, including John at the stables.

Alessandra, meanwhile, sat in the drawing room with her mother, who was cuddling Elizabeth. Isabella's countenance worried Alessandra. Despite the excitement of seeing the new home, her mother appeared uncharacteristically subdued.

"Are you well, Mother? You are very quiet today. I hope travelling here has not tired you too much."

Her mother smiled at her and passed the baby back to her. "I am well, my child, but I do feel tired. Would you mind terribly if I went to lie down?"

Alessandra felt a moment of panic. Her mother was one of the strongest women she knew and she could not remember her ever having been ill before.

"No, of course not. Margaret, could you please go with Mother and find someone to help with the assignment of a bedroom, and to make her comfortable?"

Margaret smiled at her mistress. "Of course, Miss."

Alessandra sat back on the sofa that enabled a view out over the grounds. She held Elizabeth tightly against her, a niggling level of concern growing in the back of her mind.

~~~~~

A short time later Margaret knocked and came into the room again.

"Would you like me to take her, Miss?" she asked, indicating to the baby.

"Yes, thank you, Margaret," Alessandra replied, handing Elizabeth to her. "How did my mother seem to you?" she asked, trusting the observation of the woman before her completely.

"I do not know your mother well, Miss, so I do not know how she usually is, but she does, to me, look somewhat unwell. It may be that she is just tired from the journey here, and will seem better after a rest."

Alessandra thanked her and watched her curtsey and leave the room, baby in her arms. Alessandra sat where she was for some time, thinking over how her mother had seemed since they had arrived from Edward's home two days earlier. Now that she thought about it - now that she focused on her mother instead of herself - she had to admit that perhaps her mother was not her usual self after all. With that thought, Alessandra immediately ran outside to find her father.

~~~~~

"Father," she said loudly, interrupting a conversation that was happening between Edward, John and her father, no doubt about horses and their care.

Everyone turned, surprised by the forcefulness that came from her - something so unusual for Alessandra's countenance.

"I am sorry to interrupt," she said, realising her rudeness. "But Father, is Mother unwell?"

Immediately she saw her father look grave, and look away from meeting her eyes.

"Father?" Alessandra asked again, quietly, oblivious to John moving away from them to give them some privacy for their conversation.

"Walk with me, Alessandra," he said, leading his daughter away even from Edward, who watched on in uncertainty of what was happening. When the two of them were a distance away from anyone else, he finally spoke.

"Your mother has been declining in health these past few months, Alessandra. She maintains a brave face, but she is very ill. The doctor has said she is unlikely to live much longer. I am sorry I did not tell you earlier. It has been your mother's wish that you not be told in advance. She does not want you worrying, especially when everything is going so well for you."

"But there must be something that can be done! Father, I have substantial funds now. If we find the right doctor..." Alessandra started to cry out but her father shook his head.

"No, Alessandra. We have had enough consultations and they all say the same thing. It is a natural thing to happen, my daughter. One day I shall leave also, and it will be up to you and Edward to set your children up for when you hand everything over to them."

Alessandra felt tears come to her eyes. In a rare show of physical affection, her father enveloped her with his arms and kissed her forehead. She could sense inside of him desperation to not cry. All of a sudden she could see that even though her mother who would be leaving her in the world, it must have been even more difficult for her father to contemplate his lifelong companion leaving him. With that thought, she determined to cast aside her sadness and let him lean on her, putting her arms around him and holding him tight.

"What do we do, Father, to make her most

comfortable if her time is coming?"

Her father sighed, letting some of his frustration and sadness show.

"Just love her, I suppose. There is nothing to be done medically so it is important to me to keep showing her how much I love her, and to do what I can to make her as happy as I can, for as long as I can."

"Very well. Would it be best for us to leave here and go home immediately, do you think?" she asked and he shook his head.

"No, I do not think she cares where she is, my sweet daughter. Just being near you and near little Elizabeth is enough, I think," her father said.

"And Nicholas? I can summon him here. The house is large enough to house everyone."

He looked at her with pride, knowing fully how strong his daughter had turned out to be, even though he had considered her a timid little thing before she had wed.

"Yes," he replied. "If that is possible, I think that would make her very happy, Alessandra. Thank you. Now let us walk back. Edward will worry about what is happening, I am sure. I will go and see your mother and check on her, to make sure she is alright."

They walked back. Seeing an intended look from his wife, Edward fell in step beside Alessandra to walk to the drawing room, as her father left them to find the bedchamber his wife had been set up in.

"What is wrong, Alessandra?" he asked, feeling some distress.

"My mother ... is unwell," she started to say before feeling a tear escape from her eye. She looked directly at him. "My mother is dying, Edward. She is only expected to live a short time longer. My father is keeping watch over her, but he thinks the thing that will make her happiest before she leaves us, is being with us - me and Elizabeth ... and you ... and my brother."

Edward took in what she was saying, his mind racing.

"Edward, if my mother wishes it, I would like for her and my father to stay here, and for us to stay here also, and to invite my brother and his family … to wait…"

Alessandra felt Edward pull her close to him and hold her tight. At different times he had pondered how life would be without his parents in his life. The conversation brought about that thinking again, making him desperately miss his own home. Not wanting to distress her any further, he kept those thoughts in his head, unspoken.

"Yes, my love, if you wish," Edward responded. "That sounds like a good idea."

"But do you need to get back to your parents?" she asked, mindful of his own mother now.

He shook his head. "No, they will be fine with us staying away. They will understand."

She looked up at him, appreciating now, as she had done many times since their wedding, the good man who had been chosen as her husband. Passion was the last thing on either of their minds as she pushed herself against him and into his arms, encouraging him to hold her tightly as she started to cry.

~~~~~

"My daughter, I am so proud of who you have become, and the life you are living," Isabella told Alessandra as she sat on the side of the bed. In the night her mother seemed to have begun a steep decline and now could not summon the strength to get out of bed. "You are happy with Edward, are you not?"

Alessandra nodded and tried to smile. "Oh yes, Mother! He is a good man and I do believe he loves me."

Her mother smiled back. "He does. There is no doubt about that. When a man looks at his wife as he does you, it can only be a deep love. I am glad I have gotten to meet little Elizabeth. She will be strong, like you."

They sat quietly, holding hands. Everything had
~~~~~

happened so quickly. Word had been sent for Alessandra's brother, and he and his family had quickly arrived and settled into the estate. Since then, Edward's mother and father had also arrived to provide support.

"Daughter, will you ask Edward's mother to come in to see me? I would like to talk to her," her mother requested. Alessandra nodded and quietly left the room.

Immediately she passed the request on and Edward's mother went to the bedchamber, while Alessandra settled into Edward's arms in the drawing room once more. The local physician had been and gone, confirming that her mother was in the final stages now, and would soon pass quietly.

"Alessandra," she heard a voice say. She turned to see Nicholas, her brother, looking eager to talk to her. "Could we walk in the garden together?"

She nodded and pulled away from her husband once more.

Outside, she and Nicholas walked companionably beside one another. Although it had been just the two of them as children in their family home, they had not grown up close, nor spent much time together as they each embarked on their own lives. Despite their usual distance, they were not uncomfortable with each other.

"Thank you for inviting me and my family to come and be with Mother for this time," her brother said, surprising her.

"Of course you must be here, Nicholas! She is our mother - mine and yours!" Alessandra exclaimed.

Nicholas smiled at her. He'd met his share of people who had been so driven by greed that they would not have brought any family members to such an estate, refusing to share their wealth. As he looked at his sister, he felt a strong brotherly sense of pride in the woman she'd grown to be.

"It has been nice for Victoria to see Mother one more time also, and for the children to see her," Nicholas replied.

"It is good for Mother, too. And Father. He will need our support most of all I suppose. When I try to imagine losing Edward..." Alessandra said, shuddering at the horrifying thought.

"You seem very happy in your marriage, Sister. I like Edward. He seems a very good man, and very much in love with you," Nicholas said with a wistful sound in his voice.

"Yes. But you are also happy, are you not, Nicholas? You have four children so something must work well," she said, trying to bring some humour into their sad circumstances. He looked at her and smiled, somewhat surprised by her open candour.

"I do not think we have what you and Edward have, but yes, we are happy enough. I do love our children and it is nice that they can spend this time with their grandparents. You are a good sister to let us be here."

She smiled at him and they continued to walk peacefully together, not needing any more words.

~~~~~

As days passed everyone in the family spent time in Isabella's bedchamber at some point in each day. Isabella continued to look at her daughter and appreciate the person she was to have been able to bring all of her family together for her. Even the three grandchildren, who were past the baby stage and able to run around and climb up on her bed, brought her much joy.

"You have given me the greatest gift, Alessandra," Isabella said as the two of them enjoyed some time alone. "Bringing everyone here under one roof is such a joy to me. Thank you," she continued, reaching out and taking Alessandra's hand in hers. "I was not with my mother when she passed, and I do regret that. There was no real reason that I could not have gone back to Italy, but once I was married to your father ... well, I never did get back. Take your children there, Alessandra. I have
~~~~~

written down the names of people I remember who are family, and their addresses. It has been some years since I heard from any of them so they may not still be there, or still alive, but go and see your heritage, Daughter. Promise me."

Alessandra found herself crying quietly yet again whilst holding her mother's hands tightly. "I promise I shall do that, Mother."

"Do not cry, Alessandra. I have lived a blessed life and I go happily to Him, knowing that my children are both well settled in their own lives. Please keep a distant eye on your father. He is such a strong man, but sometimes needs someone to lean on…"

Alessandra felt the hand in hers go slack and saw her mother relax back as if going to sleep. Deep in her heart, Alessandra knew that it was not sleep at all. She took one more moment of alone time with her mother before announcing to everyone else that her mother had finally gone to rest.

CHAPTER 61

The funeral, despite the circumstance being her mother's death, was a happy one. The death was easier accepted by all knowing that Alessandra's mother had been ready to leave the world they inhabited, and move on.

When it was over, everyone spoke of plans to return to their normal lives. Edward's father and mother moved back to their estate immediately, leaving only Alessandra's family in the home. Once again she found herself walking with her brother.

"I have asked Father to come and stay with us for a while, but he refuses and says he must get back to his home," Nicholas was saying with the sound of dismay in his voice. "I worry about him though."

"Yes, but his life is there," Alessandra said. "Perhaps getting back into his normal daily routine is something that he needs. I will suggest Edward and I stay there with him for a while, and see how he takes to that idea."

Suddenly Nicholas stopped and turned to his sister, taking her hands in his. "Thank you again for this, Alessandra. You have a good heart and we do not see enough of one another. If anything has come from Mother's passing, it has made me realise that I need to work harder to see family - you and Father. We must make more of an effort, no matter what fills our daily lives."

"I agree, Brother. Perhaps I shall make this our family holiday home," she said, smiling as she waved her hands around to indicate she meant the estate they were on. "It is a good, central location for all of us, is it not, for such an event?"

"It is indeed," Nicholas replied. "Although it still surprises me that Tom left it to you, one cannot argue that it is an outstanding property. We shall be glad to come to stay here whenever you invite us."

"I have to decide what I am going to do with it in the long run, but for now I shall keep it. It now holds some memories for me, of Mother…"

Alessandra started to cry once more and soon found herself enveloped in her brother's arms, for the first time in her life. She then realised that she was not the only one crying.

~~~~~

"Father, are you sure you will not come with us?" Nicholas asked his father as he and his family readied themselves to return to their home.

Alessandra saw her father shake his head and put on a brave smile.

"Thank you, my son, but I shall return to my home. I have much to do there."

Edward watched the family as they started to disassemble. Nicholas, Victoria and their children disappeared down the road to leave only Edward, Alessandra, her father, Margaret and Elizabeth.

"Well, Edward and I will travel with you, Father, and stay with you tonight, if you have no objection. It will make our journey home vastly easier if you agree to it," Alessandra said to her father. It was her way of trying to insert herself into his presence in his home, whilst making it sound like he would be doing her the favour.

"Of course. You are all welcome to stay as long as you like," he said, looking around the views once more. "It is a lovely estate, Alessandra. I believe from what the staff have told me that it was unloved for a long time. If that is true, perhaps it was always meant to come into your hands. You will love it as it should be loved, I have no doubt."
~~~~~

After they walked around, talking to the staff and ensuring everything was in place for the house to be empty for the undefined future, the five of them travelled back to Alessandra's parents' house once more.

~~~~~

Upon walking into her parents' home, Alessandra immediately felt the absence of her mother. Looking at her father, she could see that he was similarly affected. June, the housekeeper, greeted them sadly, having been an assistant of one kind or another to Alessandra's mother since they had both been young women.

Alessandra requested tea be brought into the drawing room, while she settled her father to help him relax. When he did so, he started to talk about his wife and their life together, right from when they had first laid eyes on each other. Alessandra, Edward, Margaret and June sat down and listened to the stories he told over much of the afternoon. Alessandra wondered if such an action might hurt him more but the more he spoke, the more he started to smile. She could see that he had found his way of starting to heal.

Edward watched his wife. He felt sadness for her loss but admired how she seemed determined to place focus on her father. The more Edward saw what was going on around him, the more eager he found himself to get home and be around his own parents. He found himself conflicted.

As if sensing his internal dilemma, Alessandra turned to him, smiled and took his hand, which she raised and kissed. He saw something in her eyes that he had not seen in recent times, understandably so with all that had been happening. Regardless, they sat quietly and listened and listened, until her father seemed to run out of stories to tell.

"I shall go to bed now, as I am feeling quite tired," her father said. "You are welcome to stay as long as you wish to, Alessandra. I am very glad to have you all
~~~~~

here," he continued before kissing her on the forehead and leaving the room.

Shortly afterward, Margaret left with Elizabeth. Edward and Alessandra remained in the drawing room, staring at the fire as the two of them held each other.

"You are distant today, Edward. What is on your mind?" Alessandra asked.

"My parents," he replied. "I am aware now that my time with them is possibly short, also."

"Would you like to return to your home? I do not want to leave Father yet, but I do not mind if you need to get back to your mother and father. I can follow at a later time," Alessandra said.

Edward kissed her softly. "No, my love. I thank you but I do not wish to be apart from you. Your father needs us for the moment. I can provide him with support in anything he needs help with, so I would rather be here than there, for now anyway."

"Thank you," Alessandra replied and kissed him. For a moment they looked at each other before kissing again, whilst trying not to get passionate due to where they were.

"We need to stop, my beautiful wife. Oh, how I long for you, but not here," Edward said to her with his voice deep and quiet.

"When we get home," Alessandra said quietly, without needing to finish the sentence.

He smiled softly at her. "When we get home."

CHAPTER 62

"Father, are you sure about this? You can come with us, or we can stay longer," Alessandra said to her father as he prepared to farewell them from his home.

"Oh, my daughter, you are a blessing to me. I will certainly come and stay with you when I can if that is agreeable to Edward's parents. I want to watch Elizabeth grow. For now, however, I have many things I must attend to. I shall get through them faster if I know you are all well and safe in your own home. Please, Alessandra, take your family home and I will see you in a short while."

Reluctantly, Edward, Alessandra and Margaret climbed into the carriage with Elizabeth in arms. Alessandra waved as they departed, leaving her father on the doorstep, waving after them. In her heart, Alessandra wondered if she would, indeed, ever see him again.

~~~~~

Arriving back at Chisholm Manor, they were eagerly greeted by Edward's parents who ushered them into the drawing room before they even had a chance to wash up.

Alessandra and Edward answered the many questions that were asked, but inside of both of them was a growing feeling they both knew so well. They had stayed at an inn the night before, but with Margaret within listening distance, they had withheld from pleasure. They both anticipated and knew that when they could politely excuse themselves for the night, they would not hold back any longer.

Edward buried himself in work with his father in the
~~~~~

steward's room, whilst Alessandra ensured Elizabeth was settled again in the nursery. She then put herself forward to ask her mother-in-law what she needed. Alessandra wanted to do anything to take her mind off her husband and get through the day.

When the early evening came, Edward and Alessandra excused themselves under the guise of being tired from their journey. Closing the door to the bedroom chamber behind them, Alessandra pulled him to her, fully clothed, and led him to the sofa. There she sat down and reclined back, and felt Edward immediately lie on her. As he kissed her and touched her through her clothing, Alessandra revelled in the feelings. It felt like far too long since they had been intimate together, and both were so hungry for it, they felt like they could not wait another minute.

They lay like that for a long time, indulging in the feeling of kissing deeply. It was a small thing had been overlooked for so long that Edward fell into the taste and feel of his lips moving with hers. Through his clothes, he rubbed against her, reaching out to her even through all the folds of fabric that lay between them. He withheld from rushing toward nakedness, determined to just indulge in kissing her for as long as it took to feel like they were finally caught up in what had been missing.

Alessandra felt like her heart was singing. Inside of her was the intense need to be closer to him, whilst holding and moving against each other through their clothing pushed her arousal to another level entirely.

Finally, Edward pulled away, unable to stand it any longer. He pulled her to her feet and positioned her as he slowly removed every article of her clothing. When she stood in front of him naked he drank in the sight of her. It was a sight that he felt could almost make him release without any stimulation from her.

As if just as excited, he found himself being undressed as Alessandra moved to remove every piece of fabric from his body. When they were both naked, they embraced, kissed and moved back toward the bed. Feeling it at the back of her legs, Alessandra moved up onto it and lay back, inviting him to lie on top of her, nestled within her thighs, and continuing to kiss, their mutual arousal grew more.

"Edward, please..." she groaned and he looked into her eyes to determine what she was asking him for. "Please... move inside of me."

Hearing the words he did not stop to question if she was certain but instead plunged into her. Both groaned deeply at the feeling that was familiar and yet not felt for so long. Surprisingly, although it had been so long, something about the first joining after the time apart gave him a particular strength to not finish too soon. Alessandra lay back and felt him fill her again and again as he moved into her, over and over. Edward paused when he needed to, and kissed her while looking directly into her eyes. He could feel her hands on his back, pulling him closer and deeper.

While making his movements subtle, to slow things, Alessandra became aware that the way he was moving - his very slight rocking movement against her - was resulting in her being touched in a way similar to how she was touched by him with his hands. Excited, she prompted him to keep moving in the manner. Taking his time to do so, he felt her shudder beneath him, with her tight around him. It was something that had not happened before, driving him to a point where he had to find release by plunging into her one more time.

They lay together afterward, both feeling relief and a blissful feeling in their bodies. Edward remained inside of her as he looked at her face.

"I did not know that could happen like that," she said, making him laugh in giddy happiness.

"Perhaps there is some good that comes from not joining quite so often. Do you think we should wait another few months before we do so again?" he teased her and enjoyed seeing her eyes go wide.

"No!" she exclaimed and laughed with him.

They kissed softly, caressing each other with their hands while still lying together.

"We may have just made a child, Alessandra," Edward said, seriously.

"Yes, and if we have, it will be loved as Elizabeth is," Alessandra replied.

Looking into her eyes, Edward felt such a surge of love flow over him that it flowed through to his arousal. He saw his wife's eyes grow large again as he felt himself grow again deep inside her.

CHAPTER 63

"Father!" Alessandra exclaimed as she saw who was at the front entrance to the manor. "We were not expecting you. What has brought you here? Is all well with you?"

Her father laughed at her exuberance and never-ending curiosity, which he was very well familiar with. "Daughter, I am well. I am here to see you, and to meet my new grandchild."

Alessandra looked at Edward, his mother and his father. Their expressions made her wonder if she had missed some important news. All were smiling at her, as if…

"You all knew!" she said as they laughed at her.

"Yes, Alessandra, we have known for some weeks that your father was coming to stay," Edward's father said, smiling at his daughter-in-law. "It is only right that he be here to meet little Isabella."

"Isabella?" Alessandra saw her father ask wistfully. "You named my new granddaughter after your mother? Oh, my daughter, that is … oh, thank you," he said, pulling his daughter into his arms and feeling tears come to his eyes as he kissed the top of her head.

Alessandra waited for her father to relax and regain his composure - something that she knew was always important to him - and let him move away from her as he was ready. Greetings were expressed and they made their way indoors as Alessandra looked at Edward, seeing on his face the broad grin of amusement that she knew too well.

"You kept that secret hidden well, Husband. I can see

that I will have to better hone my methods of interrogating you," she whispered to him when they were out of earshot of the older generation, in a suggestive manner that produced a deep laugh in him, and a slight blush on his face.

~~~~~

"How long shall you stay, Father? A long while, I hope," Alessandra queried her father as the two of them walked through the gardens together alone.

"It is that which I wish to speak to you about, my child. Edward's parents have invited me to live here..." he started and heard her exclaim a sound of pleasant surprise before he continued. "I am in a mind to accept their offer, as I do not mind admitting to you, Alessandra, that I am lonely without your mother. I miss her considerably, every single day."

"It is not too late to re-marry," Alessandra said.

"Oh no! I am not... no, that is not something I desire at my age."

"Then what is it that you seem uncertain about?" Alessandra asked, confused.

Her father looked closely at her, uncertain how she would take the news that he wished to convey to her.

"Alessandra you are well set up now, with this land of Edward's family, plus the other estate," he started and saw her nod. "Nicholas is not so fortunate. I believe things are very difficult for him in supporting his family, given the rent they pay where they are living. So I would like to give them our family home, Alessandra - completely."

Alessandra listened and wondered when the news that he wanted to tell her would come.

When she did not say anything, her father could see that he would have to ask her a question outright for her to comprehend what he was saying.

"How will you feel if you do not inherit any part of our family home? Would this upset you?"
~~~~~

Finally understanding, Alessandra felt her eyes go wide. "Oh Father, no! Of course not! No, of course giving Nicholas that house is a wonderful idea. It will help Nicholas and Victoria greatly, although do you think that the house is big enough for all seven of them?"

She saw her father consider the prospect of the family of his son, which indeed did look like it was unending in producing more offspring.

"Perhaps I can suggest a better solution, Father? Do you particularly want that house to stay in our family? For sentimental purposes?" she asked and her father shook his head.

"No, it is not an ancestral home. It has no importance for passing through the family line. What are you thinking, Alessandra?"

"What if I invited Nicholas and his family to live at Missinger Estate, and you sold your home and gave him the money from the sale? I have not been able to bring myself to find tenants for the estate as Edward and I do love going there to stay. If Nicholas lived there, he would be doing me a great favour by keeping it maintained and allowing us to have our own rooms in the home there. And the money from the sale of your house would keep them well provided for."

As they continued walking, Alessandra could see her father considering her idea and so she kept quiet, knowing he would do what he considered was right for everyone.

"I think it is a good idea, but you need to talk to Edward about it first, Alessandra. I know the estate is yours outright, and no part of it belongs to him, but speak to him and make sure it will not cause any disharmony between you. We get so little time with our loved ones in this world. Do not let small things build up."

Alessandra nodded and they returned to the house to once again merge into conversation with everyone else.

~~~~~

"What do you think, Edward?" she asked that night in the privacy of their bedchamber.

"I think it is a good solution for your father and your brother, and you are right, it would give some reassurance to know someone is living in it who will appreciate it and keep it maintained. With it being as large as it is, we can also keep enough rooms set up for all of us who live here," he replied, talking to her seriously about her idea. "I know that Mother and Father are both eager for your father to live here with us, and it will be good for him to have so much family around."

"Shall I arrange to speak to my brother about it, then, to see what he thinks?" she asked.

Edward could see the excitement on her face. "Yes, my beautiful, generous wife. Let me know what you need me or my father to do, and we will move forward with that plan if your brother agrees."

They lay together contentedly and quietly for a long while before Alessandra spoke, breaking the silence. "Edward?" she asked and he prompted her to continue. "Will you take me to the waterfall tomorrow?"

Edward looked at her and saw the arousal on her face at the thought, which fuelled him to tease her. "Oh! And what will we do when we get to the waterfall, my love?" he asked as he pushed her gently onto her back and began to kiss the parts of her body that he knew were her pleasure points.

Alessandra lay back, focused on the feelings he was producing in her, and forgot what she had been saying altogether.
~~~~~

CHAPTER 64

"What do you think of this idea, Nicholas? Speak plainly and honestly, please. Do not say what you think I wish to hear," Alessandra said sternly to her brother, seeing the overwhelming surprise on his face. "Father also offered to let you live in the house we grew up in, so you have that option also."

Nicholas stared at his sister, wondering why there were not more people in the world like her. Already she had done so much, letting his family stay at Missinger Estate when their mother had been in her last days, and now Nicholas and his family were staying at Chisholm Manor to spend time with their father.

"Alessandra, are you sure? It seems like a very generous gesture…"

"You are my brother, and your children are my nieces and nephews. It is important to me that Edward and I, and our children, and our parents, all have rooms established in the home there. That will leave plenty of rooms for you and Victoria to set up for you and your children, so you will not be without space. I would also like for any of us to be able to come and stay in the house when we wish to, as if it were our own home…"

"It is your own home," Nicholas said, amused.

"Yes but I am handing it to you to live in."

"But how will I repay you for this? You could be earning rent off the estate."

"I still will be, from the tenants," Alessandra replied. "You will be doing me a great service by keeping the estate running exactly as it does now, without changing anything. You also have the skills to identify any maintenance that needs to be done. Quite simply, by keeping it lived in you will be helping me immensely."

Nicholas was in shock at what was being offered to him. "I will think about it, Alessandra, but I do thank you as it is a wonderful offer. I do have to consider what Father has offered also though, as that would provide me with something to leave my children, and I do need to think about that."

"Yes, although you could invest the funds from the sale of the house…" Alessandra responded thoughtfully, whilst not wanting to put pressure on her brother.

"I am hesitant about accepting our family home from Father," Nicholas admitted. "I know it was his idea but all those memories it holds for him, with Mother."

Alessandra thought about that before answering. "Yes, but he will still have those memories, and I do not think he has offered to do it just as a token to you. I do believe he is quite lonely and will enjoy living around people. Perhaps he may spend his time divided between my home and yours."

The siblings walked further without having to speak any more, both having so much in their heads that they had to think about and consider.

~~~~~

Watching Alessandra and her extended family in their household, Edward's parents enjoyed the vitality it brought their home. They both found her father to be communicative and a welcome addition to their household, having empathy for where he was at since Alessandra's mother had died. The combination of their own two grandchildren, combined with the five that Nicholas had brought, resulted in Edward's mother in particular feeling like it was how the manor had always meant to be - full of people.

When it was time for Nicholas and his family to leave again, it was emotional for everyone, especially his
~~~~~

father who seemed particularly distressed.

"Father," Alessandra saw her brother say, in a rare moment of expression of his love. "What is it? We shall see you again soon."

"I am proud of you, my son," his father said, causing concern in Nicholas and Alessandra as they heard the words. "You are a fine father and a fine son. Thank you," he continued, moving closer to his son and pulling him into an embrace. It was something that Nicholas had rarely had in his lifetime from his father.

Alessandra saw Nicholas give her a look of fear at the action, wondering what it meant to have his father act in such a way.

"Father, you are welcome to come with us if you would like to..." Nicholas started to say but his father pulled away, with a small tear in his eye, and shook his head.

"No, Nicholas, I am fine. It has been a very happy time, all of us being together. I know that it meant so much to your mother when you and your sister were with her ... when ... before..."

All of a sudden, in front of them all, Alessandra saw her father break down in a deep flow of tears. Giving thought to how his father might not want to be seen in such a way, Nicholas immediately flung his arms around his father once more and held him tight. It was not a usual thing for the two of them to do, but finally Nicholas felt that they, as father and son, had reached a time when it was not only acceptable, but desperately overdue and, quite simply, needed.

Edward saw his parents move away respectfully and enter the house. After a brief look of acknowledgement to his wife, he followed, leaving only Alessandra, her father and her brother's family to see the demonstration of love.

"Oh my children, I miss her so much ... every single day. It does, however, make me very pleased to see both of you settled so well, and with good people beside you. Edward and Victoria are both such honest, generous and loving people. Getting to spend time with all of my grandchildren - that is a great gift that you have both given to me and your mother, who I am sure is looking down on all of us, with a great smile on her face," he said and paused before going on. "I do not know how much longer I shall have in this lifetime, so please both always remember how happy you both made me and your mother. We never wished for more children as we both loved both of you so much."

"Father," Alessandra said more forcefully than she expected. She'd become more and more alarmed with each word that had left her father's mouth. "Father, why are you talking like this?"

"Because these things need to be said, Alessandra! Your mother's passing has made me realise that I, too, may not have too long to live. We need to say things to the people we love, while we can. I give that advice to you also, my children. Make sure that you tell the people in your lives how much they mean to you. Tell them each and every day if you can, so that on that one day when they are suddenly not there, you know that they felt your love right until the very end."

Alessandra caught her brother's eyes once again. They both suspected that something was seriously wrong, either in their father's body or his mind, but said nothing.

"Go now, Nicholas," their father said. "Your beautiful wife and all of those wonderful children are waiting for you. I shall see you soon, I believe?" he asked, pointing the question at Alessandra, who nodded in return.

"Yes, Father, you will travel with me and Edward when we go up to Missinger Estate, and we shall settle in to welcome Nicholas and Victoria when they move there," Alessandra replied.

"Very well then. Go safe on your journey, my son."

Nicholas knew he was dismissed so climbed into the carriage with the rest of his family and Alessandra and her father watched them slowly and quietly disappear from sight.

~~~~~

"I worry about him, Edward. He is despondent, as if he is giving up on life," Alessandra said as they lay in bed that night, holding each other tightly.

Edward nodded in response. "Yes, I can see it also. I suppose it is understandable, given how much he loved your mother. Certainly, I cannot imagine how I would be if anything happened to you, but what do we do about it?"

"I do not know," Alessandra replied.

"I will talk to Mother and Father about it when I can do so alone. Perhaps tomorrow you could take your father out for a walk after breakfast, to get him out of the house."

"Yes I will do that, and then you and your parents can have some time alone together," Alessandra continued, suddenly aware that her family must sometimes seem like such an imposition on his family.

"Oh, no, my beautiful wife. I did not mean for that reason. If you and your father take a walk, I shall be able to see what my parents' input is to how he is feeling."

Edward looked closely at her and saw her tears beginning.

"Thank you, Edward. I am so fortunate to have you…" she started to say. Edward pulled her even closer to him and no more was said.

~~~~~

"I do not know, Edward," his father said when Edward brought up the subject the next morning. "I agree, he is very unhappy, but what can we do?"

All three were quiet as they thought about options.

"Could a change of scenery not perhaps help?"

Edward heard his mother say quietly. "A trip to Bath can do wonders for anyone. Has he visited there before? Seeing something new might reinvigorate his mind."

"Yes. It is worth suggesting I suppose," Edward said. "Certainly, making the suggestion could not hurt. I will talk to Alessandra when they come back from their walk."

As if sensing the discussion between Edward and his parents had ended, Alessandra and her father walked in then, making the conversation flow naturally.

"Ahh, there you are," Edward's father said, smiling at both. "We were just discussing how lovely Bath is at this time of year. How would you like it if we were all to go and look at some of the sights there? Perhaps we could even visit the baths. They are very good for one's body, you know." He worded the question to everyone but directed the question most particularly at Alessandra's father, who looked up with just a twinge of interest on his face.

"Bath! Do you know, I have always wanted to visit there. My physician has mentioned the waters on many occasions as therapy for one complaint or another."

Edward's mother smiled at him, pleased her suggestion may have been a good one.

"Shall we all go, then? We could arrange to rent a house to rent that will fit all of us in. Alessandra, would the children be pleased to visit Bath also, do you think?" she asked her daughter-in-law to divert the conversation.

"They will," Alessandra said, excited. "Oh, it is a wonderful idea!"

And so it was arranged.

CHAPTER 65

After settling into what would be their home for the week, Alessandra and Edward immediately ventured into the central part of Bath, while their parents moved off toward the Roman Baths.

In a moment of sadness, Alessandra thought back to the last time she had been there. That had been when Tom had approached her again, and the first time she had met his wife, Katherine. Edward looked at his wife and immediately understood why she was quiet. When Alessandra sensed him looking at her, she turned to him and smiled. It was an effort to try to at least temporarily forget the man from her past who had changed her life so much.

"Do not feel bad for thinking about him, Alessandra. He made an impact on you, and now with you being able to provide a home to your brother at Missinger Estate, Tom will always be in our memory," Edward said softly to her, holding her gaze even as they moved forward. "Certainly I cannot fault the man for wanting you to love him. He did not act with decorum or sense, but I certainly can understand why he loved you so."

Alessandra felt a tear come to her eye, thinking about her young friend dying so early on in his life.

"I do not think that he did love me, Edward. I believe he just got lost in his thinking somehow, but you are right - we cannot forget him. It would be disrespectful to do so. There are also other aspects of our being in Bath before that did not involve him, and I would much prefer to think of those while we are here," she said with the suggestive tone that he knew so well by now. Watching his face as they continued to walk - seeing him also remember the entire day they had spent completely alone in their room - she saw that he too could visualise the joy of having had that time together.

Edward looked deeply at her and blushed. It was something that did not happen often, but on occasion she took delight in encouraging in him.

"My beautiful wife, you are once again trying to make it so that I have no choice but to stop right here," he said, holding her arm firmly and halting them in their walking. "Put my arms around you and hold you close so that other people cannot see what you are doing to me," he continued, smiling at her in humour. "Now I am going to kiss you," he said and did so. "And hold you … and I am not at all going to think about you and I doing such things," he continued light heartedly whilst attempting to sound stern.

Alessandra could feel against her. It served as proof that although he was making light of the conversation, he only seemed to become more aroused with the more he spoke. It made Alessandra begin to giggle excessively.

Seeing Alessandra giggling and so carefree fuelled Edward but he determined to concentrate on anything else. Eventually, he felt his body relax and able to begin walking again, but not before giving her another stern word, spoken in fondness.

"You know not to speak to me in such a manner in public, Alessandra. Do not do it!" he said, making her giggle even more.

~~~~~

Over dinner in their new surroundings, all family came back together once more and Alessandra was overwhelmed by the difference in her father.

"And did you know..." he kept saying with great excitement, sharing every small piece of history he had
~~~~~

learned about the location.

Alessandra heard less of what he was saying in words, than what she saw he was expressing in his mannerisms. Upon watching him, she found herself relieved of some of the stress she had held unknowingly deep in previous weeks. She realised then the depth of concern she'd had, worried that he was going to give up on life and leave her also.

After dinner, Margaret brought the children in, who their grandparents fought over for cuddles and smiles with. Edward watched everyone in the room, happily studying the combinations of each child with each grandparent. He wondered how his life had become so full, with so many people around him, after his isolation as a child himself. As he looked at Alessandra he saw her smile at him. At that moment he silently wondered if she was yet eager to become pregnant once again. Sensing in his body the thought of that affecting him, he immediately dismissed the idea, but not before his wife saw it on his face.

~~~~~

"Yes," Edward heard his wife whisper to him as they lay naked together, already satisfied from the touch of each other's hands and lips.

Lying on his back with her cuddling into his shoulder, he moved so that he could look at her face directly, and smiled at her.

"Yes ... what, my lovely wife?" he asked, knowing something was churning around in her mind. He saw her look at him in a particular way that made his body immediately reactive once more.

"Yes, I want you inside me again, Edward. I want us to make another child. It is time."

"Are you sure, Alessandra?" he asked and saw her look at him with so much love he could feel his heart pound heavily.

"Yes," Alessandra replied. "I am rested and I love
~~~~~

Elizabeth and Isabella, but I do want us to have more children, Edward. Do you have any objection?"

Edward kissed her deeply and then pulled away, revealing his desire in his eyes as he began to manoeuvre himself on top of her. Finding himself stopped, he looked at her in surprise, but then his desire moved to another level as he found himself pushed back onto the bed, and his wife moving onto him, down on him. He then felt nothing except the sensations she produced in him from her movements.

CHAPTER 66

In the summer the annual hunt was held at Chisholm Manor Estate. This was the third such event that Alessandra had seen in her lifetime, but for Edward and his parents, it seemed to have always been something that occurred every year, naturally, as if it were the house itself that made sure it happened.

As Alessandra sat outside under a makeshift tent for cover and protection from the sun, she placed her hand on her belly, feeling fluttering inside.

"How are you feeling, Alessandra?" Edward's mother asked from the chair beside her.

"I am well, but this one feels different, like it is moving differently from how Elizabeth and Isabella did," Alessandra replied.

Margaret listened quietly without speaking. She relaxed nearby on a blanket in the shade, with the two young children with her - one a baby and one at the age where crawling and exploring were well underway. Now instilled completely in the nursery and no longer doing any of the household chores she always had done before Alessandra had given birth to Elizabeth, Margaret realised how happy she was in her work, having such wonderful people as her employers.

Suddenly Elizabeth made a sudden move to crawl away, and Alessandra saw her mother-in-law immediately leap up and pick her up, making her granddaughter laugh as she was lifted high off the ground.

Watching on, Alessandra enjoyed seeing how

Edward's mother invested time into Elizabeth. For someone who only had one living child, Alessandra thought to herself, she is so wonderful with children. And the thought made her go on to concede how strong her mother-in-law was, to have yearned for children as she had told Alessandra many times she had, and still go on, raising Edward so well, and being a loving wife to his father.

Her thoughts were diverted by seeing her father come toward them with a smile on his face.

"What a happy scene this is, with five such lovely ladies before me," he said happily, making Alessandra smile sincerely at him. He sat down on the rug next to Margaret and started to talk in baby language to Isabella before turning and redirecting his attention to his daughter.

"How are you, Daughter? Is that little one going to arrive today, do you think?" he asked, smiling while glancing meaningfully at her belly. "It is surely time, is it not?"

Alessandra smiled shyly at her father. "Father, you know she is not due quite yet."

"She? Oh, how can you be so sure?" he asked, looking content and happy before turning back to Isabella and resuming his baby talk with her once more.

Everything seemed blissful and peaceful until suddenly one of the riders came galloping right up to them.

"The doctor - someone must go for the doctor at once!" he said with the greatest urgency in his voice.

Margaret jumped up instantly. "I will alert the housekeeping staff and ask them to go with you on your horse, if you agree. They can direct you to the physician's location."

Isabella was passed to her grandfather before Margaret ran to the main house. In the meantime, however, Alessandra and her mother-in-law became stricken by the urgent request.

"What has happened?" Alessandra asked urgently, immediately feeling her body tense up at horrific possibilities about Edward appearing in her mind.

At the same time, the question that escaped her mother-in-law's mouth was, "Who is hurt?"

The rider took in the picture before him and instantly regretted having ridden in quite as he had. In particular, knowing that Edward's wife was so pregnant, he immediately worried about what would happen when he gave the news, but knew he had to.

He dismounted and came up to the women, both fearful of what they would be told. His sight settled on Edward's mother.

"I'm so sorry," he started to say. Alessandra saw her mother-in-law go white. "Mr Chisholm - your husband - has fallen. It does not look good, Mrs Chisholm."

Alessandra's father quickly stood and handed baby Isabella to Alessandra before taking Elizabeth from her grandmother's hands. At that moment, Margaret ran back to them with a footman beside her and addressed the rider.

"This is Paul. He will ride with you and direct you to the physician so you can request he come."

The two of them quickly mounted and soon disappeared, leaving everyone in the group silent in shock of the news, and the unknowing.

Alessandra suddenly felt a pain in her belly but desperately tried to keep it to herself, knowing Edward's mother must be most distressed at that moment. After a few minutes, however, she could not help but let out a cry. Immediately Margaret moved to her, took Isabella from her and Elizabeth from Alessandra's father. With one child in each arm, she looked desperately at Alessandra's father, trying to encourage him to help with either of the women in front of him, but soon saw he might not be able to help.

Surprisingly, seeing her daughter-in-law in pain seemed to wake Edward's mother from her daze. She quickly moved to Alessandra, helped her up and encouraged her to walk to the manor. By the time they reached the front door, it was evident the baby was coming. Chaos descended as housekeeping staff quickly readied the birth chamber and Alessandra was made comfortable. The pain left her in a daze, like something was not right with the child. Others watched as a fever seemed to catch on her and Alessandra started to drift in and out of a fitful sleep.

Meanwhile, downstairs in the foyer, the doctor arrived but as yet there was no sign of Edward or his father.

"Where is Mr Chisholm?" he demanded, having believed he had a patient in the manor who required urgent attention. The rider, who had initially alerted them to the fall, appeared once more and immediately left to take the doctor to the location where Edward's father was.

~~~~~

"Alessandra," she could hear a voice calling to her from far away. When she found the strength, she saw her mother-in-law beside her and the midwife standing behind. "Wake up, child. You have a job to do."

Alessandra tried to process the words but could not understand what was being said to her. All she wanted to do was sleep. When a strong pain ripped through her body she was reminded sharply of where she was and what was happening - she was in labour. The midwife came forward and talked to her sternly.

"Come, now, Mrs Chisholm. You have done this twice before and you know what needs to be done. This little one is eager to come into the world and is waiting for you to deliver him. Now gather your strength and push!"

~~~~~

Edward's mother was torn between wanting to support her daughter-in-law and help her grandchild into the world, and suspecting that before the day was out, she would be heartbroken over whatever had happened to her husband. Downstairs she waited at the window of the drawing room, looking with the hope of seeing someone - anyone - come to the house to give some news. Behind her, Alessandra's father sat quietly, bringing her cups of tea and small amounts of food to try and help her relax, but in her mind and her heart she knew the love of her life was already gone from her.

Suddenly in the distance, she could see a parade of guests who had come for the hunt. At the front of the procession was Edward. All rode their horses slowly. As they came closer, she could see her husband. He was in front of Edward but not sitting up. Instead, his form was slung over Beauty.

"Oh!" Edward's mother cried out.

The sound drove Alessandra's father to jump up from his seat and move to her side. He did not try and tell her everything was going to be alright. Even from where he was standing, it looked as if the worst had happened.

Shortly afterward, Edward walked in alone, having requested the guests to go to their rooms for a short time so he could talk to his mother alone. He immediately walked straight to her and put his arms around her. She could see he had been crying.

"Oh my son, is he…" she began to ask.

Edward pulled himself together, looked directly at her and nodded in response to her question. "Oh Mother, he was doing so well one minute and then a fox jumped out in front of his horse and I do not know why it was startled by it, but it reared and Father was thrown backwards," he started to say, feeling himself start to sob once more.

"Where is he, Edward?" his mother asked, preparing to see the body of her loved one.

"He has been laid in a bedroom upstairs."

Edward held out his hand to his mother and she took it. It was something that had not happened since Edward had been a small child. He was glad she let him lead her to the bedroom. Upon entering, immediately her eyes fell to her husband and the physician beside him.

"Mrs Chisholm," the doctor said as he walked toward her. "I am so sorry for your loss. He was a great man."

She walked up to the bed and looked down. He looked so peaceful to her. She stood beside her husband, remembering so many wonderful things about their life together. With clarity, she could remember right back to being told by her family in Italy that she was to wed a gentleman in England, and the moment she first laid eyes on him. A part of her wanted to be angry that he had gone out on the hunt this year, given his increasing age, but it was something that he loved. She could not be angry over that.

Although his face had much changed since when they had first met, she still considered him handsome as she leaned down and kissed his lips one final time. Briefly, she wondered why she had wasted so much time worrying about all the silly little things that she had when time together was so brief. At least she had Edward and his family…

Suddenly Edward saw his mother look up, and turn to him, a desperate look of urgency on her face, combined with the realisation of having forgotten about her daughter-in-law.

"Edward - Alessandra!" she exclaimed cryptically.

It wasn't much of a message but that was all it took for Edward to leave the room and run down to the drawing room. He expected to see her there, even though she had not been there minutes earlier.

"Edward," Alessandra's father said as he walked in, surprised to see his son-in-law again so soon.

"Where is Alessandra?" Edward commanded, visibly

distressed.

"She is in the birthing chamber," her father began. He needed to say no more as he watched Edward run from the room without looking back.

Running up the grand staircase, Edward found himself overloaded by emotion. It was one thing to lose his father, but was he going to lose his wife on the same day?

CHAPTER 67

Through a misty mind, Alessandra could hear voices. They sounded like they were in the distance, talking. She could hear them mentioning her name so knew they must have been talking about her.

"She is very weak, but with enough sleep, she may recover well enough," one voice said.

Alessandra, in her daze, tried to comprehend what they were talking about.

"He is a healthy lad," said the second voice, sounding happy but concerned at the same time. "But what a sad day to have arrived in this world, with his grandfather..."

Just as Alessandra felt herself begin to drift off to sleep once more, she heard the door open forcefully and a third voice talk loudly. The voice reached her and she started to try to call out to it, but her mouth would not speak.

"My wife is in labour?" the male voice asked loudly to anyone who would listen, before a softer, quieter one replied.

"Sir, she has already done her work," Margaret replied.

When Edward looked more closely at Margaret he realised that the bundle she was holding was not Isabella at all, as he had immediately assumed. He peered into the face of the little person being enveloped and felt his emotions overflow once more. He looked up at Margaret, who answered a question that had not been voiced.

"It is a boy, Sir," she said. "He appears to be very healthy but the mistress…"

Edward's eyes tore away from the angelic face of his newly born son and turned suddenly to the bed in the room. Seeing his wife looking so lifeless, he immediately thought the worst. Sensing his distress, the midwife spoke up.

"She is exhausted but she will recover," she said. "She needs to sleep now but this little one does need to feed. With your permission, I do think we should try and let it."

Edward tried to concentrate on what was being said to him, and eventually nodded in full understanding.

"Yes, of course. Shall I take him?" he asked. Margaret handed the baby into his arms, wondering again at how much of a loving, hands-on father he was, compared to many other men.

Edward looked at the small face once more as he carried him over to the bed. Sitting on the bed, Edward gently undid his wife's nightgown to allow just enough access for the baby to feed. Carefully he held both of them in his arms to facilitate it. Looking at his wife's face, he could see how much the birth had taken out of her. He held back tears, determined to remain strong, at least until his son had fed.

As the baby began to suckle, Alessandra felt the familiar sensation and woke to look down. It surprised her that Edward was beside her and a new baby was at her breast. It took her several minutes to remember that she had given birth.

"Edward," he heard her breathe out as her hand came up and touched his face. "I am sorry. I seem to have rushed…"

Edward smiled at her through tears. "Oh my love, we have a son and look at him. He is beautiful."

Alessandra indulged in the new knowledge and the new feeling of love inside of her, before remembering how the day had begun.

"Edward, someone was hurt," she said and looked into the eyes of the man she loved. As she became fully awake she noticed how sad he looked and how red his eyes were. "Oh, no! Your father?" she asked. Edward nodded before breaking down completely.

"Margaret, can you take him please? He has fallen asleep," she called out so the baby could be put down in his bed. "And could you please both leave us alone and ask that no-one disturb us?"

After they were alone in the room, despite the strong exhaustion she felt, Alessandra put her arms around her husband and let him cuddle into her like a small child, weeping heavily and loudly.

"Oh my love, I am so sorry," she said and then sat silent, letting him speak - or not speak - as he wished.

Edward found himself wrapped in his wife's love. He indulged in it. Having watched her go through the same thing when her mother had died the year before, he knew she had a sound understanding of what he was feeling, but it was more the strength he gained from her through her holding him that soothed him. After a long time, he pulled away from her. He had a conflicted look on his face.

"My mother…" he started to say but immediately felt disloyal about leaving his wife.

"Your mother needs you, Edward. Go to her … please," Alessandra encouraged.

She saw a look of relief pass over his face before he kissed her deeply once, started to walk away, and then returned to kiss her even more deeply. When he finally left the room Alessandra felt overwhelmingly saddened by the news of her father-in-law. In contrast, she also remembered the small person lying in a tiny bed not too far from where she was. She smiled with the decision of what his name was meant to be.

"Charles."

CHAPTER 68

News of the extraordinary day at Chisholm Manor Estate spread quickly. People came from around the entire area to pay respect to both the new master on the birth of his son, and to say farewell to the old master.

Edward watched his mother closely, aware of the bittersweet contrast of the two things that could happen in one day - one life extinguished as another began. During the funeral service, she clung to him, as much emotionally as physically. Alessandra held back in everything, ensuring her husband did not feel divided.

Of comfort to her mother-in-law seemed to be Alessandra's father, who had not too long since lost his own lifelong love. Alessandra would see them huddled together in different places - the drawing room, the gardens, and even her favourite spot - the glass jungle room.

~~~~~

"The estate is now yours, Edward, to command as you wish, but I do advise that you consider things carefully before making any changes. Do not rush in. Take your time and assess what urgently needs to be done, and what can be put off. This is a full-time job and it will take much out of you if you let it. Do not let it take you from your family too much. It can be lonely as a wife to the master of a great estate like this one if you do not work together to manage everything so it all works well," Edward heard his mother say as he turned to look at her.

They were sitting in the drawing room alone.
~~~~~

Alessandra and her father having gone out for what was now a routine of a daily walk through the gardens together in the late afternoon sun.

"Did you feel like that, Mother? Lonely?" Edward asked, not sure if he would cause offence, but curious after her choice of wording. Four years earlier he would not have dared be so intrusive into his mother's private life, but since his marriage - and particularly since his father's passing - the two of them seemed to have moved forward as adult companions, as much as mother and son.

She looked at her grown son and recognised once more how much he had grown, and what a fine man he had developed into. She couldn't have been prouder of him already being a father to three children, all of whom appeared healthy.

Edward saw his mother smile sadly and nod after a period of time, during which he considered she might be letting memories flow over her.

"Sometimes I did, when things were going on that your father would have to deal with. There were many times when he would be gone from breakfast until bedtime. Yes, at different times it did seem like a lonely life, but those times were far outweighed by the many, many more when he was here," she said and paused before continuing. "You appear to have a full, loving marriage, Edward. As you start to get busier in the estate, make sure you and your wife monitor how you are both feeling. I know Alessandra is very strong. I have no doubt she will run the household well whilst continuing to be the loving mother that she is but do not let the busyness of the two of you result in space between you."

Edward considered what was said to him and nodded, lowering his eyes as he pondered the advice. Already he had started to feel pressure on him as he took on the many roles that his father had played before him. So far the evening routine of he and Alessandra spending time with the children, and both of them putting them down to sleep for the night, had not been affected at all by his workload. Equally unaffected was he and Alessandra retiring to their bedchamber together in the evenings to talk together about their day before going to sleep. Since the birth of Charles, neither of them had made any move toward physical intimacy. Every day was so full that sleep was a priority every night. Edward also knew that with his wife breastfeeding their son several times a day, while running the household largely on her own now that his mother had taken a back seat there, Alessandra was as exhausted as he was when they came together in the evenings.

Thinking about his family he felt a sudden desire to be around his children, so stood up.

"Would you like to come to the nursery, Mother? I feel the need to hug my children," he said and immediately saw her smile and stand up with a renewed sense of energy about her.

"I would like that very much, Edward. Yesterday when I was playing with little Elizabeth she…" Edward's mother began and was soon making him laugh as she told a small story about one of Elizabeth's increasing adventures in exploration of her surroundings.

~~~~~

A month later, Edward and Alessandra found themselves settled into a routine that was busy but not stressful. Edward spent much of the day around the estate, visiting tenants and discussing different aspects of agriculture with them. After several weeks of the routine, he started to finally find it easier to not see his wife at all between breakfast and the evening meal.

Alessandra similarly resolved to put her head down and treat the work as a job, doing everything she could between breakfast and their evening meal together, whilst making time each day to feed the baby, spend
~~~~~

time with Isabella and Elizabeth, and enjoy an afternoon stroll with her father.

"You are always so busy, Daughter," her father said to her one day on their daily walk. "If you need help with something, please do not forget that I can help. You only need to ask."

"Father! No, you do not need to do anything while here except relax and enjoy yourself," she said, horrified at the thought of her father taking on any of their work.

He stopped walking and turned to her. "Alessandra, I have worked all my life, in one way or another. It is difficult sometimes to not have anything I am required to do. Please, if you or Edward need assistance with anything, promise me you will let me know so I can help."

Alessandra looked closely at him, noticing suddenly how much he had aged since her mother's death. She conceded that perhaps it was difficult for him to not have any vocation anymore.

"Thank you, Father. I certainly shall ask for your help when I need to, and I will talk to Edward and ensure he does also."

CHAPTER 69

As the four-month anniversary of his father's death passed, Edward found himself starting to feel very lonely. He knew his wife was there for him and yet he could not bring himself to bother her with his desire for her. Night after night he kept quiet and focused on simply holding her close.

As always in the evenings, he and Alessandra put the children down to sleep after extensive time hugging each of them and then moved to the privacy of their bedchamber.

On this evening, he sensed something about his wife was different, as if she had something serious on her mind. He put his arms around her and held her in front of the fire before taking her hand and leading her to the sofa. There they reclined back and held hands, sitting close.

"What is it, Alessandra?" he asked gently, finding a surge of panic inside of him.

Alessandra looked at him as if only just realising he was there. "Oh, it is nothing, Edward. My milk has dried up much sooner than it did with Isabella and Elizabeth, that is all. Margaret has already weaned Charles onto cow milk," she said and put the matter out of her mind, determined as she was to not talk about trivial things when Edward was so exhausted at the end of each day. "I am sorry. Please tell me how your day was. Did you sort out..." she continued, encouraging him to speak about his tasks of the day.

~~~~~
~~~~~

The next morning, after breakfast, Alessandra felt withdrawn and alone. As difficult as it was to acknowledge to herself, she knew she missed Edward. She tried to formulate some kind of plan to have some real time alone with him. The idea initially seemed impossible, until she considered her father's offer the day before.

Midway through the day she entered the drawing room and found her father in pleasant conversation with Edward's mother. Alessandra decided to be bold and approach both of them for help.

"I would like to ask both of you for assistance with a matter," she started. She could feel a slight blush on her face beginning but determined to see the request through.

"Of course Alessandra, how can we help?" her father asked, jumping up quickly, as if it were an emergency.

"Oh, Father. It is not something that requires immediate attention, but..." she started, feeling very awkward before she found her resolve once more. "I would like - if the two of you would not mind - to go away to Bath with Edward for a short time. I..." she continued, now feeling the full force of her 'beetroot face', as she had come to refer to it over the years.

Alessandra saw her father look at Edward's mother knowingly, as if the two of them had already discussed such a plan. When he looked back at her, he smiled broadly. "Alessandra, that is a wonderful idea."

"Yes, go tomorrow, Alessandra, with our blessing," Edward's mother said. "Do not worry. The estate will be fine in the hands of me and your father. You and Edward have been working so hard that you deserve it."

Alessandra could not hold back her smile as she moved to give each of them a hug.

"Thank you!" she exclaimed excitedly, making them both laugh. "I shall sort things out now." Before she left the room she turned back to them with a sly grin on her face. "Could we perhaps keep this a secret until breakfast tomorrow?" she asked. Both parents nodded, smiling.

~~~~~

That night in bed Edward sensed that his wife was keeping something from him. He did not want to pressure her, given all that she was dealing with, so once again went to sleep feeling content to be with her, but at the same time feeling a slight sense of loneliness, like he was losing her.

~~~~~

After breakfast the next morning, Edward stood up to excuse himself but found himself commanded by his wife, unexpectedly.

"Sit down, Edward … please."

He did so, looking at all of the faces at the table and realising that something was going on that he had not been made party to.

"You shall not be going to work around the estate today," Alessandra continued, pretending to be stern in her voice. "I have quite another job for you to do."

Edward looked at his wife. He was ready to comply with whatever she needed assistance with, but when he looked into her eyes he saw something he had not seen in a long while.

"What can I help you with, my lovely wife?" he asked, sensing she was somehow teasing him in her mock seriousness.

"You can help me with packing enough clothing for you and me, for two nights."

Edward sensed his mother and Alessandra's father both looking at him. Turning his attention away from his wife he saw how much they were both smiling. Upon seeing his further confusion, all three people before him started laughing quietly.

"What have I not been told?" he asked in good humour.

"You shall go with your wife, Edward, and enjoy two

nights in Bath with her. Do not worry about the estate. We shall look after it and we are quite qualified to handle anything out of the ordinary, should it happen," he heard his mother say, smiling at him. "Your children are in good hands, and the estate is in good hands. Do not argue. Just do as your wife bids."

Alessandra watched her husband's face change through different emotions as he looked at each person in the room. When his eyes settled on hers, she saw he was inwardly pleased. It made her happy.

"Go!" Alessandra's father insisted. "You are young and you are in love. Do not waste another moment."

~~~~~

As the door closed behind them in their bedchamber, Edward found himself shy for the first time since their wedding night. Sensing it, Alessandra moved to him, put her arms around him, and kissed him deeply.

"Husband, let us go and say goodbye to our children, and then be off," she said to him, making him instantly aroused and hard just by the look in her eyes.

Edward blushed and smiled at her. "I cannot go to the nursery right at this moment, Alessandra," he said, making her giggle for the first time in months. As he listened, he remembered what a wonderful sound it was to him - and how much he had missed it.
~~~~~

CHAPTER 70

Shyly the two of them entered their rooms in their Bath accommodation. When the door was closed behind them they took a moment to look around their suite, with its small lounge and dining area, and bedroom beyond.

Edward still felt shy but was so heated he could hardly think. When he looked at his wife he found deep inside him a level of eagerness he had not quite felt before. Once more she approached him, put her arms around him, and kissed him, not holding back on the level of desire she felt.

Leaning against her, Edward finally found his confidence. He took his time undressing her, indulging in seeing every tiny piece of her skin as it became visible. As he did so, Alessandra teased him, using her hand to reach out and brush against him. It was evident he was already very hard and ready. The sensations increased in Edward until he felt like he might not be able to hold back any more from climaxing. Determined to not let that be the case, he held her hand still.

"Alessandra, it has been so long and I am already on fire. Please..." he started to say as he removed the last item from her body. He felt her start to undress him. It seemed not soon enough that they stood naked together. He gently pushed her backward into the bedroom and positioned her on her back on the bed. Before joining her he took a moment to look down on her and take in the beautiful sight before him.

Alessandra held out her arms to him and welcomed him, her own arousal well advanced also. She kissed him over and over, enjoying the sensations that had been missing since before their last child had been born. Every part of her body felt like it was longing for him. She revelled in feeling him start to kiss her everywhere. When he reached her core, his tongue moving on her, she exploded in orgasm quickly, surprising both of them, and then making her giggle.

Edward slid up her body and kissed her again. He desperately needed to find relief. As he looked into her eyes to silently ask what she wanted, he immediately felt her hands on his hips, pulling him closer so he could sink into her. Alternating between closing his eyes to kiss her, and looking down into her face, he felt the familiar warmth engulf him and immediately shuddered inside of her.

He lay like that for some time, enjoying the sensations flowing through him. When he opened his eyes he saw her smiling at him. Alessandra reached out her hand and stroked his face, alternating this with kissing him briefly on the lips, over and over.

"You are right, Edward. It has been too long … and I have missed you too much," she said.

Edward felt his heart sing. In recent months the feeling of loneliness had started to creep in, even though he had tried to keep it at bay.

"I have missed you too, Alessandra. Always I want you," Edward responded. "I never stop wanting you."

She smiled at him further. "I feel the same way."

He pulled out of her and lay beside her, pulling the covers over the two of them. As he pulled her tightly against him, they lay on their sides, looking at one another.

"Thank you, for arranging this," he said to her, feeling shy once again. "I did not want to rush you after the birth."

"I know, and I thank you for always being so considerate toward me, Edward. We have both become so busy, but we must not let that stop us from being close like this. I do not want it to stop. I love you too much."

Edward was overwhelmed in emotion all of a sudden. Feeling a tear come to his eye, he leaned in and kissed her again before they indulged in a period of much, much slower lovemaking.

~~~~~

Lying back on the bed, both finally feeling sated, Edward laughed.

"Oh my wife, what you do to me!" he said, bringing his arm up and covering his eyes as he lay on his back, making her giggle again. It was a sound he loved so much. "I ... we ... must rest!"

Alessandra looked at her husband, pleased to see him so happy once again after a period of time where everything had seemed so very serious. Over their 48 hours away together she did not want him to ponder about the sadness that had occurred, or give thought to any worries around the estate. She just wanted to scoop him up, hold him close, and reassure him that everything was alright.

Edward pulled his arm down, away from his eyes, and turned to her. He was still in awe of her as a wife, even with having been married almost four years. As he thought about the possibility of having made another child, he found himself thinking about Alessandra's hardship with the birth of their son.

Alessandra had watched Edward's face and saw it change. "What is worrying you, Edward?" she asked, knowing something was weighing on his mind.

"I cannot bear the thought of losing you," he said simply, making her heart swell.

"Why are you thinking about that now, Edward? This is a happy time," she replied.

Edward considered not telling her his concerns, but fought his indecision about it and spoke.
~~~~~

"The last birth was taxing on your body," he said quietly, looking away.

"Edward, during any birth I could leave this world - but on any day I could leave this world, as could you. Do not let us think too heavily about it. We must make the most of the time that we do have together."

"But, do you particularly want to be with child again?" Edward asked.

Alessandra took time to think about that. "I am happy with the three children that you and I have, and I will be happy if we have more. I would rather put it in nature's hands if we are meant to keep having children or not. But if you wish for us not to join anymore…"

"I have always been happy having this time with you, even if we do not join," he said and his mind wandered to the specifics of procreation.

As if reading his mind, Alessandra spoke. "What if we tried joining without making a child, Edward?"

"Yes," he replied simply, that very possibility having just entered his mind.

They turned on their sides toward one another, with thoughtful looks on their faces.

"The baby-making aspect is your … juice, is it not?" she asked. Edward smiled at her terminology and nodded. "What if you stopped that from being in me?" she continued. Edward could see difficulty on her face as it became redder and redder before him. "If you … pulled out of me … before…"

Edward sensed what she was saying and considered teasing her about her 'beetroot face', as he had heard her call her current discomfort before. Instead he let it go, not wanting to make her in any way uncomfortable.

"We may have already made a child today," Edward said, his voice almost a whisper.

"Yes, but we also may not have. Could we perhaps try it?" Alessandra proposed. "If a child still comes, then we shall embrace them and love them just as we love

Elizabeth, Isabella and Charles."

Edward studied her, relieved. The birth of little Charles had shaken him up and left him concerned about Alessandra being with child every year. It was a thrilling idea that conception could be avoided while they still enjoyed the excitement and pleasure of moving together. As he thought that, he saw Alessandra's eyes move and her face light up in a smile once again. He also realised that he had once again become hard.

"Shall we try now, then?" Alessandra asked, smiling at him. "It might be something we need to work on to perfect, after all."

Edward laughed with her and moved on top of her, nestling between her legs before he slid into her, and moved with her. When he felt close to climax, he pulled out of her and immediately felt her hand on him, touching him as she had right from their wedding night. As a result, he climaxed over her belly. Instead of resting at that point, he moved backwards and let his tongue and lips caress her until a few minutes later, he felt her muscles contract against his mouth. When he came up he saw her smiling brilliantly at him.

"Should we eat, Husband? This could be a long night," she said with a sly grin.

Edward laughed out loud at her before finally dragging himself out of bed and starting to get dressed. "Yes, my beautiful wife. I do believe we may both need some replenishment now!"

~~~~~

They ate out that evening and enjoyed the feeling of being alone but in society. It was such a rare thing for them to do. Edward enjoyed seeing the great appetite his wife exhibited, and her enthusiasm for trying foods she had not tried before.

"Do you think your mother and my father are alright in the manor?" Alessandra asked, more to herself than him, but Edward responded.
~~~~~

"I do. Mother knows almost every aspect of what has to be done, and even though your father has not run such a big property, he is experienced and knowledgeable about all facets of it," he said and paused for a moment, thinking. "To be honest, Alessandra, I think it might be good for both of them to have the responsibility. I know we do not need them to actively do anything, but I think they are both people who would rather not be idle, in body or mind."

"Perhaps we should leave more often then," Alessandra said, giving him a knowing smile that instantly affected him. In response, he fondly gave her his warning 'do not look at me that way in public' look, which made her laugh softly at him.

~~~~~

"What would you like to do today, my love? Visit the shops? Go and bathe in the Roman Baths?" Edward asked his wife the following morning, after what seemed to him to have been a very long night, and active morning.

Alessandra lifted her head from his chest and looked demurely at him, making Edward laugh once again. "Or perhaps stay here all day?" he asked, teasing her as he lay on his back, pulling her with him so she was lying on top of him.

Kissing his lips, Alessandra relaxed forward so that she lay along the length of his body. She felt his hands move to caress her back, hips, buttocks, and back to her neck and shoulders. Edward didn't touch any part of her that easily aroused her.

Alessandra found herself loving just focusing on all the areas of skin he was caressing. After a while, she let out a sigh of contentment, which made him smile as he looked at her face.

"You are so beautiful, Alessandra," he said all of a sudden, seriousness in his voice. Alessandra looked into his eyes, appreciating how often he told her that, even
~~~~~

though she knew she had no prettiness in her whatsoever. "How would you like to visit your ancestral land in Italy?"

The question came as such a surprise that Alessandra blinked, wondering if she had indeed heard it. She immediately sat upright and Edward moaned at the sight before him, already forgetting what he had asked. His hands automatically reached out and started to caress her breasts, enjoying the shape of them, and how well his hands fitted around them.

Alessandra wanted to question the question, but behind her felt him growing, as she indulged in the feelings once again being awoken in his caresses of her breasts and nipples. She moved back and over him before lowering down, a move she had not done for many months.

"You will need to tell me when to stop, Edward," she said huskily, enjoying fully the feelings inside of her. While she moved up and down on him, he let one hand lightly flick across one nipple, while he moved his other hand down so he could stroke her where he knew she most loved, and heard a loud moan come from her. The sight before him was breathtaking - the way her body moved and felt, and the look of desire on her face. When she opened her eyes and looked down at him he knew he would not last long, but for her was determined to. He let his mind wander, and his eyes close, so that he would not yet climax. Soon he felt her squeezing him tightly in small bursts as she let out the moan that told him clearly that she had had her orgasm.

"Move off me, Alessandra," he said.

Alessandra immediately pulled off, leaving Edward bare for only a moment before she moved back and he found himself engulfed in her mouth, where he instantly found relief. He did not know the number of orgasms he'd had in the preceding 24 hours but could feel that with each one, the intensity was getting stronger, almost to a point where it was unbearable. It made him resolved that he did indeed need to not stay in that room with his wife for the entire day and night to come.

CHAPTER 71

Edward and Alessandra walked around the shops of Bath, looking in windows and inside the stores themselves. It was a pleasant distraction from what was really on their minds. Store by store, they sought out gifts for everyone at the manor. It would not be long until it was winter, and that would also be the time of Christmas.

"We shall find gifts for all of the staff and tenants also, Edward. I would like to make sure they know how much they are appreciated," Alessandra said, making her husband feel proud. He had never heard of any estate master doing such a thing, but liked the idea as he did indeed appreciate the level of work that was involved in running such a large property, and the skills the staff individually had.

"That is a fine idea, Alessandra," he responded, appreciating again the generous nature of his wife. He suspected that many women would have been far more interested in what they could get, rather than what they could give to others.

The two of them enjoyed themselves, thinking of different people and what each might like. As they moved from store to store, Edward realised it was the first time the two of them had indulged in such an activity as buying items for other people. Their lives were so entwined at the estate, and with their children, that such a simple pleasure had been overlooked. His mind ventured back to a thought he'd had that morning about visiting the land where Alessandra's mother had grown up.

When they returned to their room later in the day he raised the subject once more as they sat on the sofa in front of the fire, watching the flames.

"What do you think about the idea of us going to Italy?" Edward asked. "Would you like to see if you have relations there?"

Alessandra blushed slightly, remembering the question from the morning, and the moments of love that followed. Edward did not tease her, knowing exactly how her mind was working.

"I think I would like that very much," Alessandra replied. "Mother wrote down names and addresses for me. It would be nice to see where she came from and who those people were. But how long would that take, Edward? We could not leave the children or the estate for very long, nor could we take the children with us. Could we?"

"I agree it would take great planning and thought to travel so far. Shall we talk to our parents about it and see what they think?" he asked and Alessandra nodded.

For that afternoon they did not move toward anything sexual at all, finding new joy in sitting, fully clothed, in front of the warm fire. Whilst holding one another, they talked and talked. After dinner, however, Alessandra turned to him and smiled shyly at him.

"Tomorrow we are returning home," she said simply.

Edward nodded. "Yes."

"Then we shall be busy once more, unable to have time like this," Alessandra continued.

"Yes," he said, touching her hair and face gently with his hand.

"Please make love to me now, Edward," she said.

She did not need to say anything more. Edward smiled, wanting to only please her and make her feel beautiful and loved.

CHAPTER 72

Edward watched his wife run inside the manor house as soon as they pulled up in the carriage. He could sense Alessandra's urgency to get to the nursery and see the children. He took his time, going into the drawing room first to greet his mother and Alessandra's father.

"Oh, my son," his mother exclaimed as she ran to him and hugged him in a rare show of affection. "How are you? And where is your wife?"

Edward laughed, loving how happy his mother seemed. In fact, to him, she almost seemed to be glowing.

"Alessandra has gone directly to the nursery, Mother," Edward said. "I will go and join her shortly, but I wanted to see you both first, and ask if there is anything that needs my attention directly."

"No, Edward," he heard Alessandra's father say. "All is well here. In fact, you probably could have stayed away longer if you wished it."

Edward laughed at his father-in-law. "I do not think Alessandra could stay away longer than two nights. She was very lonely for the children while we were away, I believe. I shall leave you both now and go to the nursery also," he said and started to move away before turning back to them. "Thank you once again for making our time away possible."

Alessandra's father looked at Edward's mother and they smiled at one another, imagining in their minds how much their children might have enjoyed their time alone.

~~~~~
~~~~~

"Oh, Edward! Look! I do believe little Elizabeth and Isabella - even little Charles - have all grown while we have been away," she said happily, making Elizabeth smile in pride. Now three years old, she was already finding her own personality and particularly enjoyed the times when she could see and talk to her mother.

Edward looked at each of his children before kneeling to hug Elizabeth. He then lifted Isabella onto his knee as he sat down in one of the chairs in the nursery.

"I do believe you are right, my lovely wife. My beautiful daughters, in particular, to seem to have grown much over the past two days," he said, holding his youngest daughter close to him. Although still too young to be able to have a two-way conversation with, when he held her on his knee and she looked directly at him and smiled, his heart caught.

"Margaret let me hold and feed Charles," Elizabeth said shyly in her almost-three language that took some concentration to understand at times. As she spoke, she moved tentatively toward her mother, who, as wished, picked Elizabeth up and pulled her into a warm hug on her lap.

Alessandra looked over at Margaret, who was smiling broadly at the family scene in front of her. The two women exchanged an affectionate glance.

"And how did you like that, Elizabeth? Were you scared?" Alessandra asked.

Elizabeth looked at her mother with a look of surprise on her face. "Oh no, Mother! He was a good baby and did not frighten me at all!"

Edward laughed softly at his eldest daughter, enjoying watching her start to develop into a small person now. In his current position, surrounded by his children and the wife that he loved so much, he felt like he must surely be the luckiest man in the world.

CHAPTER 73

"I think it is a wonderful idea, Alessandra. You know it was a wish of your mother's that you should see where she was born and lived until she came to England," Alessandra's father said later as they all sat in the drawing room.

"But how long would it take? I do not think it can be a feasible plan," Alessandra said sadly.

Edward's mother spoke up, understanding the conflict of the young mother.

"What is it that concerns you, Alessandra? Your father and I are happy to watch everything here, and if you do not wish to be away from the children for so long, you can take Margaret and one of the other household staff with you."

Edward watched his wife during the conversation. He did not want to push her into doing something she did not wish to do, but equally did not want her to miss any opportunity if she did wish to go.

"I do not know how long it would take," Alessandra replied quietly, suddenly unaware of how people even got to Italy, it seemed such a far way off.

"I believe you will need to get to Dover. From there you can cross the channel to Calais, in France, before making your way to Venice, where your mother was from. I should think you would need to take at least three weeks," she heard her father explain, causing panic in her.

"Three weeks?! Oh no, that is too long. We could not possibly..." Alessandra started to say but her mother-in-law cut her off.

"Yes, you can! Alessandra, your father and I are here, and we are both glad to have an occupation. It would be wise to make use of us while we are both here and physically able to help you both."

Alessandra looked at Edward, who in turn was looking intently at her.

"What do you think, Edward?" she asked him, desperate for some guidance.

"I think that it is a good idea. Three weeks is not too long, and as Mother said, we can confidently leave the estate in the care of her and your father. It would be nice to see where your mother came from, would it not?"

"But is it something you wish to do also, Edward? It is such a long way to travel if you do not want to…"

"Yes!" Edward exclaimed. "I have never been away from England at all, and I would greatly enjoy travelling … with you."

"What of the children though? Would it not be nicer to wait until they are all old enough to come with us and learn of their history also?"

"Perhaps, but we can always go again at a later time. The children were fine without us here when we went to Bath, and I am sure they will be fine for a few weeks, at the age they are. If we wait too long then they will be of an age where they are running around the estate, and I that think would wear my mother and your father out!" Edward said, adding some humour into the decision making process.

Alessandra looked closely at him, seeing his passion for the idea in his eyes. The idea of spending three weeks alone with her husband was a thought that would not have been visible on her face to the older generation in the room but was very clearly seen by Edward.

"Very well, let us do it," she said, seeing her desire mirror back at her from his eyes. "Let us arrange it and go before I lose my nerve."

CHAPTER 74

The ship at Dover was postponed overnight due to bad weather, leaving Alessandra and Edward stranded in the port overnight. It already seemed like a long day, having travelled here from their home, but when they found a room for the night, that did not stop them racing to fall into each other's arms with vigour and energy.

Their idea to try and not cause the creation of a child so far appeared to be working. Even their first day in Bath, before they had talked about it, did not seem to have been fruitful, as Alessandra had bled since then. When they had first married, and at different times since, they had refrained from joining and both had been happy with alternative ways to pleasure, but Alessandra felt particularly close to Edward when they were moving together, joined. She relished the new possibility of doing so without conceiving. It was liked so much by Alessandra and Edward that sometimes he felt like he simply could not get enough of her.

"We must sleep, my love," he smiled at her fondly, feeling exhausted after their journey and active lovemaking. "Come, settle here in front of me with your back to me and let me hold you so you cannot tempt me further with your lips," he said in amusement but with determination to be refreshed for their journey on the sea the following day.

"I love you, Edward," he heard his wife say sleepily before he felt her start to relax, her back to his chest.

"I love you, too, my beautiful Alessandra."

~~~~~
~~~~~

"Oh!" Alessandra exclaimed as she felt the first movement of the sea as the ship began to leave port. She looked at her husband and saw excitement mirrored on his face. They laughed together at the new sensations, neither having been on the water before. Soon they were well away from the land and enjoyed feeling the salty wind on their faces, neither in any hurry to go indoors.

After a light meal, they went to the cabin that was theirs for the one night. Once settled in for the evening, both found themselves curious about how things might be in closeness with the ship moving as it was. It fuelled Edward. He undressed himself and his wife quickly, using his initiative and hunger without waiting for any sign from her.

Alessandra recognised his level of passion and let him lead the way. She happily lay back on the small but comfortable bunk and welcomed him inside her.

As he moved, Edward concentrated on the different feelings the ship movement invoked in him. There was a sense of not being in control, as their bodies were moved slightly this way and that. It excited him greatly. Looking at Alessandra's face, he could see that she too was finding it a new source of excitement and pleasure. He took his time, pulling out when he needed to, but stopping her from touching him when he did, before he moved back inside her for another short period of time until he would pull out again.

"Oh, Edward," Alessandra breathed out as she felt him move back in once more. It was the first time he had moved in such a way - filling her up for a time before removing himself. She felt like she was undergoing an entirely new experience. "I think we could do this all night," she said.

Edward laughed and kissed her before sliding back in again.

CHAPTER 75

Travelling through France on their way to Italy, Alessandra found her naturally curious nature undergoing an in-depth growth in her level of knowledge. Everywhere they went, she asked people so many questions. In doing so, she kept Edward amused and feeling that he could not love his wife any more than he did. She was a constant inspiration to him in so many ways. He found himself extremely proud to be the man standing next to her, dining with her ... making love to her. Every night she showed him how much she loved him, and the time together without the regularity of household chores pushed their closeness to another level.

In Venice, they made their way to the first address on her mother's list. There they found themselves in the company of her mother's sister. She was an elderly woman who Alessandra and Edward both calculated must have been much older than Alessandra's mother.

"Oh, my dear! How wonderful to meet you at last. Your mother and I did keep in touch for many years, but then real life started to get in the way of writing, for both of us. I have not heard from her for ... oh, at least 10 years I think," the woman said to Alessandra as they settled in a room like Alessandra had never seen, with its level of opulence. She and Edward had to strain to listen carefully, as the accent was far more intense than the lesser accent her mother had spoken with.

"Oh, but Aunt, do you know that ... my mother..." Alessandra started to say and the older woman leaned in to touch her hand lightly.

"I do know that my sister passed away, Alessandra. Your father sent word when it happened," she said and paused before continuing, looking closely at Alessandra. "You look much like she did at your age."

Alessandra shook her head. "Oh no, my mother was very beautiful."

The older woman touched her hand once more. "Yes, Alessandra, she was … as are you."

Quickly Alessandra changed the subject, knowing it was not true but not wanting to offend. For the rest of that day they talked and talked. Edward and Alessandra both enjoyed hearing about the life of her mother, from childhood right up until the time when Alessandra was born.

"She loved your father so much, sometimes I was quite jealous. Both of our marriages were arranged by our parents, and I loved my husband enough, but what your mother had with your father was something much, much more. I can see that you have that in you, too, Alessandra - I see the way you and your husband look at each other. Enjoy it, embrace it, and work hard to keep it so."

~~~~~

Over the following week, Alessandra met her cousins. She and Edward felt like they were in a new world, being taken to see opera and dining in the most exquisite buildings they had ever seen. When it was time to start their return journey, Edward sensed her sadness.

"We shall come back again, Alessandra. When the children are a little older, we will come back as a family," he assured her and felt her rest her head on his shoulder in their carriage.

"Yes, let us do that, but I should like to have more children by then," she replied softly. Edward pushed her away gently so he could study her face. For several minutes both remained silent, deep in thought whilst looking into one another's eyes. "Will you … tonight
~~~~~

…?" she asked and heard him breathe out deeply.

"Yes."

~~~~~

On the return ship journey, Edward took his time pleasuring her, kissing her everywhere and using his hands and tongue to bring her easily to orgasm with the level of arousal she already had. He revelled once more in how it felt to be inside of her whilst the ship moved in its erratic way. More and more, he found that they both enjoyed the extended time that could happen with his withdrawal when he needed to, and then moving back inside her. Knowing Alessandra had said she was ready for them to try and conceive again, they moved together until he climaxed heavily inside of her.

"Oh, my darling," he breathed out heavily as he felt himself have the orgasm, feeling the great moistness inside of her.

Alessandra held him close to her, appreciating their current level of freedom would soon end. Their time together in Italy she had appreciated so much. She equally loved the need she constantly felt to be close to him, touch him and have him move inside her. She was ready to go home, though, she found. She missed her little ones and longed to see them and to hold them.

Edward pulled out of her but stayed lying on top of her, kissing her lips and looking into her eyes. "What is it?" he asked when he saw the emotion on her face.

"I am looking forward to seeing our babies," she said, letting out a small cry.

Edward smiled at her indulgently. "Oh, my beautiful wife and mother of my children, we will be home soon. Once we arrive at Dover it will be a short time indeed."

She smiled at him. The love she felt made her pull his head down and kiss him again before pushing him onto his back. She took much time to pleasure him with her hands and mouth, over and over, before sitting astride him and taking her time to move up and down on him.
~~~~~

Edward watched her move, thinking that he would never in his lifetime see anything so beautiful as what his wife looked like right then.

332

CHAPTER 76

Pulling up to the manor, they saw both of their parents on the front doorstep, along with Margaret and the children. Edward laughed at his wife's excitement as she started to squeeze his hand tightly, and move around on the seat.

As soon as the carriage stopped, Alessandra threw herself from the carriage and ran up to where her children were. She knelt to pull into her arms, Elizabeth, who had reached out with her arms for a hug. The look on Elizabeth's face said clearly that she'd hoped she would receive the desired arms of her mother around her.

"Oh, how much I have missed you, Elizabeth! Are you well?" Alessandra asked and felt her daughter nod against her.

Alessandra hugged her tightly again before kissing her forehead and then standing to take Isabella from Margaret, and holding her close.

"Oh my, how you have grown, little one! And so heavy now!" she laughed, so happy to be home.

Beside her, she saw Edward kneel and pick up Elizabeth to hug her. "How have you been, my beautiful daughter?" he asked her gently

Elizabeth shyly responded. "Good, thank you, Father."

Edward laughed softly at her timidness and kissed her cheek. As always with Elizabeth, he determined not to push too hard with her to speak. He had already discovered that his oldest daughter also suffered from 'beetroot face' whenever the attention was put onto her too much. He'd also perceived it was something she was starting to be embarrassed about. Not wanting to bring too much attention to her, he held her tightly against him until she was ready to let him go.

Finally, Alessandra heard her mother-in-law usher them all inside. They settled in the drawing room, Alessandra with baby Charles in her arms and Elizabeth cuddling into her side, and Edward with Isabella on his lap. Once comfortable, Alessandra and Edward told all about the adventures they'd had, and the family they had met.

"Oh Father, it was so wonderful meeting my aunt. She told me so much about Mother's upbringing. It was extraordinary hearing her speak," Alessandra said.

Her father enjoyed the vision of his daughter looking so completely happy. For a moment he thought back to the early days of his marriage to her mother. Increasingly, he also felt an ever-growing sadness that slowly he was forgetting what his wife had looked like.

As he sat next to Edward's mother, he felt her reach out her hand and squeeze his, as if perceiving that moment to be a sad one for him. Edward saw the action and the look that passed between the two parents. It caused a confusing array of feelings in him. He had never seen his mother be affectionate toward anyone other than his father so it initially caused a slight amount of anger. Then he saw the look in his mother's eyes and knew he could not be angry at her. Looking at her objectively, he could see that she was still a beautiful woman. He expected it must have been incredibly lonely with his father not around.

Before he could dwell on it any more, the moment passed and was forgotten.

~~~~~

As the day moved on, Alessandra and Edward went with Margaret to the nursery, to settle the children down
~~~~~

for the night. Once there, Alessandra found herself pulled into a hug by Elizabeth.

"Please do not go, Mother," she asked in her timid little voice.

Alessandra gave her an extra hug and kiss. "I am not leaving again, Elizabeth. Your father and I are back to stay now. When you wake up tomorrow, we will still be here. Now cuddle down there in your nice warm bed and close your eyes."

Edward stood near the door, waiting for her, but Alessandra felt inclined to stay for another moment with her daughter, to make sure she was alright. When she was sure Elizabeth was relaxed and falling asleep, Alessandra stood up and walked to her husband. After placing her arms around him, they stood in a quiet hold for some time, looking at their children before quietly leaving the room.

"I enjoyed our time away immensely, but it is also good to be home, Edward," Alessandra said as he started to help her undress. "I do, however, wish I weren't so tired."

Edward smiled at her and kissed her softly. "Well, it has been a very active few weeks, my love," he said. Alessandra accurately understood his double meaning and stifled a giggle. "Perhaps tonight, in our own bed, we might … rest."

Alessandra laughed with him while blushing slightly. "Perhaps."

CHAPTER 77

"I do not understand, Mother. What do you mean you are leaving?" Edward asked, uncomprehending of what was being said to him. He and Alessandra had been home for several weeks. During that time it had seemed as though everything had returned to normal, and everyone was happy.

She looked at her son. In him, she still saw a man she would never consider handsome but who had made her so proud because of the man, the husband and the father that he was.

"Alessandra's father wants to go and live at Missinger Estate with his son for a while, to spend time with him, and he has invited me to join him."

"But you have a home here," Edward said.

The two of them were talking in the 'glass jungle room', away from the rest of the family.

Edward heard his mother take a deep breath, and let out a sigh. "Edward, you are settled with your own family now. While you and Alessandra were away in Italy, I found myself missing your father deeply. Alessandra's father was there. We are good companions and we have both lost our loved ones so we each understand that loss. Why should it surprise you that we wish to spend more time together?"

His mind wandering, Edward found it difficult to feel happy about what was happening. Regardless, he did not want to express displeasure to her. Not when she had given him so much in his lifetime.

"Do you ... love him?" he asked as one final

question, trying to understand.

"I think I am beginning to, yes. I have been lonely, and he understands that loneliness very well. It makes things easy between us. When I look at you and Alessandra, I do, in the depths of my soul, want to find that again before I leave this world, Edward. I want to feel loved."

Edward did not say anything more, and they sat together peacefully, each thinking about their own views and their own needs.

~~~~~

At the same time, walking out in the garden, Alessandra found herself drawn into a similar discussion with her father.

"I love her, Alessandra. I did not think I would love anyone again, but when it was just the two of us here, I found her to be a good person to lean on in my loneliness," he said but somehow the news did not surprise his daughter at all. "I do also want to spend time with Nicholas while I can, so moving to Missinger Estate is the easiest way for me to do that."

He stopped walking and took both of his daughter's hands in his. "Say something, Daughter. I do not wish to upset you."

Alessandra looked at her father and smiled at him. "Oh, Father, no! You have not upset me. After all you have been through, it is only natural that you should want companionship. If Edward's mother is the lucky woman to secure your attention, I am very happy for you both," she said and they started to walk once again. "And it is only fair that you go and spend time with Nicholas. I have had you all to myself all this time. It is certainly time he had his turn."

~~~~~

That night in bed Edward was assertive in his attentions to her, as if driven by an even greater need than normal. As he lay down next to her, she looked closely at him, wondering what he was thinking.

"How do you feel about the news of our parents?" she asked him tentatively, not wishing to upset him.

He looked at her and pulled her closer.

"I must admit, it does make me feel a little … strange … but I cannot be upset at them. Whenever I think of losing you, I can imagine the deep feeling of loneliness they each must feel at times, so I know that I need to be happy for them. For now, it is just … odd."

They lay quiet but Alessandra determined that he would not go to sleep with that conversation the last thing in his head, so moved herself to kiss him everywhere - his lips, his neck, down to his nipples and over his belly, before taking him in her mouth and giving him the kind of pleasure he had not taken for some time.

"Oh, my love…"

CHAPTER 78

The final goodbyes were said. On the manor doorstep Alessandra and Edward each hugged their parents tightly, not knowing when - or if - they would ever see them again.

Alessandra's father laughed at his daughter.

"We will not be that far away, and it is your house we will be staying at, Alessandra, so come and visit us there. This is not goodbye forever, my child," he said, hugging her once more.

As the carriage rode away, two lost souls stood and watched it disappear in the distance. When they could not see it anymore, Edward turned to his wife.

"The house will not be the same now, with it just being you and I, my lovely wife. And our three children, of course," he said, turning and giving her a full hug, holding her tight.

"Not for long I do not think, Edward," Alessandra said, quietly in his ear as she returned the hug.

He breathed her in - her scent, the feeling of her cheek on his, the feeling of her breasts against his chest - and he started to feel aroused at being so close to her until the words sank in.

"What are you saying?" he asked, pulling away abruptly. "Who else is leaving?"

Alessandra laughed at him joyfully and he was entranced by the happiness on her face. She did not answer him, but let him think about things in his own time, as she started to kiss him all over his face, smiling brilliantly all the while.

Edward pulled away again and looked at her with a grin beginning.

"You are … with child?" he asked and saw his wife laugh out loud.

"Oh, yes," Alessandra replied. "I am very certain, my wonderful husband. Our family of three will soon be a family of four."

Edward looked at her, knowing he should feel simply happiness at the news, but somehow it fuelled him more. He dismissed the idea of doing any work for the rest of the day as he took his wife's hand and led her inside and upstairs to show her exactly how happy she made him.

The End

OTHER BOOKS
BY
ANN M PRATLEY

HOONIGAN
ANN M PRATLEY

HOONIGAN

Tristan Clarkson has woken up, over and over, bound to a chair and unable to see. He has no idea where he is, or why he is in the situation he's woken to. His memory is vague, protecting him from recent events that will eventually haunt him for the rest of his life. He wants to remember, but at the same time his mind acts as though he really, really doesn't. Initially he's confused. With each waking, his memory clears that little bit more, as do his senses. He soon becomes aware that the very person who has abducted him, is in the room with him, determined to make Tristan pay for something he cannot even remember.

Meanwhile, in a hospital nearby a patient has been taken. With the help of FBI Special Agents Ashley Power and Tim Moore, an investigation begins into where the man has been taken, and who would have reason to remove him. With the patient having already been weak from time in a coma, time is of the essence in finding him alive.

Hoonigan is a blend of crime and suspense, intermingled with the strength of friendship, and the awakening of one father's realization of just how much his son really means to him.

CHRISTIAN
(FREEDOM OF FLIGHT SERIES - BOOK #1)

Twenty four year old Christian Shaw has a good life. He's had a rocky ride with being charged for a crime he didn't commit, but he's come out on the other side, older and wiser. He has good friends who've stood by him. He has family who love him. However there's something about Christian that he's never understood. There's something about him that sets him apart. It has made him not want to get close to anyone.

Now someone's appeared unexpectedly. To his surprise, she's just like him. Even more importantly, she has the knowledge to help him understand more about the strange existence he lives. But is she as nice as she appears, or could she have a darker reason for seeking him out and devoting time to him?

Providing an insight into one man's strange journey of coming to grips with who he really is, 'Christian' tells a story of courage, friendship and crime solving intrigue.

BRANDON
(FREEDOM OF FLIGHT SERIES - BOOK #2)

For fifteen years, Brandon McStevens has held himself away from everyone he knew prior to the day he turned fourteen. That day changed his life forever. Something happened to him that he can't explain to anyone. He feels ashamed and embarrassed. The only way he's ever been able to move past that and live, has been to find somewhere else to reside.

Since leaving his family home, he has continued to live in a small cave. Nestled high above a small coastal community, he has come to spend most of his time enjoying the ocean … oh, and up in the sky. He doesn't know how it happened. He doesn't know *why* it happened. All he knows is that despite understanding how much hurt he must have caused when he left home all those years ago, he now lives the only existence he can imagine.

He's never met anyone like him. He's never *seen* anyone like him. Until that day when that woman and her dog saw him change, no-one had ever seen or heard of him doing that. To this day he regrets having shown himself like he did. But time passed and it has all been forgotten … or has it?

Certain he's the only one like himself, he's surprised when two people come looking for him … and have much to tell him. Finally the time will come when he no longer has to feel like a freak of nature … or so alone.

FORBIDDEN CONFLICTS SERIES

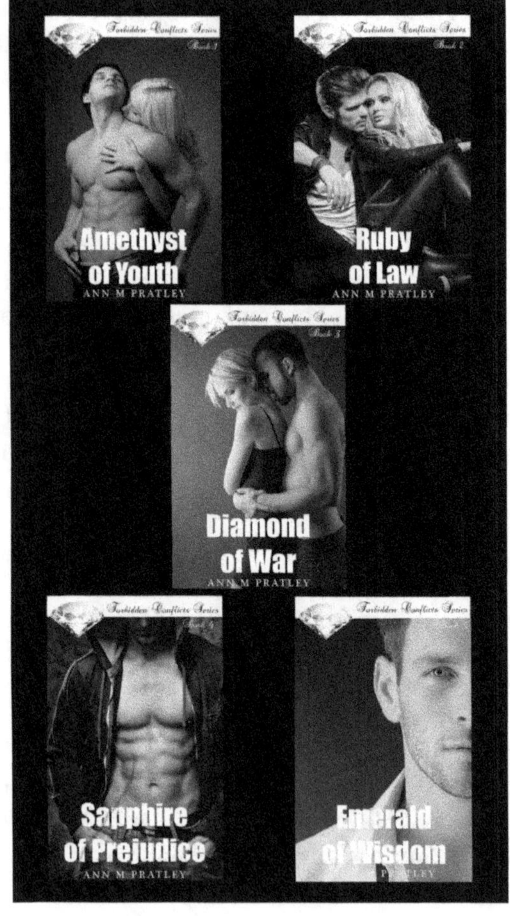

Crime Families • Passion • Suspense

AMETHYST OF YOUTH
(FORBIDDEN CONFLICTS SERIES - BOOK #1)

The youngest member of the Stonewarden family, Charlotte (Charlie), is 18 years old. As with everyone in her family when they reach that age, she's been told that when she turns 19, she'll be recruited into the family business. She has her warning that she has one year to do anything else she wishes to do - travel, study, work. Whatever she wants to do, she has 365 days to do it. On her next birthday, her life will effectively stop being her own.

But Charlie wants nothing to do with the business. The youngest of six, with five older brothers, she wants a different life. Maybe if the family business was something normal like a retail shop or a business centred around trade, she'd feel differently. There are people who say that her family's long term history of robbing from the rich and providing to the poor is a good thing. To her, all she can see is that they are thieves. Plain and simple.

Her view is further secured when she and her older brother, Max, are shot at in a local supermarket. Seeing Max lying in blood and later lying unmoving in hospital in a coma, pushes her further in her resolve to find a way to not take part in the activities of her father and brothers.

At the shootout she is saved by a checkout operator, Ash. Whilst building their friendship Charlie will learn things about her family that she didn't particularly wish to know. She will hear more and more that she can't share with Ash, and the more she learns, the wider the gap will become.

In years she's young, but having lost her mother when she was only nine years old, Charlie has an older soul. The possibilities she'll be presented with during her one final year of her own, will push her in her considerations of how she really wants her life to be. She wants one thing. Her strict ex-military father wants another. The dynamics of her new friendship will pull her in a third direction.

How will she chose what's right for her? And what would she have to do to break free from the chains that she can see her father wants to place around her for the rest of her life?

REVIEWERS SAY:

"This was a good clean romance with plenty of action to further the story along ... will make you ponder about life's situations, their actions and reactions, and how the decisions of past generations can affect the current ones. You'll be glad you read it!"

"... loved this book! It took me by surprise--great from start to finish! I don't normally read crime family dramas, but I love NA/coming-of-age novels. Charlie is on the cusp of being inducted into her family's Robin Hood-esque biz, but she doesn't want that. She isn't sure what, exactly, she does want...just not THAT. Her connection with Ash furthers that disconnect, and they stumble through the beginnings of young love together. Of course, secrets and family craziness threaten their romance at every turn. ...It's an awesome start to the Forbidden Conflicts series!"

"A wonderful read. A timeless push and pull between our own wants and our family's wants. Will she follow the path her family wants or will she follow her own path? Read the book to find out."

RUBY OF LAW
(FORBIDDEN CONFLICTS SERIES - BOOK #2)

For generations the Leadbetters have lived off crime. For as long as any of them know, fathers and mothers have taught sons and daughters how to succeed in the criminal world, primarily through theft.

Phillip Leadbetter is 29 and has devoted his whole life so far to doing what his father and mother have told him to do. The sacrifice for doing that is that he still lives at home and he hasn't yet met anyone who he believes could accept the man that he is, because of his family.

One night a potential tragedy brings him into the path of Daisy, an up and coming professional in the legal sector. Seeing him as her knight in shining armor, she can't stop thinking about the rugged guy who saved her. She's also very pleased when fate brings their paths to cross again.

Getting to know one another, both leave out major details about who they are. She doesn't want him to know she's a lawyer because some people just don't like lawyers. He doesn't want to tell her about his family and their long history of criminal activity.

How then will things turn when they meet up in a courthouse, each learning in that moment who the other really is? How will they deal with the fact that she is on one side of the law, and he is very definitely on the other?

DIAMOND OF WAR
(FORBIDDEN CONFLICTS SERIES - BOOK #3)

James Stonewarden is a playboy. He has been since the moment he first started to notice girls. He loves them all, and they all love him. Why would he want to get himself into a relationship?

Sasha Leadbetter's a hot-headed young woman, known to the law for her quick temper and harsh ways. She isn't one to mess with - especially with the way she keeps a blade in her pocket. To her it's her security. It's something that makes her feel safe and comfortable. She's had it for so long that it's nothing for her to pull it out and hold it to someone's throat without any conscious thought.

Unaware of who each other are, or how their families are distantly interconnected through crime, the chance of James Stonewarden meeting Sasha Leadbetter is slim. But it happens.

A playboy and a young woman who has the mentality to kill. What kind of recipe could that result in? And what will happen when James identifies a car at Sasha's family home, that matches the description his sister Charlie gave after the supermarket shooting months earlier?

THE GOLDEN DESIRES
(THE GOLDEN DESIRES SERIES - BOOK #1)

He wanted to escape. They needed to survive.

When Isabella starts to dream of a stranger, she's awakened inside with feelings she has never felt before. She knows he's not someone she's ever seen before, and he is not of her village. He is a stranger, and she's desperate to determine if he is real or he is a part of her imagination.

Far away a businessman desperate to escape the noise and stress of the city, embarks on a journey to find peace and the solitude he increasingly needs and desires. But at his destination he will find much, much more.

REVIEWERS SAY:

"I found myself drawn to keep reading ... almost as if reading a compelling action/adventure because the pacing was so excellent. And... ahem... the love scenes are quite well written, too ... I look forward to reading the sequel..."

"The author paints such a vivid picture of life in this idyllic community that one begins to think it may actually exist ... extremely well-written ... perfect for anyone who is looking for a romance with a hint of paranormal mystery."

"The concept behind this story was intriguing and very sexy ... Fireworks and all out romance, followed by some interesting obstacles, but they are overcome, because well...it's love. What I loved about this read was the fairytale like narration with a sci-fi/fantasy kick; it made me feel like I was part of the story..."

"... magical quality was a nice twist, delving into the realm of fantasy romance ... the author's style was well suited to the tone of the world she has created. Did it leave me hungry for the next installment? Absolutely!"

THE GOLDEN SUPREMACY
(THE GOLDEN DESIRES SERIES - BOOK #2)

What is lying in wait, eager to destroy them?

Over distance and time they met and fell in love, choosing to live together in an ancient village of peace and harmony. And then the battle had happened. A fight between good and evil; the warmth of fire and the cold of ice. They thought they had won. But had they?

Trent and Isabella start to feel that the entity that had tried to destroy them, might not have been defeated after all. But rather, perhaps it is lying in wait for another opportunity to strike.

What is it?
And who is its puppet now?

THE GOLDEN UNITY
(GOLDEN DESIRES SERIES - BOOK #3)

Cesare is the golden child of the village. His brilliant yellow hair is unlike the color of anyone else's. He is a cheerful child who in the eyes of some, can do no wrong.

Esmeralda is the product of two biological parents who have something buried deep within them. Something that makes them easy to manipulate by the being that has not given up on wanting to destroy the ancient village. The young lass with the blue-black hair is looked upon as an alternative child. She captures attention and intrigues the villagers. When they look at her, sometimes they feel like they're looking at a puzzle that confuses them and they cannot solve. It's impossible to determine why but there's just something *different* about Esmeralda.

Despite them being opposites in nature and appearance, the two have grown up together as best friends, just as their parents did before them. The goodness of Cesare showers a level of kindness and friendship on Esmeralda that she has never been able to turn away from. The difference of Esmeralda has always held Cesare's attention. Between them they have found a balance that holds them together as friends.

But what will happen as they move into their time as young adults? They are unknowing as yet that they are meant to be paired, whilst at the same time they are meant to be adversaries.

What does the puppet master have planned now? And how will these two gifted youth react to someone trying to manipulate them against their will?

A third strike from the puppet master. Will it win in its plan of attack this time?

ANN M PRATLEY
Total
FREEDOM
ANN M PRATLEY
Total New
BEGINNINGS

TOTAL FREEDOM
(TOTAL FREEDOM SERIES - BOOK #1)

For Debbie King, life began feeling like it was all too difficult, she would never achieve, she would never have friends, and she would simply never fit in. But when she meets someone new who seems just like her, with low self-esteem and no belief in themselves and what they have to offer, Debbie finds strength to focus more on them and less on herself.

So begins an incredible journey of friendship and love that will be tested by other people entering their world, and the shared passion they have for their musical talents and career together. It is a deep friendship that will be tested over and over again by events and an ongoing uncertainty over what their relationship really should really be like.

REVIEWERS SAY:

"The overall story was great and hooked me right in. I had to stay with them for the entire journey ... you know it's a good story when you wish it didn't have to end."

"... an incredible job developing complex characters that are emotionally scarred and then allowing the reader to really understand their pain ... a terrific coming of age story surrounding a triangle of young characters, Debbie, Craig and Steven."

"Covered a lot of different things that can happen as we grow and was appealing for that reason."

TOTAL NEW BEGINNINGS
(TOTAL FREEDOM SERIES - BOOK #2)

In her early adulthood Debbie made a choice. She had two men who loved her. She chose one. She lost the friendship of the other.

Twenty years on, horrific tragedy strikes. Mother to three grown children, she has to find the strength to be there for them, while pushing her own grief aside. Dealing with the loss of the man who has been by her side for two decades pushes her into depression. Every day seems harder to deal with than the last. The feeling of loss is further heightened by finding her husband's lifetime of journals. Hesitant at first to look inside them, she eventually does. Almost instantly she regrets that decision. In the years of her husband's writing she reads things that lead her to seriously question whether she ever really knew him at all, or if they had actually been strangers for two decades.

The combination of the loss of her husband, and the uncertainty about who he really was, pushes her to retire into a dark room and have no desire to leave. She wants to shut out the world. She wants to not believe what she knows in her heart is reality.

With her youngest daughter, Poppy, still living at home, Debbie is eventually pulled from the darkness by her daughter's pleas. Finally the dark days start to fade and Debbie can start to see the sun shining once more. Finally she can find the strength to keep going. Finally she can start to move into a period of recovery and growth. Finally she can accept that it's okay to accept help and lean on others.

As she starts rediscovering her ability to embrace life again, results appear from her daughter's determination to help her mother. Someone from her past is brought back into her life. A friendship is re-established. It's time to let go of the past and begin a new future. It's time for total new beginnings.

Did you ever hear the words in your head … 'what if'? What if you chose one path earlier in life but later had the chance to walk down the path previously unchosen? Would you?

PAINFUL DELIVERANCE SERIES

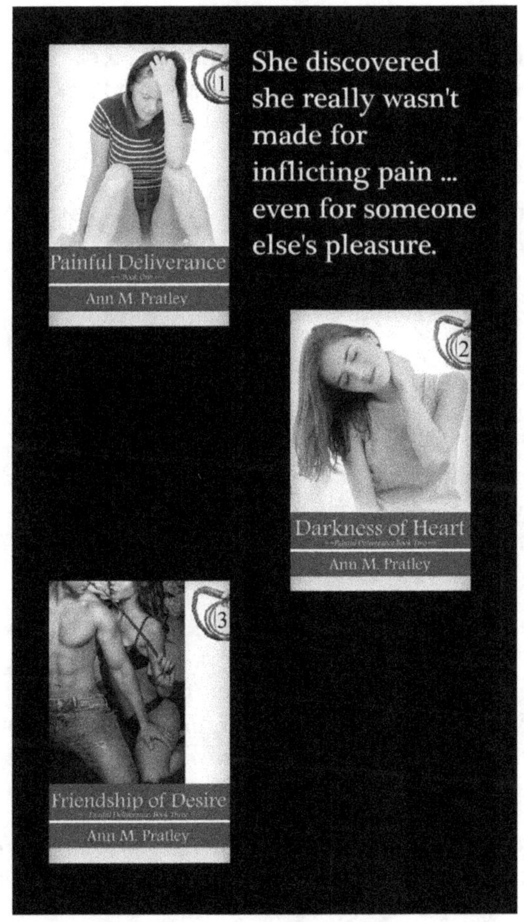

Obsession • Romance
Psychological Trauma

PAINFUL DELIVERANCE
(PAINFUL DELIVERANCE SERIES - BOOK #1)

She just wasn't made to inflict pain.

She knows it is nothing abnormal. She knows others enjoy it. But with every new level of pain he directs her to deliver to him, Alexis feels another piece of her soul die. He has wealth and he has power, and she knows he won't easily let her go.

But she has to leave. Escape. Move on. Forget. She has reached her limit of what she can do. The plans are in place to get away. She just has to hope that wherever she goes - whoever she meets - she won't find herself in exactly the same situation again.

DARKNESS OF HEART
(PAINFUL DELIVERANCE SERIES - BOOK #2)

She thought he'd stopped looking. He hadn't.

She got away from him to start a new life. She moved on. But in his mind, he still loves her and needs her. He still believes that she loves him. That she is meant to be his. That he is meant to be hers.

He will not give up searching for her. He will not give up *fighting* for her. He will pursue her and stop at nothing to get her back. But it will come at a cost … a sacrifice much greater than he will see coming. A sacrifice that will finally wake him up and bring him back to stark reality.

REVIEWERS SAY:

"… author did a great job of making brief references from the first book. Lincoln, Lexi and Alexis are back, though perhaps the most complex character is Diana … definitely written for a mature audience … the author is a great storyteller and writes with an easy to read style … certainly writes a more interesting and readable story than many best-selling authors. It's very easy for me to recommend this book with 5 of 5 stars."

"This story continued the journey of Alexis, Anthony and Lincoln while giving us a new perspective into the repercussions of Lincoln and Alexis's relationship: from the POV of Lincoln's wife Diana! I loved her addition to the story's … kept the tension of the story just right, balancing the calm new life Alexis has been building and keeping the reader engaged."

"It is a book of courage, the courage to leave everything you know behind, the courage to change, the courage to face your fears, and the courage to face the unknown."

FRIENDSHIP OF DESIRE
(PAINFUL DELIVERANCE SERIES - BOOK #3)

Tom and Samantha. Feisty friends from childhood who feel like they know each other inside out, until the day comes when one of them suggests they go to a BDSM club together, and become formal play partners. Pushing the limits of what each of them can individually stand in their lifelong friendship, they attract and repel like magnets, until the time comes when they must choose how they will relate to one another - and what kind of relationship they will go on to have in the future.

Whilst on this journey of discovery, the two of them meet and make a new friend - Alexis. A young woman with a hidden and secretive past, and a mystery surrounding the relationship she has - or has had - with a renowned business entrepreneur who begins to integrate himself into Samantha's life, unknown to any of them whether he has done it for him, or for her … or for Alexis, being the mysterious link from his past.

ABOUT THE AUTHOR

Ann M Pratley has a great passion for writing and words, and enjoys writing fiction where the characters take on a life of their own through the writing process.

~~~~~~

If you enjoyed this book, please do consider leaving a review at Amazon.
Reviews are so important to new authors.
www.amazon.com/Ann-M-Pratley/e/B01GAO60PS

~~~~~~

Sign up for my monthly newsletter to receive news of sales, freebies, new releases and the opportunity to read advance copies of soon-to-be-released books!
authorannmpratley.wixsite.com/writingisbliss/contact

~~~~~~

If you would like to make contact with me, please:
Follow Me On Twitter
https://twitter.com/ReadMyBooks1

Visit my Goodreads Author Page
goodreads.com/author/show/14777236.Ann_M_Pratley

Visit My Facebook Page
https://www.facebook.com/authorannpratley

Thank you,
Ann M Pratley
~~~~~~